DEBRA WHITE SMITH

Brittan

HARVEST HOUSE PUBLISHERS

EUGENE, OREGON

Cover photos © Jim Whitmer Photography; Brian Booth / Trainstock, Inc. / Alamy

Cover by Dugan Design Group, Bloomington, Minnesota

Published in association with the literary agency of Alive Communications, Inc., 7680 Goddard Street, Ste #200, Colorado Springs, CO 80920. www.alivecommunications.com.

BRITTAN
Copyright © 2008 by Debra White Smith
Published by Harvest House Publishers
Eugene, Oregon 97402
www.harvesthousepublishers.com

Library of Congress Cataloging-in-Publication Data

Smith, Debra White.
Brittan / Debra White Smith.
    p. cm.—(Debutantes ; bk. 3)
ISBN-13: 978-0-7369-1931-9 (pbk.)
ISBN-10: 0-7369-1931-7 (pbk.)

1. Debutantes—Fiction. 2. Women detectives—Fiction 3. Houston (Tex.)—Fiction. I. Title.
PS3569.M5178B75 2008
813.'54—dc22

2008016209

Printed in the United States of America

08 09 10 11 12 13 14 15 16 / LB-NI / 11 10 9 8 7 6 5 4 3 2 1

PROLOGUE

"Okay, let's do it," Lorna said, and Heather and Brittan fell in beside their friend. The trek to the vehicle was as uneventful as a Sunday afternoon stroll. The night smelled of damp earth and warm summer dew and reminded Lorna of her grandparents' farmhouse where she'd spent summers.

The three amateur sleuths silently slipped through the night like three panthers focused on their mission, determined to succeed.

Lorna reached the police car first. She paused until Heather and Brittan were at her side. Then she reached for the windshield wiper. Even though Brittan insisted the vehicle had no alarm, Lorna planned to handle the wiper with the greatest delicacy. If an alarm were in force, a mere touch or lift of the wiper usually wouldn't set it off. A slap of the wiper against the windshield might, if the alarm's sensitivity was set on high.

Here goes, she thought and gritted her teeth as she lifted the wiper. The sound of distant traffic and the shrill chirps of crickets slipped through the night. Lorna placed the ziplock bag beneath the wiper, making sure the single long-stemmed red rose lay at a strategic angle. She gently settled the bag against the windshield and pulled away from the vehicle. Everything was simple. Easy. "The Rose," as the three anonymous sleuths were called in the media, had made another clue delivery. Now they only had to walk back to the black Dodge, drive from the neighborhood, and the job was complete.

Everything was perfect...predictable...until two cats darted across the yard and began a screaming duet. A canine backup singer piped in.

"Oh no," Heather groaned.

The front porch light flicked on.

"Duck!" Lorna hissed and dropped into a squat.

Her friends joined her in the police car's shadow as the house door bumped open.

"All right already." A sleepy male voice sailed across the yard. "It's just cats anyway." A dog with the bay of a St. Bernard erupted into the yard. He sounded as if he were serious.

Lorna figured he was probably the size of a squirrel and wouldn't know what to do with a cat if he caught one. But that didn't stop him from flinging attitude all over the far side of the yard.

When the cat rampage ceased, Brittan squeezed Lorna's arm. Lorna glanced to Brittan and then toward Heather. Both friends' expressions said the same thing, *Let's go before the dog loses interest in the cats.*

Lorna inched up until she glimpsed the man's shadowed form in the doorway. He yawned, scratched his head, and gazed toward the sound of the barking dog. Glancing behind her, Lorna scoped out the best route. Pointing toward the darkest section of street, Lorna whispered, "Let's get outta here."

Brittan hunched over and led the way. Lorna and Heather followed. They scurried across the street to the clump of trees that shielded the street from the streetlights' glow. The three friends stepped into the oak patch, pausing long enough to ensure they'd been undetected.

The man still stood in the door. The dog was trotting back from the yard's shadowed edge.

Lorna released her breath and turned toward a path through the park.

"Hurry!" Heather whispered. As she glanced back she saw the dog stop where they'd just been squatting.

"Oh no! It's a German shepherd," Brittan whispered. "What if he's trained to track?"

"Are you kidding?" Lorna turned. "Of course he is. He's probably an official police dog."

"Yes," Heather whispered, "but unless his owner gives him the order, he probably won't leave the premises. They're *trained*," she emphasized.

"It doesn't sound like he waited for any order to be disturbed over the cats," Brittan whispered.

"Rocky!" a male voice commanded. The man stepped out, and the front door slapped shut.

Lorna's attention shifted to the bare-chested officer. Rob Lightly for sure. His hair was mussed, and he wore pajama bottoms. The dog trotted to his master, who bent to scratch his ears. "What's the matter, boy?" he asked. "This isn't like you."

The dog wagged his tail but whined.

"Those cats fight all the time," Rob mused and scanned the neighborhood.

Lorna grasped Brittan's hand on one side and Heather's on the other. The silent message between the three friends was *Wait!* The slightest movement could alert the skilled dog.

Rocky's whine escalated into a short bark.

His face drawing into a frown, Lightly strolled toward his car.

Eyes widening, Lorna held her breath as the cop neared the vehicle and stopped. He placed his hands on his hips and studied the windshield. Next he rounded the vehicle and leaned over the ziplock bag. After several seconds of examination, he gingerly pulled the bag from beneath the wiper and opened it. The first object he pulled from the bag was a single long-stemmed rose.

"Oh my word!" he exclaimed and whipped around to examine the street. After gazing directly at the clump of trees, he pulled the documents and photos from the bag. Hurrying toward the porch light, he fumbled through the papers and photos before commanding, "Rocky, inside!"

The dog trotted to his master's side and through the door his owner opened. Rob searched the neighborhood once more before closing the door.

"If he's what his reputation says," Brittan whispered, "he'll be back out here in 5 minutes—at the police station in 15."

"Let's scram!" Lorna whispered, and all three hustled toward their vehicle. Within three minutes, they'd cruised to freedom and couldn't wait to see tomorrow's headlines.

ONE

"Rare Incan Necklace Still Not Found," Brittan Shay mumbled. She sat rigidly at one end of the couch as she skimmed the front page article from the *Houston Star*. Reporter Duke Fieldman detailed the heist that had taken place three months ago. The rare gold and pearl artifact, featured at the Houston Museum of Fine Art, had been nabbed during an Ancient Incan exhibit. The thief had left a single long-stemmed red rose in the place of the necklace. So not only had the thief stolen a priceless treasure, he or she had also implicated the Rose as the perpetrator.

The whole ordeal had left the people of Houston reeling and made national news. Duke Fieldman's article "Defending the Rose's Honor" had been syndicated. He'd staunchly stated that he believed the Rose was being mocked by a clever criminal. For a full week the media was rife with speculation that the Rose had turned from solving crimes to committing them. Brittan and her two best friends were aghast, but they disciplined themselves not to jump into the middle of the media storm. As much as they wanted to solve the case, they deduced that this criminal might be throwing them a challenge and that if they acted rashly their identities might get revealed— which was probably what the thief wanted. Besides, the FBI's strong detective team seemed sure the necklace would be found.

Brittan bit at her cinnamon gum. *But it's still missing!* she thought. She lowered the paper and gazed out her new house's massive window that faced toward the shoreline of Lake Houston. The growing tension in her gut would not be relieved. As risky as it was, Brittan was beginning to think the Rose didn't have a choice.

What if this thief strikes again and leaves another rose? she worried. *If he keeps getting away with this, eventually everyone will be convinced the Rose is really a criminal.*

"Wait a minute!" she whispered. "How do I know the thief is a man? Maybe it's a woman." She narrowed her eyes. "A sly, wicked woman who wants to ruin us." Her fingers flexed. The paper crumpled in her dampening palms. The shoreline blurred as Brittan's emotions raced into overdrive.

"We've got to stop her...or him!" she exclaimed and tossed aside the paper. "We've *got* to!" Brittan stood, her fists at her sides. "Whoever you are, you just might ruin our party if we don't do something!" She strode toward the window lining the living room's west wall.

Just then she caught sight of another enemy. It smothered Brittan's growing irritation with a different concern, this one much closer to home. The long-haired dog that had harassed her all week romped past her pier and plunged into the waves along the shoreline like a carefree icon of supreme mutt-ness.

"Good grief! It's that same stupid dog again!" Brittan glanced toward the fresh row of geraniums she'd planted yesterday—for the second time. The first time the floppy-eared mutt spied the red flowers, he saw an invitation to frolic. The geraniums he didn't dig up, he rolled on—and that was *after* he'd flung Brittan's garbage all over the curb the day before. Both times Brittan chased the obviously well-fed scoundrel from her yard.

Today she went for the only weapon she could think of—a broom. Brittan's housekeeper kept this home as spotless as her penthouse, and everything was always in its place. As expected, the broom rested in the utility closet. Armed and ready, Brittan marched toward the door. But when she gripped the knob, common sense overcame her ire. Brittan set the broom near the door and moved to the huge window.

The perpetrator jumped in and out of the wavelets created by a barge motoring past the bay. His golden coat glistened with diamond-like droplets. The more he gleefully romped, the more he looked like he was in a high-priced dog food advertisement.

When Brittan bought the lake house last fall, she knew it would need a lot of improvements. She'd committed her time and money to creating a showplace that rivaled the Garden of Eden. The crumpled geranium lying cockeyed on her cobblestone sidewalk demanded she protect "Eden's" splendor.

But that won't stop the problem, she reasoned and rested her hand on the windowsill. Narrowing her eyes, Brittan drummed her fingers against the frame. The dog obviously had an owner who cared a great deal about him—enough to keep his coat groomed and his diet healthy. The enthusiastic pet didn't appear to have a care…or need in the world.

"Okay," Brittan grumbled, her lips tight. "I think it's time for a *lit-tle* communication." She walked into the kitchen and placed the broom back in the closet. Moving to the counter, Brittan opened a drawer and pulled out a linen hand towel. A quick glance toward the silver-plated pencil holder on the counter confirmed that the permanent marker was where she placed it yesterday. Brittan pulled it out and whipped the cap off. Leaning over the towel, she wrote, "Your dog destroyed my geraniums yesterday and scattered my trash the day before. He's on the trail again today. If you don't keep him in your yard, I'll call animal patrol. This is getting irritating. Keep your dog home!"

She straightened, eyed the message, and then added one final line: "If he's creating mayhem in my yard, what's he doing in the other neighbors' yards? For his own safety, keep him penned up!"

Brittan laid the marker on the counter and marched into the great outdoors. The cool morning breeze tangled its fingers in her hair, causing her to brush her bangs away from her glasses. As she suspected, the rascal was romping from the lake, straight toward one of her flower beds. Today he had "eat the elephant ears" in his eyes. Brittan glanced toward the broadleafed foliage beneath the massive oak. A blue jay swooped in and fluttered to her nest in the branches above. Brittan recalled the bird dive-bombing the gardener while he cared for the elephant ears. Mr. Snowden had braved the attacks to pamper the foliage like newborns ever since they emerged two months ago in March. Their lavish growth testified to the attention he gave them.

"And I'll be a pickle if I let you destroy those too," Brittan mumbled under her breath. Purposefully keeping her voice friendly, she edged toward the dog and called, "Here, boy! Come here, fellow!"

The villain stopped. Tongue lolling from his open mouth, he cocked his head, lifted his ears a bit, and looked at Brittan. Soon he lowered his ears and backed in the direction he'd come from.

Afraid she'd lose the opportunity, Brittan upped her calls to frantic. "Here, boy!" she pleaded and bent forward. "Come on! Come here to Brittan! Come on, boy!"

The dog twitched his tail and then lay down and rolled over. Brittan hustled forward but slowed when she was a few feet away. The dog whined and wagged his tail. When she looked into the liquid-brown eyes, he seemed to say, "Please love me. I want to love you."

For the first time Brittan's softer side stirred. While she wasn't an animal fanatic like her friend Heather, Brittan still liked them. She'd even thought about getting a small house dog a few times. Sighing, she knelt beside the flower-bed destroyer and scratched his damp ear. His soft fur smelled of fresh shampoo despite the dirt on his paws.

"I bet the reason you get away with so much stuff is because you're so pretty," she crooned.

"Woof!" he agreed and squirmed for more strokes.

Brittan slipped the linen cloth under his loose collar and tied it in a knot. Then she noticed the collar tag and turned it so she could read the name. "Elvis. Humph! Whoever heard of naming a dog Elvis?" Brittan noted the phone number on the tag.

"Woof!" Elvis replied and added a congenial lick.

"Hold still!" she commanded and stroked his neck. Brittan brushed the hair out of her eyes while taking a few seconds to memorize the number.

Finally she released the dog. "Okay, enough bonding! Time for you to go home!" Brittan stood and waved south, the direction the dog had come from. "Go home!" she encouraged.

Elvis hopped up, ran around Brittan, and panted for playtime.

"No, no!" Brittan scolded. "Go home! Time to go home!"

With a commanding squawk, the blue jay plunged from her nest, straight toward Elvis. The dog was so intent on begging for more strokes, he didn't spot the bird until she was nearly on top of him. With a jump backward, the dog focused on his airborne attacker. He lowered his tail and scrambled toward the lake. When the bird detected victory, she upped her efforts and went for Elvis' ears. Yelping, the dog ran toward the pier, and then took a hard left and continued down the shoreline.

Chuckling, Brittan trotted toward the lake and watched the dog race from her yard, across the next one, and straight toward a man standing near another pier in the distance. Brittan started to turn and leave, but on a whim, decided to wait. If the man was the dog's owner, she wanted to know that he got her message.

She glanced toward the blue lake streaked with gold from the mid-morning sun. For a few seconds her angst vanished. The water rippled into infinity while a trio of seagulls soared. Even at ten o'clock the wooden lawn chair called Brittan's name.

She eyed the chair, longed for the solitude of her Eden, but refused to give in. Brittan was attending a tea in honor of her friend Heather Winslow in an hour. She needed to change out of the soft shorts and T-shirt and into something a little more appropriate for the high-society gathering honoring the bride to be. Brittan didn't have any time for lounging today.

Crossing her arms, she gazed toward the man who welcomed Elvis with a jovial back rub. The dog's merry bark was all the evidence Brittan needed to affirm the tanned stranger in blue shorts was Elvis' owner. Resting her hands on her hips, she watched with satisfaction as he untied the cloth from the dog's collar. After briefly skimming the note, the man gazed up and down the bay. Finally his eyes rested on Brittan.

Without a blink, she waved and hoped he took her hint; or rather, her whack over the head. If he didn't understand *that* message, he was beyond daft. Squaring her shoulders, Brittan strolled back toward her house. From this vantage she admired the effects of her planning and labor. Even though the home was 25 years old, each room featured huge windows that gave the place an ultra-modern appeal. The strategic landscaping heightened the effect.

Sighing, she picked up the broken geranium that had been lying on the rock and eyed the blue jay, now accosting a squirrel. "You certainly stay busy," Brittan mused and moved toward the glass doorway.

"Excuse me? Miss!" A deep voice rose up from the shoreline. Brittan turned toward the voice to face a man. At this closer vantage, his features were vaguely familiar, but she couldn't imagine why. While the guy had certainly looked trim at a distance, now his lean form would best be described as athletic.

Brittan tossed the geranium aside, slipped her hands into her pockets, and maintained a disinterested persona. He was most likely married. Most of the good ones were. Besides, he obviously owned Elvis and probably was not happy with her right now.

His assured grin bordered on annoying as he waved the cloth and called, "Did you write this?"

"Yes," Brittan replied and pressed her lips together. She had no intention of giving the guy any indication that she wasn't serious about the dog issue.

As he casually strolled into her Eden, Brittan stood her ground and never wavered in her appraisal. Elvis appeared on the edge of the yard, but inched back when he spotted the blue jay still harassing the squirrel. Normally Brittan would have chuckled, but she couldn't afford to show a glimmer of weakness.

The closer the man came, the more details Brittan noticed…and the more she found to appreciate. His eyes were as disturbingly blue as his hair was provocatively curly, and this added to Brittan's need to up her resolve. To top it off, he even had dimples! No way was she going to give into feminine weakness and return his grin. She balled her hands in her pockets and locked her knees.

"I see that you aren't all that happy with me right now." He lifted the cloth.

Brittan raked her mind for why the man looked so familiar but hit a block. She was simply too taxed with the effort of trying to decide exactly how to respond.

"Well, would *you* be happy if the roles were switched?" she finally asked.

"Not at all," he purred and extended his left hand in offer of a handshake.

She eyed his ringless hand and tried to determine why he hadn't offered his right hand. Brittan also debated whether or not she should ignore the offer. There was no sense striking up a friendship with someone whose lack of responsibility had upset her life the last few days.

"I'm Rob, by the way," he coaxed. "Rob Lightly. And I won't bite." His smile broadened.

Brittan's resolve momentarily wavered, and she found her hand enmeshed with his. She recognized the name but was so distracted by the handshake she couldn't make her mind home in on why she knew it.

"And your name is?" he queried while maintaining his hold.

"Brittan Shay," she supplied and wondered if she was going to involuntarily hop through every hoop the man held up.

Before his grip loosened, Rob tilted her hand upward, darted a pointed glance toward her fingers, and then smiled into her eyes.

"So...you aren't married!" he stated like he'd just won grand prize.

"Nope." Brittan snatched her hand away, crossed her arms, scowled straight at him, and fully understood why he'd offered his *left* hand. There was *no way* she was going to let this turn into a pickup. "But having to deal with your dog makes me wish I was." She lifted her chin and tapped her toes.

"Ouch." Rob winced. "Look...I'm sorry." He glanced toward Elvis, now distracted by his own tail. "My father lives three houses down." He waved to the right. "Elvis is his dog. I come over on my days off and take him for walks. Lately he's been escaping his pen. I was just in the process of fortifying the gate. When he's not in his pen, he stays inside with my dad. My dad is a Vietnam vet...lost his leg in the war." A protective edge sharpened his words. "Elvis is good for him."

"Oh," Brittan mumbled. She stopped tapping her toes and uncrossed her arms.

The protectiveness she heard in his voice now became evident in his expression. Apparently Rob's dad was an invalid who needed Rob's support as much as Elvis' company. She thought about asking more about his father's condition but decided that would be prying.

A breeze ushered in the smell of the lake and cleared her senses. As her defensiveness subsided, Brittan gradually recalled why the guy's face and name was familiar. Last year she and Heather and

Lorna had alerted a Houston precinct captain to an animal cruelty case in typical "rose" fashion.

Two years ago, the three Houston debutantes made a public name for themselves when they secretly left their first rose in the offices of *The Houston Star,* which was owned by Brittan's family. The rose was accompanied by evidence that revealed the identity of an internet scoundrel who'd hacked into the Houston banking system. Soon after, they'd solved a case of who murdered Houston's mayor. And last summer's headlines involved "the Rose" uncovering a scheme to frame an innocent pastor for internet pornography.

Now Brittan was face-to-face with the Houston precinct captain, a rose recipient. Before last year's delivery, Brittan saw the guy's photo online and was impressed to say the least. She recalled wondering if he was married but lost hope of him being single when she saw a jungle gym in his yard the night they delivered the rose. However, his ring finger was as void of a wedding band as hers, which made Brittan wonder about the jungle gym.

"Anyway, here's your cloth back," Lightly said.

Brittan took the cloth and waited for the man to dismiss himself.

Instead he said, "Sure, I'd love to," with an enthusiastic nod. "I thought you'd never ask!"

"What?" Brittan cocked her head.

"Oh? Didn't you just ask me in for a soda or tea or something?" He touched his temple. "Or was I just wishing so hard I hallucinated it?" His blue eyes sparkled with as much mischief as admiration, and Brittan couldn't stop her full-blown grin no matter how hard she tried.

"Let me get this straight," she said and adjusted her glasses. "Your dad's dog is driving me nuts, and I'm supposed to reward you with a nice chat over a glass of iced tea?"

"Of course!" he said. "And while you're at it, why not throw in a doggy bone for Elvis too." He rested his hand on his chest. "It's the *least* we can do."

Brittan's exaggerated sigh couldn't have been more flirtatious if she tried. "Did you graduate from Southern charm school or *what?*" she teased and waved her hand.

"Yep. I graduated at the top of my class. Does it show?"

"Not in the least," she drawled and tried to remember why she'd been so exasperated with the man. In the face of his devil-may-care smile, she couldn't imagine anyone being aggravated at him for more than a few seconds.

"Maybe it would be good to get to know my neighbors better," she acquiesced. "And if your father needs help, maybe I could be available on the days you aren't here."

"Maybe you could come and take Elvis for a walk even."

Brittan chuckled. "And why don't I pay you for the privilege while I'm at it?" she chided.

"What a great idea!" Rob agreed. "Twenty dollars should cover it."

"Ha, ha, ha," Brittan replied and forgot all about Heather's tea.

TWO

"No, no, no...move it to the left a little more."

José Herrera nudged the birdhouse to the left and glanced over his shoulder in the hopes of seeing satisfaction on his petite mother's face. Instead, she puckered her lips, squinted, and didn't look any happier than she had 15 minutes ago when they moved the birdhouse from the other display window.

"I think it needs to go back in the other window," she finally said.

He groaned but stopped short of cursing. Maria Herrera, a devout Catholic, had washed his mouth out with a bar of Dial soap when he was 12, and he'd never cursed in front of his mother again. José could still taste the stuff at 35. If it weren't for the fact that he needed her craft store chain for his extracurricular activities, he'd have given in to a verbal tirade and stormed out two hours ago.

Decorating a craft and gift shop with two old ladies was a long way from his idea of a stimulating Friday. But this was the sixth Houston area store he'd helped her and his aunt with. This store, located near the elite section of Lake Houston, would probably prove to be the best cover yet. José was willing to do just about anything to get the setup finalized. The sooner that happened, the sooner he could start trickling his special project money through the store's account. His mother blindly trusted her son with her money. While he'd never touch a penny of hers, he had no scruples against using her accounts to launder his funds.

"Go on! Go on!" Her reddened lips tight, she shooed him toward the other display case.

José picked up the waist-high birdhouse and stand and walked back to the other case. Only after he placed the item next to a display of decorator baskets, exactly where it had started, did his mother give the final nod.

"Perfect!" she crowed. Her back erect, she whirled toward a stack of unopened boxes like a gypsy dancer doing fancy footwork. Her skirt swished around her ankles as she stopped at her next project—a box full of potpourri that was already making the place smell like honeysuckle.

José thought the sickening odor was almost as annoying as doing the tango with the birdhouse.

His dowdy aunt, wearing a double-knit sweater pulled up to her double chin, bustled in. Except for the fact that their wide-set Spanish eyes were the same, the two sisters barely resembled each other. His aunt was as low fashion as his mom was high.

"We got the coffee!" Aunt Julia crowed and lifted a package. "It came to the post office box."

"God be praised!" Maria exclaimed. "We're in business."

The two widows sold the same French vanilla coffee at every one of their locations, and they always kept a pot brewing for any shopper who wanted to try a cup. Shortly after Aunt Julia opened the box, the smell of vanilla mingled with the scent of honeysuckle. With the two ladies clucking like hens over their coffee, José slipped past a display of antique picture frames toward a storage room in the back.

If the latest deal went down as planned, he'd have another hundred grand by tomorrow morning. He planned to stagger the deposits into every craft store account over a two-week period.

From the accounts, the money would be used to purchase "inventory" from several false suppliers José had set up. The end result was clean money in his pocket. So far the setup had worked beautifully for five years. And every time his mother and aunt opened a store, José's horizons broadened.

He jiggled the key ring in his trouser pocket before extracting the keys and unlocking the storage room that only he had a key to. After a glimpse over his shoulder, José stepped into the musty room, snapped the door shut, and clicked on the light. The framed antique photo propped against the cluttered shelf looked like a piece of his mother's inventory. But the photo was hiding a rare, gold and pearl necklace he'd nabbed.

The theft had made national news three months ago. Leaving the red rose at the scene had sent the media into a whirlwind of speculation. José chuckled and savored the satisfaction. He could only imagine what the Rose must be thinking. He'd hoped the challenge would send that smart aleck looking for him. Then he would outmaneuver the cocky sleuth and arrange for public exposure and disgrace. Whoever was behind the Rose, he or she deserved having their face rubbed in media mud.

José had two cousins, both Aunt Julia's sons, both as close to him as brothers. The youngest was now doing time in federal prison because of the Rose. Juan had been having a good time when he hacked into Houston's banking system and shut down commerce for a day. Little harm was done, but the FBI didn't seem to agree. If the Rose hadn't tipped off the *Houston Star,* Juan would still be free...and possibly assisting him and Eduardo in their enterprise.

Despite José's public challenge to the Rose, there'd been no response. It was almost as if the Rose hadn't registered that he'd issued a challenge.

Either that or the detective is too smart to fall for the trap. Maybe the Rose is as smart as you are, a nagging voice added. José's fingers tightened around the frame. "Never!" he vowed. "No one has ever outsmarted me—and no one will!"

He scowled at the faded old photo and forced himself to stop playing mind games. That was probably exactly what the Rose wanted. José's fingers relaxed against the frame. He needed to focus on moving the ancient Incan necklace. He'd worry about the Rose later. The dealers and clients he supplied goods to had long ago stopped being surprised at the rare finds José provided. With the help of cousin Eduardo, "the connector," they'd built a repertoire of wealthy clients eager to own rarities without asking bothersome questions.

José kissed the top of the frame. Business was booming. Thievery had never been more profitable...or beautiful.

Brittan gassed her Jaguar and checked her Rolex. In the presence of Rob Lightly's warm smiles, she'd forgotten about Heather's tea until the event was scheduled to begin. Rob had told her a few things about himself that Brittan already knew, such as the fact that he was a precinct captain on the Houston City Police Force. Before he left, he secured her phone number. Brittan had even dared to give him her cell number. She couldn't ever remember a more enjoyable hour in Eden, even with Elvis-the-geranium-slayer romping along the shoreline.

It had been years since she slowed down long enough to have a relationship with a guy. Even the few college flirtations she'd indulged in, Brittan had been far too practical to let any relationship get serious. That would have distracted her from maintaining a 4-point grade average. Now that college was two years in the past, she'd begun to wonder if she'd die a pragmatic old maid. Granted, her dad and mom continually introduced her to men whose families were on the "approved" list because they had sizable fortunes.

One or two had even been imports from European aristocracy. But Brittan had yet to meet one who interested her beyond a brief handshake.

Now both her best friends were engaged. Heather Winslow's wedding to reporter Duke Fieldman was a few months away. Lorna Leigh and Mayor Michael Hayden were the talk of Houston. The ring on Lorna's finger would choke a rhinoceros. The glow on her face was as striking as Heather's. And every day Heather's wedding grew nearer, Brittan felt more and more left out.

She rested her hand on the gearshift and steered around the corner, past the strip of specialty shops that catered to the wealthy residents on this side of Lake Houston. The Mediterranean restaurant and upscale convenience store anchored the klatch of retailers. As she drove past Pizzazz, a slinky number in the dress shop window caught Brittan's eye, and she wondered how much the knee-length dress cost. It was absolutely *her*. Made of ecru-colored satin, the piece offered a feminine impression without detested frills.

"You're on my list, baby," Brittan whispered and glanced down at the beige suit she wore. Her friends often teased her about wearing only shades of beige, black, and army green. Despite their observation, Brittan couldn't help being drawn to the most basic wardrobe colors. After all, they made sense.

She adjusted her glasses and slowed for the intersection she needed to cross before merging into heavier traffic. After darting another glance toward the dress at Pizzazz, the new shop next door caught her eye. The sign read "Herrera's Crafts and Gifts." A decorative birdhouse filled the display window, and Brittan imagined it nestled beneath a tree in Eden. Images of the rabid blue jay setting up camp inside reaped a snicker.

Dismissing the items until later, Brittan pressed the accelerator and zoomed into the intersection. Instantly a flash of silver appeared in her peripheral vision. Brittan instinctively slammed

on her brakes and snapped her focus to the right. A sleek Volvo slid
to a squealing stop as her Jaguar's bumper mashed into it. Brittan's
seat belt bit into her ribcage before she was flung back against the
seat and held tightly in place.

"Oh no!" she shrieked and pounded her fist against the steering
wheel. The car responded with a pleasing purr, uninterrupted by
the upheaval.

A striking Latin alighted from the other vehicle. Whipping
off his sunglasses, he slammed the car door, quickly surveyed the
scene, and stormed toward the Jaguar.

She glanced at her watch again and noted she was already 30
minutes late. If she didn't get to the tea soon, she'd miss most of it.
She looked back outside. The *last* thing she needed was an angry
encounter with someone who ran a stop sign. As much as she
wanted to jump from the car and stand her ground, she took a few
deep breaths, counted to three, and schooled her features into a
placid mask.

Recalling something about a soft word turning away wrath,
she was thankful she had the presence of mind to actually apply it.
By the time the guy reached her vehicle, Brittan had hit the button
and the automatic window was rolling down.

"Hello there," she said in a voice calm enough to slow a stam-
peding bull. When she threw in her special smile, guaranteed to
charm the spots off a giraffe, the guy visibly cooled before her eyes.
"It appears we've got a problem, huh?" She snapped open her car
door.

He stepped aside for her to get out. "You better believe we do,
lady!" he huffed. "You plowed straight into me."

"Did I?" Brittan laid a hand on her chest and stopped herself
short of insisting *he* was the one who'd violated the traffic law.
After all, *she'd* been stopped long enough to decide to purchase a
dress *and* a birdhouse. But Heather's tea was calling, and Brittan
didn't have time to argue over who was to blame. It was easier to

smooth over the incident and come to an agreement on compensation later.

"Well look," she continued and glanced toward the line of cars now creeping past the scene. "Why don't we just exchange numbers and talk later today?" Brittan stepped toward the front of her car and noted that the damages to both vehicles were minor. "Sometimes in cases like this, it's best to just cover the cost of the damages out of our own pockets. That stops the cost of insurance from going through the ceiling." She shrugged and turned down her bottom lip. "I mean, we could go head to head over whose fault it was, but where does that get us? The best I can tell, there are no witnesses." She waved toward the passing cars. "Or at least none who cared enough to stick around and testify. If the police come, we'll probably both get tickets."

She offered the guy another measured smile, gradually realizing he wasn't any worse on the eyes than Rob Lightly. While he wasn't as tall, he was every bit as trim and alluring in his simple jeans and oxford shirt. Brittan had always had a thing for Latin men. Her very first boyfriend in junior high had been from Guatemala. But for the life of her, she couldn't remember his name right now.

Sighing, he rubbed his forehead, glared at the bumper, and then back at Brittan. "What's your name?" he asked, his eyes softening.

"Brittan Shay." She extended her hand.

"I'm José Herrera," he responded during the shake. "Live around here?"

"Yes. I own a lake house just around the corner. It's my getaway when I get tired of the city. And you?"

"I live west of Houston. But my mom owns the new craft shop." He pointed toward the strip of stores.

"Oh, where the birdhouse is?" she asked.

"Uh, yeah," he said through a frown.

"I was just planning to buy it for my yard."

"Figures," he grunted. "You were looking at the birdhouse and didn't see me. I swear!" He lifted both hands. "I *hate* that birdhouse!"

Brittan narrowed her eyes and bit her tongue when she checked her watch again. Heather's tea had been in progress 35 minutes.

"Look," she said and marched back toward her driver's seat, "let's just exchange numbers and talk about it this evening, okay? I've really got to go. I'm already late for a reception for one of my best friends."

"So that's why you're all dressed up and look like a million bucks," he quipped.

Brittan paused before bending toward her purse. "Yep," she said as her face warmed a bit. The look in his eyes implied he was every bit as appreciative of her appearance as Rob Lightly had been. His hair glistened in the midday sun, and his unexpected smile took on a dazzling quality that nearly made Brittan forget the tea all over again.

Good grief, sister! she scolded herself. *Give him your number and get out of here!* She reached into her purse's side pocket and pulled out a calling card that simply had her name and cell number on it. She rarely gave out the cards, but was glad she had them when needed. She straightened, handed the guy the card, and said, "Call me after five, okay?"

"Sure." He removed his billfold and pulled out a card of his own. "And here's *my* card as well."

Brittan took it and read the inscription: *José Herrera, Manager, Herrera Craft and Gift Shops*. His contact information was below the name. "So you manage the birdhouse?" She chuckled.

"Yep. And I've already moved that baby around today more than I ever want to remember. I hope you *do* buy it and put me out of my misery."

"Okay, I'll just do that," Brittan agreed, and she realized she was grinning every bit as flirtatiously as she had at Rob Lightly.

"You know..." he hedged and glanced toward his vehicle, "it might be best for us to talk about our little fender-bender over dinner. Have you tried the Mediterranean place?" He pointed toward Beynards. "They have excellent sea bass."

Brittan blinked and tried to comprehend the full meaning of this guy's invitation. A horn's blast from across the intersection insisted she make her decision and kindly remove her body *and* her car.

"Okay," she heard herself agree. "What if we meet at six?"

"Sure!" he agreed. "And if you like, I can let you into the craft shop afterward so you can get that birdhouse."

Another horn demanded compliance. "It's a deal!" She dropped into the car.

Smiling, José hustled back to his car.

Brittan rolled up her window and thought, *What a day* this *has turned out to be. I haven't met a guy who caught my interest in months, and now great guys are dropping out of the sky!*

THREE

Brittan slipped into the Leighs' ballroom behind a group of ladies dressed in mid-afternoon finery. Heather stood in one corner, amiably chatting with one of Houston's most prestigious matrons, whose diamond earrings were nearly as big as the tulip bulbs in the chandelier. The occasional clink of fine china punctuated the low hum of feminine voices refined by the best social training. The place smelled of weak coffee and pastries and an occasional whiff of someone's expensive-beyond-belief perfume. While many of her contemporaries went for the exotic, imported stuff, Brittan always settled for Chanel No. 5. It suited her.

She sighed and closed her eyes as tension drained from her shoulders. She'd nearly violated a dozen traffic laws to get here. By the sound of the angry horns on the freeway, it was a small miracle she hadn't been involved in another fender-bender. She opened her eyes in time to see a waiter cruise by carrying a tray laden with little morsels. Brittan's stomach reminded her she hadn't eaten since breakfast, and she motioned for the man to come her way.

The cucumber sandwiches he offered looked about as satisfying as a toothpick, but Brittan didn't turn them down. Once her napkin was filled, she munched away and wished for a slice of pizza the size of the Empire State Building. *These little parties are real bummers when a gal has a serious appetite,* Brittan noted.

She glided from her corner to the one near a harpist strumming her instrument. Brittan looked around and decided no one had missed her. That problem aside, she concentrated on why the stoic harpist seemed so familiar. Then she recalled getting caught snooping in Mayor Michael Hayden's apartment. Brittan had been there because she suspected Michael was involved in framing an innocent pastor for pornography. Her suspicions had been completely unfounded, but Brittan had single-handedly destroyed the special evening Lorna planned for Michael, replete with the present harpist. The fiasco had nearly caused their breakup. Almost a year later, the memory still made Brittan wince. She wondered if the harpist remembered her.

Brittan ducked into another corner. That's where she found Lorna. The former tennis pro looked as calm as Brittan was rattled. Her shoulder-length brunette hair, trained into a flip, was a demure complement to her linen pantsuit, the color of ripe peaches.

"So *there* you are!" her friend chided. "Heather and I were wondering if you'd copped out on us."

"Not on your life," Brittan replied. "I was just...delayed." She glanced away.

"What? Did you finally meet the guy of your dreams and plan an elopement?" Lorna teased.

Brittan's attention snapped back to her friend. "No, not at all," she stated without lifting a brow. "I met *two* guys of my dreams and planned a date with one tonight. The other," she shrugged, "he's promising to call later."

Lorna's eyes bugged. "Are you serious?" she whispered.

"Am I ever serious?" Brittan replied and popped one of the microscopic sandwiches into her mouth.

"Oh my word!" Lorna gasped. "You haven't had a boyfriend in… forever. We didn't even think you really wanted one."

"Who says I want one?" Brittan defended, but didn't admit that she was beginning to *pine* for a great boyfriend and potential mate.

Lorna pressed her lips together and cut Brittan a glance that said, *You think I believe that now?*

"Remember Rob Lightly?" Brittan asked.

"You mean the precinct captain Rob Lightly? The guy we, um," she glanced over her shoulder, leaned closer, and whispered, "left the rose for last summer?"

"Yep. Well, believe it or not, his father lives a few houses away from my new house. Remember that dog I've been ready to assassinate?"

"Yes." Lorna nodded and lifted a fragile teacup to her lips.

"Well, he belongs to Rob's dad. The guy's an invalid. When Rob visits his dad, he lets the dog out now and then because the pooch stays inside with Mr. Lightly a lot. The dog's name is Elvis, by the way."

"Elvis?" Lorna laughed, causing two matrons to turn disapproving gazes their way.

Brittan shifted so that her back was facing them and rolled her eyes. Sometimes these events were just *too* stuffed-shirted. She gazed toward Heather. Petite and blonde, she wore her social smile with skill. Few would suspect it was a mask for her more relaxed personality. Idly Brittan wondered if any of these elite females were aware that the bride-elect held a black belt in karate and could take down men three times her size.

"So what about the other guy?" Lorna asked.

"Oh yes. *Him.* I actually had a fender-bender with him on the way over here. His mom owns a new gift shop in the little shopping center by the lake."

"And?" Lorna lifted her brows.

"His name's José Herrera. And yes, he's very much of the Latin persuasion. *Oo-la-la!*" Brittan wiggled her brows. "Short story: He asked me to dinner tonight. I agreed."

Lorna snickered and tucked her hair behind her ears. Her sizable diamond solitaire twinkled with the message that this gal was looking forward to a wedding of her own. "This is absolutely unbelievable," she gushed.

"Well believe it, sister," Brittan shot back. "I'm having a *very* good day." She winked.

"...and there's still no word on where the necklace is?" A woman's low voice sliced through Brittan's thoughts. She glanced to the left and spotted two women stopping near the fireplace.

The youngest looked like an Ethiopian princess with dark skin and delicate features. Her red suit completed her image of perfection. She set her teacup on the high-gloss, antique mantel and said, "No word. The detective has been on it for three whole months and is starting to make noises like it might be gone for good."

Lorna and Brittan exchanged glances.

"Have you seen today's headline?" Brittan whispered.

"Yep," Lorna whispered and cast another discreet glance toward the ladies.

Brittan followed her lead. The redhead was as polished as her darker companion, but not half as beautiful.

"I believe the lady in red is Matrice Bishop," Lorna observed. "She's on the museum's board of directors with my mom."

"Hmmm..." Brittan inserted her last cucumber sandwich into her mouth and thoughtfully chewed. "Sounds like the investigation isn't getting anywhere." She peered into her friend's eyes and waited for Lorna to follow her thoughts.

The brunette lifted her teacup to her lips and gazed over the rim at her friend. "It *has* been a while, hasn't it? You know my mom's the chairman of the board," she reminded Brittan.

"I know."

"Want me to go ahead?" Lorna asked.

The three friends had brainstormed about Lorna pilfering information from her mother's files, such as the access code to the museum's alarm system. Because of their hesitation, Lorna had yet to do anything about pouncing on the case.

"Let's talk with Heather," Brittan said. "I'm thinking it's time."

"Me too, me too," Lorna said in a singsong voice.

"And what are your thoughts on the Rose connection?" the redhead asked.

"I have my doubts," Matrice admitted. "Whoever took the necklace is probably just playing mind games."

"Those kind can be the scariest."

The three debutantes hadn't attempted to solve any cases since last summer when they'd uncovered the conspiracy to frame a young pastor for internet porn. Brittan, Heather, and Lorna usually stayed incognito after solving a major case. Other than Lorna's and Heather's fiancés, no one knew they were the Rose. Both Michael Hayden and Duke Fieldman vowed by their lives they wouldn't tell a soul.

"What I don't understand," the redhead continued, "is why anyone would want a rare necklace they couldn't display. I mean, if they *did,* the necklace would be spotted and confiscated."

"Well, there are some who just enjoy the thrill of purchasing the unattainable." Matrice crossed her arms. "They don't mind that they have to keep the item locked away for viewing only by a chosen few. As long as they can make a handful of contemporaries go green, they're happy. Besides, some don't care if anybody sees it. There's just this wicked thrill that goes with owning something rare—something they really aren't supposed to own."

Brittan gazed toward the long table, laden with all kinds of drinks. Coffee and tea claimed one end while cold drinks were on the other. She longed for one of the tall fruit punches topped with a tiny umbrella, but didn't dare move from her spot. By silent consensus, she and Lorna casually observed the crowd while gleaning all they could from the ladies' conversation.

During a lull, Brittan mused about a person who would steal precious artifacts. She imagined a James Bond sort of character... only more dangerous. Despite her mind's insistence that she should never align herself with such a man, Brittan found herself mesmerized by his ability to confiscate rare and guarded artifacts. The deed would require a great deal of planning and intellect. But then, most successful criminals were exceedingly smart.

Our job is to outsmart even him, she thought and smiled. The very idea of discovering who took the Incan treasure stimulated Brittan's creative energy. If they did solve the case, it would make international news and vindicate the Rose's honor.

※ ※ ※

Rob Lightly pulled his Dodge truck into his driveway next to his patrol car. He eyed the jungle gym his cousin's family had left behind when they moved to California. Herb and his wife, Paige, had four kids, all under eight. When Herb's engineering firm transferred him to California, Herb and Paige offered Rob the chance to rent their home. He'd readily agreed. Herb had promised to have the jungle gym removed by the time Rob took up residence. But as a true procrastinator, he had yet to follow through.

Rob glared at the apparatus and wondered if it was time he took matters into his own hands. More than anything else, he was tired of mowing around it. With a sigh, he put his rig into park, turned off the Kenny G CD, and crawled out of the truck. He'd barely let himself into the brick home's front door when his German shepherd, Rocky, dashed out of the house and straight toward his favorite oak tree.

"Okay," Rob said through a chuckle. "I guess I did leave you inside a little longer than usual."

With business taken care of, Rocky trotted back to his owner and sniffed his leg like he always did when Rob had been with Elvis.

"Smellin' a little competition, are we?" Rob asked and scratched the dog's ears.

Rocky licked his hand and then trotted back into the house. Rob always liked to tell everyone that Rocky owned the home and he was just his guest. Rob stepped into the living room. Other than the collection of Civil War swords mounted across one wall, the room was void of anything except what was absolutely necessary—a big screen TV, a sofa, two recliners, and a narrow coffee table big enough to hold a large bowl of popcorn. Rob shut the door and eyed last night's empty pizza box lying next to one of the recliners. He'd been off yesterday and today and had given most of that time to his father—except for the time spent watching the Yankees game last night.

He shoved his keys into his pocket and walked straight to the bookcase that held his college textbooks and a crime and punishment series that had proved enlightening on several cases Rob had worked. He reached for the large family Bible on the top shelf and inserted his fingers between the pages where a piece of wax paper protruded.

The Bible fell open to a single long-stemmed rose Rob had placed there last year. The Rose had left clues to an animal cruelty case on his patrol car's windshield. He hadn't told anyone he saved the flower. The act made him feel like a sentimental fool. Now nearly a year later, the flower was a reminder of the night Rob had discreetly followed a sedan from his neighborhood, to downtown Houston, and then to the parking garage of the Shay Building. He never told a soul that before he'd busted the animal cruelty case, he'd tracked the Rose.

That night he hadn't gotten a good look at the car's occupants. He only knew there were three people inside. By their size, he deduced they were women. He hadn't followed the car into the garage because he wanted to expedite the arrest of the jerks who mistreated dogs. Even if Rob hadn't been a police officer, that was one group of men he'd have strung up for their heartless crimes.

Sighing, he lifted the dried rose to his nose and sniffed. The faint smell brought Brittan Shay's Asian features to mind—dark hair, glasses, and a bright smile.

After busting the animal cruelty case, Rob ran a check and discovered that the Shay Building was full of executive offices...and had a penthouse on the top. That penthouse was occupied by Brittan Shay and her friend Lorna Leigh. When he ran the license plate number, Rob discovered it was a Hertz rental vehicle. He pulled a few strings and got Hertz to affirm what Rob's gut was already telling him. The car was rented to Brittan. Common sense told him one of the other members of the Rose was Brittan's roommate, Lorna. The third person in the car that night was still a mystery.

Rob laid the rose back on the wax paper and narrowed his eyes. This morning when he saw the Asian doll watching him as he read her message on the cloth, he knew his strategy was finally showing results. When Rob's dad, Simon, suddenly decided he needed to move away from the neighborhood he shared with Rob, he insisted that he move out to the lake. He'd picked out three lake houses before the idea even had time to settle with Rob.

When Simon asked Rob's opinion on which house he thought was best, Rob scouted out the neighborhoods and spotted Brittan Shay consulting with a landscaper. At first glance, he could hardly believe the woman really was *the* Brittan Shay. But when he ran a check on the address, Rob discovered he was having a *very good* day. Because all three of the lake houses were equally well-built and in good locations, Rob suggested his father buy the A-frame on the east shore...close to Brittan's place.

After a few weeks of no chance meetings, Rob began to ask God if He could arrange a meeting. Finally he decided that maybe

God wanted him to take a step in faith. He was on the verge of meandering Brittan's way to introduce himself when she sent the message via Elvis. Rob figured that was invitation enough. For months now thoughts of the Rose meandered through his mind as he followed Brittan Shay and Lorna Leigh in the society pages. Lorna was obviously attached to the mayor, but Brittan was the one who'd caught Rob's eye. He'd always been attracted to Asian women. Occasionally he dreamed of meeting Brittan. Today his dreams came true. To top it off, he was able to confirm what he was 99 percent sure of. She wasn't married or engaged.

Rob snapped the Bible shut. He hadn't told another soul he knew who the Rose was. Something inside insisted he should honor her... their...desire to stay incognito. He'd sensed their thrill in leaving the clues because, well, he was an investigator himself.

Rob reached into his shirt pocket, pulled out the card with Brittan's number on it, and kissed her name. "I'll give you a day or two to think about me," he mused. "And then I'll get into your space."

FOUR

Brittan stepped into the Mediterranean restaurant's foyer and was impressed with the place's upscale decor, replete with an original oil painting by artist P.C. Mosier. Her mom, a European art connoisseur, had purchased one of his pieces last year. This particular painting depicted a street in France with a restaurant and a man playing an accordion. The gold plate attached to the frame read *Street Music*.

She was a long way from being the art expert her mother was, but she did appreciate the effect the man's work had on her. He had an uncanny way of creating a 3-D effect that made the painting look as if it were seconds from bursting into real-life movement. She lightly stroked the edge of the canvas frame, relishing the feel of true art.

The delicate smells wafting in the restaurant seemed to ooze from the painting and caused her stomach to rumble. Brittan had only grabbed a few nibbles at Heather's tea and hadn't eaten since. If not for her finishing school training, she would stuff her face the minute the food was placed in front of her tonight. But she would follow protocol and eat with restraint.

Hovering near the hostess stand, Brittan smiled at the dark-haired woman who appeared to have stepped from the folds of a

Middle Eastern novel. Her black hair was piled high and made her dark eyes appear exotic, but the woman's features were strangely pointed, just stopping her from being beautiful.

"Do you have a reservation?" the woman questioned.

"No, I don't." Brittan shook her head. "I'm here to meet—"

"I'm sorry, but we're full this evening," she replied without a blink.

The door opened behind her, and Brittan turned to face the reason she was here. José Herrera looked even more dashing in a navy blue suit and scarlet tie than he had in his jeans and oxford shirt. "Hello, Liza," he said as he swooped into the place like he owned it. "I believe you have me down for two." He stopped beside Brittan and lightly rested his hand on her shoulder.

"Yes, of course," Liza said through a smile that couldn't have been more enchanting.

Brittan lifted her brows a bit and wondered if José had that effect on every woman. He'd certainly snared her attention, even after he'd crunched her fender.

Which is supposed to be the reason we're meeting, she reminded herself and followed the hostess through a maze of cushioned chairs and intimate tables and into an alcove, kept private by stucco walls on three sides. *But it feels more like romance,* she added.

"Perfect, Liza," José approved, and the hostess dismissed herself.

He stepped toward one of the chairs and pulled it out with the flourished practice of a gentleman. The appreciation in his eyes suggested this meeting really *was* about romance.

Brittan settled into the chair and placed her sequined evening bag near her feet. After Lorna's party, she'd hurried back to Pizzazz and purchased the dress in the window. Glancing down at the glistening fabric, the color of champagne, Brittan admitted that the tailored look was perfect for her...and this evening out.

A blonde waiter appeared, bowed, and began to recite the list of specialties. He concluded the spiel and presented a menu to each of them. "I'll be back in a few minutes to take your order," he stated.

Brittan wasn't the least bit surprised at the creative entrées or the prices that went with them. She eyed the gold ring on José's right hand and recalled his Volvo. Apparently he had a few dollars tucked away here and there.

"I'll start with a crab cake as an appetizer," José announced after glancing over the menu, "and then have the sea bass. What about you?"

"Sounds good to me," Brittan agreed and put aside her menu. "It's been ages since I had sea bass. I'm assuming it's served on a mound of mashed potatoes."

"You got it," José said through a grin and placed his menu on hers. "So tell me about yourself, Brittan Shay."

Her heart began a gentle pounding in the face of his sensual appraisal. She wondered how many women he'd captured with those dark eyes and full-lipped smile. At the moment, Brittan felt like she was the only woman in the world to him.

Her sensible side suggested she needed to grab the glass of cold water the waiter was now serving and splash it over her face. There was no sense in getting swept away by some guy she'd had a wreck with mere hours before.

Besides, her common sense insisted, *you don't even know if he's a man of faith.* If he didn't share her faith, there was no reason for her to waste her time. Despite what she'd hinted to Lorna, Brittan would only get serious about a man who shared her beliefs.

This is about the wreck first, she scolded herself. *As for romance... love takes a backseat until I know where he stands on his worldview... and who has his heart.*

"Aren't we supposed to be discussing the wreck?" she asked and wondered why her logic did nothing to slow her heart rate.

"Oh, that." He waved away the idea. "I talked to the guy at the body shop today. It's only going to take pennies to fix. I'll be glad to cover yours as well. There's no need to get insurance involved. Don't you agree?"

Brittan nodded and recalled saying something similar to him this afternoon. "I didn't have a chance to have my car looked at yet," she admitted. "But I thought the same. I don't mind covering my expense if you cover yours."

"Then it's a deal," he declared and extended his hand across the table.

She chuckled through the handshake.

"Now, where were we?" He rested his elbows on the table, loosely wove his fingers together, and gazed toward the ceiling. "Ah yes, I was asking you to tell me about yourself." He leaned closer, and this time there was no doubt that José Herrera had romance on the brain.

"Let's start with *you*," Brittan countered and picked up her ice water. She allowed the frigid liquid to weave a path to her stomach and cool her heating pulse. This guy had enough magnetism to melt a slab of steel. "Tell me about *your* life."

"I manage the craft and gift shops my mom and aunt own. There's not much more to it than that. It's a very boring existence. Or at least it was until this afternoon." He threw in a wink.

"For some reason I don't think your life is boring," she drawled.

He covered his heart with his hand and lightly complained, "But you hurt me with your skepticism, Senorita."

For the first time Brittan detected a faint tinge of a Spanish accent. *And that*, she concluded, *was feigned.*

"But I *am* boring," he insisted. "I work all week for a slave-driver mother who has me move birdhouses from one display window to the next and back again and only leaves me weekends to myself. I do my laundry on Saturday, and on Sunday, of course, I am a good man. I go to church."

"Church?" Brittan asked.

"Yes, of course." His earnest smile hinted that he believed *everyone* should go to church. "I attend a tiny church near my home west of Houston. It's not my mother's first choice for me, but the people love me, and I love them."

"I'm in the same boat. My friends and I attend a smaller church that my parents don't quite think is good enough." Brittan leaned forward. "But it fits our needs," she added. "I'm practical, but I'm still a woman of faith."

"Yes." José nodded. "I could tell. You have that…" He tilted his head, "That look about you."

Brittan sat straighter. "Thanks," she said and squared her shoulders. "I'm not perfect, but I do believe in Christ and try to follow Him."

"Already we have so much in common," he crooned. José smiled into Brittan's eyes and wondered how long it would take to compromise her faith. He *loved* finding nice young women who were a little *too* good and a little *too* sure of themselves.

When he'd seen her Jaguar at the intersection today, he'd purposefully waited until she pulled forward so he could ram his vehicle into hers. Yesterday he'd misjudged the distance between his bumper and a brick wall at the shopping strip. The result had been a crunched fender that someone would have to pay to repair. José had already planned to find someone to collide with to file a claim on *his victim's* insurance. His rule in life was to never pay for anything when he could get someone else to take the blame…and fork over the bucks.

But once he got a good look at Brittan, José changed his plans. Some things were worth paying for. And a chance to tango with the likes of Brittan Shay was alluring. Before he was through, José predicted Brittan would fall just like a dozen others before her.

I give her two months, he mused. That was a little longer than most, but there was a glint in her eyes that suggested she was a tad

bit stronger than his usual prey. Aside from that, her highly polished appearance and cropped, black hair screamed of money. And
José liked money. A lot. Enough to steal what he wanted when he
wanted. Enough to con an heiress into compromising her faith and
swindle her in the process.

When the waiter arrived to take their order, José served up a
practiced smile that usually ensured women were wilting within
the hour. But this woman squared her shoulders, broke eye contact,
and focused on the waiter.

Instead of waiting for him to place their order, she said, "I'll have
the sea bass, please, and the calamari for an appetizer."

José lifted a brow and allowed the waiter to note her request
before offering his. Brittan just might be a bigger challenge than
he realized. A thrill zipped through his gut. *The greater the challenge,
the greater the victory,* he mused. That was his motto in stealing forbidden artifacts…and women.

Once the waiter left, José decided a different breed of woman
just might require a different method of seduction. He settled back
into his seat and watched as Brittan indulged in the toasted bread
and pesto the waiter provided. Even though she casually placed a
bite into her mouth, her first chew was somewhat eager. That led
him to believe that even the strictest of social training couldn't
override her desire. *She must be hungry.* He hid a smile and hoped
her other instincts were as strong.

"You're starving," he commented.

She slowly swallowed and narrowed her eyes. "Why do you
say that?"

"Either you're very revealing or I'm very observant," he replied
and allowed one corner of his mouth to tilt upward. "Which is it?"

"I vote for you being very observant," she replied.

"You're also very smart, aren't you?" He lifted his water glass.

She lowered her gaze and suavely went for another morsel.

Hmmm…no comment. Most women would have dimpled into

a simpering fit at that point. Apparently Brittan was comfortable enough with herself not to quaver when receiving compliments.

By the time the fish arrived, José decided the last thing he needed to do was give Brittan the slightest hint of his goals. If she suspected, she'd mercilessly dump him and never look back.

After dinner he opened the restaurant's door for her, and they stepped into the cool evening breeze. José wondered if this was a woman he might have to marry to meet his goals. The thought troubled him a tad. He'd never planned to include that deed in his life. Marriage was the same as a locked cage. He eyed her cream-colored jaguar. Even with a crumpled fender, it oozed money and power.

But if it's a solid gold cage, maybe it wouldn't be so bad, he reasoned. Besides, he was so good at covering his tracks, even Brittan Shay would never suspect he did what he wanted when he wanted.

Normally at this point José would take his victim's hand and give it a warm squeeze. Instead he barely brushed her elbow with his fingertips and nudged her toward the parking lot.

"Oh wait!" she exclaimed. "You said you'd take me to your mom's shop and let me buy the birdhouse."

"Yes!" He pressed the heel of his hand against his forehead. "How could I have forgotten?" He lifted both hands to the heavens and repeated his mother's favorite phrase, "God be praised! At last I can get rid of the thing."

Brittan's low-toned chuckle sharply contrasted with the high-pitched giggles of the airheads he usually dealt with.

"Come on!" He motioned toward the shop. "We'll take care of this sale pronto! I'm ready to burn that birdhouse!" José unlocked the shop and ushered her inside. The smell of honeysuckle potpourri made him sneeze. "Sorry," he apologized. "It takes me a while to acclimate to the aroma Mom insists on having in her stores."

"No problem," Brittan replied. "I kind of like it." She pivoted to face him and smiled into his eyes. "I assume it's potpourri?"

José nodded.

"Maybe I'll look at it while I'm here."

He purposefully kept his smile slow and a little sexy—just not too much. "You can look at anything you like, lady."

Her expression never changed. Then her focus slid to the birdhouse in the display case.

Hmmm, he thought and couldn't remember a pursuit that had intrigued him more.

José reached to flip on the lights but hesitated. "I think I'll leave the lights off," he said. "I don't want anybody thinking we're open."

"Good idea." Brittan nodded.

Besides, it's cosier with the lights off. He locked the store door as the evening sun was lowering behind a bank of purplish clouds, providing just enough glow to put the kiss of intimacy in the shadowed shop. José had been told he looked particularly alluring in the shadows, and he planned to take advantage of every opportunity to impress Brittan.

FIVE

"This is absolutely perfect!" Heather cooed as she slumped into one of Eden's lawn chairs. She slipped off her spiked sandals and wiggled her toes in the grass.

Brittan settled in the chair across from Heather and hid a frown. For years she puzzled over why both her friends were so determined to destroy their feet with lethal shoes. She always chose sensible loafers, reasonable pumps, or classy flat sandals for summer. The cooling grass tickled her toes that were strapped by golden leather.

Lorna claimed the seat between Brittan and Heather and kicked off her own spikes.

Brittan briefly wondered how many years would lapse before both her friends were supplementing a podiatrist's house payment.

That afternoon they'd all gone to the bridal boutique for Brittan and Lorna's fitting for bridesmaid dresses. When the clerk pulled out matching spiked heels tall enough to cause a nosebleed, Brittan had drawn the line. Heather had finally agreed to compromise. The pumps she settled on were still a bit tall for Brittan's taste, but she didn't think her feet would be ruined if she wore them for one evening.

The three friends had topped off the trip with dinner at Mario's, one of Houston's favored Italian restaurants. Brittan loosened the button on her linen skirt's waistband. She'd eaten way too much and felt like an overstuffed Christmas turkey.

Heather slumped against the back of the chair and stretched her legs, clad in a slinky pair of slacks. "I promise, by the time the wedding gets here, I'm going to be too worn out to walk down the aisle. Mom is *obsessed* with turning this into the social event of the century."

Lorna wiggled her engagement ring, and the bluish diamond sparkled in the evening sun. "Believe it or not, my mom and dad are fine with Michael's idea that he and I get married in the Bahamas."

"Sounds like the smart move to me." Brittan rested her elbows on the chair's armrests and made a tent of her fingers. "The media treats you guys like you're the king and queen of Houston. No telling who'd crash your wedding if you have it here."

"Tell me about it!" Lorna complained and tugged at the neck of her knit blouse. "Just about the time we think we're shaking the media, a camera goes off in our faces. Good grief!" She lifted both hands. "People need to get a life. If they're bored enough to obsess over us, they need to volunteer at a nursing home or at least do something humanitarian. We're not Prince William and Kate Middleton, for cryin' out loud!"

"Ah, but Michael Hayden's not just any mayor," Heather said without opening her eyes. "And you're not an ordinary fiancée. He looks like a movie star, and you're an accomplished athlete. What do you expect?" She shrugged, and her blonde hair slinked around her shoulders.

"Yes, Heather, and it would appear that your mother is determined to make a celebrity out of Duke," Brittan mused and shifted against the weight in her stomach. "Ever since he signed that contract on the novel series, she's been…uh…enthusiastic."

Heather chuckled. She opened her eyes and slid a sideways glance toward Brittan. "Thanks to your dad, Duke is now an 'acceptable' mate for me."

"Thanks to *Duke,* from what I understand," Brittan admitted. "Dad was worried sick some other publisher would gobble him up before our editor moved on the series. Dad says Duke's a *very good* writer."

"Well, *I* think so." Heather rested her hand against her chest and sat straight in the chair. She gazed toward the lake, now lapping at the shoreline as the eight o'clock sun dipped below a bank of clouds brewing on the horizon.

Brittan followed her gaze and recalled a similar sunset two nights ago after her date with José. She eyed the birdhouse nestled in the elephant ears and hid a smile. By the time they left the store, José had been looking like a love-struck schoolboy. She'd remained cool externally and gave him no indication of just how much she was warming up. No sense in appearing *too* eager. That would take away from the chase.

She hadn't mentioned José to her friends much, only casually indicating she'd enjoyed her date. Brittan sensed their curiosity and nearly laughed out loud when, during dinner, she caught them nodding at each other after she mentioned seeing a guy who resembled José.

"So…what are we thinking about that Incan necklace situation?" Lorna sat straighter in her chair and glanced toward Brittan and then Heather. "Should we go after the thief?"

"Do you think that's what he wants?" Heather worriedly eyed Lorna. "I thought that's what we decided."

"But it's been three months, and they still haven't found him," Lorna replied.

"His guard is probably down by now," Brittan speculated.

"Do you think he's still in the area?" Heather questioned.

"There's only one way to find out," Brittan said in a sing-song voice.

"Where do we start?" Lorna stood, paced toward the water, and swiveled to face her friends. The evening breeze, laden with the scent of the lake, tossed her hair about her face. She looked like a model posing at a photo shoot.

"I think we ought to go to the museum office, tell them we're the Rose, and ask who they think took the necklace." Heather's words dripped with sarcasm.

Lorna rolled her eyes. "What if I get the alarm system's access code from my mom's files? Then we can sneak in and copy the surveillance cameras' digital files."

"That works." Brittan scooted to the edge of her seat. "If I can get in and take a look at the police department's investigation files, we could go on from there."

Heather and Lorna looked at her like she'd suggested they rob a bank.

"You mean you'd actually *do* that?" Heather squeaked, her blue eyes rounding.

"Well…if it's for the good of society, yes." Brittan shrugged. "I mean, I got into the murdered mayor's computer, right? And Lorna borrowed that old man's computer last year so we could go through it for clues on the porno case."

"So what are you planning?" Lorna asked, crossing her arms. "Borrow the FBI computer system, comb through it, and return it?"

"Uh, no." Brittan gazed toward a sailboat skimming the rippling water. "I'd probably try to access the local police files. From what I understand, one of the Houston investigators is working closely with the FBI. If I can gain access to that person's office and computer…" She nibbled at her thumbnail and studied the sailboat.

"Is it just me, guys, or are we getting braver?" Heather remarked. "I mean, we started out uncovering a hacker from afar. Next thing you know, Lorna breaks into some guy's pickup in broad daylight and lifts his laptop. And now," she waved toward Brittan, "you're talking about going through police files. At this rate I might be the only bride in Houston who spends her honeymoon in jail!"

"And who went undercover at city hall?" Lorna challenged. "And let's not forget your little trip through the woods last year when you got up close and personal on that animal cruelty case." She wagged her index finger back and forth. "You got close enough to take digital shots of those guys. If they'd seen you, they probably would have killed you! I nearly swallowed my toes!"

"Don't you mean you nearly swallowed your *tonsils?*" Brittan squinted and gazed up at her wide-eyed friend.

"No. I don't have any tonsils," Lorna explained, her face impassive. "They were removed when I was ten."

Heather giggled. A chuckle burst from Brittan.

Lorna crossed her arms and huffed. "Okay, you got me…*again!*" she complained and tapped her toes. "Are you happy?"

"I promise, I think you should just change your name to Madame Malaprop and be done with it."

"Ha, ha, ha," Lorna drawled.

A distant barking mingled with the soft hum of a fishing barge trolling offshore. As the barge moved farther from shore, the barking grew nearer. Finally Brittan was jolted into the realization that the bark sounded somewhat familiar. She recalled hearing that exact bark three days ago when Elvis chased the neighbor's cat up a palm tree. The idea of Elvis erupting into Eden sent Brittan to her feet.

"Oh my word!" she mumbled. "He's back."

"Oh look!" Heather exclaimed. "He must be part golden retriever. Isn't he just gorgeous?"

"Yes, and you should see what he keeps doing to my *gorgeous* yard," Brittan groused. After her little chat with Rob, Brittan hadn't caught one glimpse of Elvis. She attributed that to Rob being more conscientious about his father's pet. But now she wondered if Rob was slipping up in the worst way. Elvis loped straight into Brittan's yard, his nose pointed toward the geraniums...again.

"What is the deal with you and those flowers?" Brittan asked. On the verge of scolding the animal, she recalled Rob mentioning that Elvis was his father's canine "nurse," for lack of a better word. The pooch was living his life cooped up and probably needed some wild escapades to keep from getting cabin fever.

Brittan sighed. "Come here, Elvis!" she called. "Come on, boy!"

The dog stopped and looked straight at Brittan. Dubiously he wiggled his ears, panted, twitched his tail, and then stepped toward her.

"Come on, guy!" Brittan encouraged, and suddenly Elvis romped straight at her. Expecting him to stop, she bent toward him...just as he jumped. The result was a tangle of paws and arms and legs that tilted Brittan sideways and then sent her sprawling. Her shoulder hit the ground first, and her breath swooshed out on a surprised grunt. No sooner had she flopped onto her back than Elvis was there, straddling her and licking her face.

Enveloped in the moist essence of doggie breath, Brittan squealed, "Stop!" and pushed at the dog.

Elvis responded with another lick.

"Brittan!" Heather exclaimed. "Are you okay?"

"Yes!" Brittan bellowed and shoved against the canine. After a strong hand reached for the dog's collar and hauled him off her, Brittan peered up into Rob's face.

His grin couldn't have been more audacious. "Looks like Elvis is in love," he commented. "Sure you're okay?"

An all-too-familiar chuckle accompanied Elvis' panting, and Brittan shot Lorna a glare. Lorna covered her mouth and studied the grass.

"Elvis!" Heather encouraged and then whistled.

Rob released the dog, who bounded toward this new interest while Rob offered Brittan a hand. She gladly accepted the assistance and rose to her feet. Brushing at her new linen skirt and short jacket she sighed over a few grass stains. "Ah well, easy come, easy go," she mumbled.

"I'll pick up the tab on the cleaning," Rob offered.

"No, that's okay," she replied. He responded with a deepening grin that made Brittan wonder how she'd let José Herrera blot out the memory of Rob's dimples. Brittan had given little thought to Rob since her date with José. Even though she hadn't dismissed the guy, he had yet to intrigue her. Brittan *did* have a thing for Latinos, and Rob couldn't help that his gene pool was Caucasian.

"Looks like I'm going to have to bite the bullet and have him sent to obedience school." Rob placed his hands on his hips and gazed at the dog now basking in Heather's attention.

Brittan eyed her friend. "She's got such a way with animals," she admitted and shook her head. "I promise, she could talk a grizzly into giving up a boatload of trout."

"Maybe I should send Elvis home with *her* for a couple of weeks," Rob teased.

"Seriously, she's a board member of the regional humane society. She could probably hook you up with a good animal trainer."

"And I'm guessing you'd be willing to pay for it?" Rob smirked and reached up to pull a blade of grass from her hair.

Brittan smoothed at her hair, honestly appraised him, and finally decided to blurt out the truth, no matter how cute his dimples were. "Yes. Who trained your German shepherd?"

"How'd you know I have a German shepherd?" Rob asked.

Brittan froze. After a second she glanced at the ground and frantically searched for her brain. It must have fallen out when she took that tumble. Otherwise she'd have never blundered so badly. She just let Rob Lightly know she was privy to personal information he'd never told her.

"Uh…" She snatched at the first thing that came to her mind, "Did you tell me the other day?"

Rob knitted his brows and gazed at her for a few puzzled seconds. "Did I?" he asked.

"Well, I somehow know, don't I?" Brittan lifted both hands and shrugged. This was going beautifully. She wasn't lying, but at the same time she was wiggling her way out of confessing that she'd seen him and his dog before.

"Hi! I'm Lorna Leigh." Lorna strategically wedged her way into the conversation and extended her hand toward Rob.

He took it and smiled through the shake. "Nice to meet you, Lorna. I'm Rob Lightly."

"Yes, I figured as much. Brittan told us she met you a few days ago." Lorna cut a glance at Brittan that said, *Have you lost your mind?* "She told us all about Elvis," she added and chortled at the dog.

"Yes, he does get around." Rob inserted his hands into his shorts pockets and snickered. "Actually, I've already trained him," he added with a special grin for Brittan. "He sniffs out pretty ladies and leads me straight to them."

Brittan's cheeks warmed, but she refused to reveal one hint of the effect of Rob's blue-eyed appreciation. Because she was half Asian, her skin tone didn't easily reveal blushes, and Brittan had learned to hide any hint of chagrin with a blasé expression.

Lorna, on the other hand, wasn't half as couth. She wiggled her eyebrows at Brittan and didn't even try to hide the gesture from Rob.

Brittan thought part of Lorna's brain must have fallen out too.

"So…" Rob turned toward Heather, who was wrestling with Elvis.

"Oh, this is my friend Heather Winslow." Brittan gestured at Heather, who stepped forward. While Rob was shaking Heather's hand, Brittan leaned close to Lorna and mouthed, "He's on the police force, remember?" She looked into Lorna's eyes and knew she understood the unspoken message. Rob was being *very* friendly, and he just might be the way to gain access to police files.

SIX

As Rob shook hands with Heather, he noticed her ruby engagement ring and recalled seeing a big write-up in the paper about her engagement to the newspaper reporter turned author—Duke someone. Rob deduced that he'd just encountered the third member of the Rose.

Apparently Brittan was the only one of the three who wasn't engaged. The other two had nabbed men in key positions in Houston society. Heather had her newspaper reporter and he'd read that Lorna was involved with the mayor. What great cover. After all, Lorna would simply be a "nice little mayor's wife." Who would suspect she was part of the Rose...or that the reporter who wrote about the Rose was married to a member?

Very convenient. Rob cut a quick glance at Brittan. He briefly wondered if he might hold appeal simply because of his position. If he and Brittan were to become a couple, that would allow the Rose to have access to the police department.

He eyed Heather and then Lorna and wondered if their current engagements were driven by love. Both young women looked as guileless as Easter rabbits. Rob hoped neither of them had made cold-hearted moves to marry key men to further their Rose endeavors. If Brittan showed interest in him, he hoped it was for himself, not his job. He glanced toward the rippling water and decided it was best to proceed cautiously. No sense getting his heart ripped out because he fell too fast and discovered in the aftermath that Brittan was choosing him only because he was a cop.

Heather cleared her throat, and Rob realized they were trapped in silence. He focused on Heather again.

"If you don't mind, I'll take Elvis for a walk," she offered.

"That's fine," Rob agreed. "I left his leash at home. I was just supervising his free time." He looked quickly toward Brittan. "Well, more or less," he admitted. "He's got a mind of his own. I don't know if Brittan told you, but he keeps getting out of his pen even though I've had it repaired. He's a canine Houdini. I really hate to leave him cooped up in that tiny yard all the time."

"You're very thoughtful," Heather said through an admiring smile. "A lot of people aren't half as considerate when it comes to animals."

"Thanks. I'm not a rabid animal rights activist, but I do have some very strong opinions about respecting them. I'm a precinct captain with the Houston PD. I worked that big animal cruelty case last year." He looked straight into Heather's eyes and didn't blink. "Do you remember it?"

She glanced away and bent to scratch Elvis's ears. "Yes, of course. I'm on the board of the regional humane society so we were all thrilled with how that turned out."

"Brittan just told me you might know a good dog trainer." He squatted and clapped for Elvis. The dog responded with a jovial romp, and Rob stroked his silky fur.

"Of course," Heather agreed. "I'd be glad to recommend someone."

Rob placed his hands on either side of the dog's face. "Are you ready to go for a walk with Miss Heather?" he asked.

Elvis' eager woof was answer enough.

"Well, go on!" Rob encouraged. "Go for a walk!"

"Come on, Elvis!" Heather encouraged, and the dog gleefully followed her toward the lake. As Heather trotted away, Rob realized she was barefoot. He caught sight of a pair of spike sandals near her chair and couldn't blame her for shedding them.

"Rob, I'm going inside to get some drinks. Want one?" Lorna asked.

Rob swiveled to face Brittan and her friend. "Sure!"

"I should go too," Brittan said and stepped toward the house.

"No, that's okay, girlfriend," Lorna chimed in with a wink. "I've got it. I know where everything is."

Brittan shrugged and said, "Okay. Suit yourself. What do you want, Rob?" She turned toward him. "I've got sodas and—"

"Do you have iced tea?"

"Sure. Bottled okay?"

"Perfect." Rob gave her the thumbs-up while Lorna hurried from the yard. He smiled toward Brittan. She returned the grin before an uneasy silence settled between them.

Rob had just arrived at his dad's when he saw Brittan's Jaguar pull into her driveway. After a few minutes with his dad, he used taking Elvis for a walk as an excuse to get out and hopefully encounter Brittan. When Elvis tried to go south, Rob called him north—straight toward Brittan's yard. He hoped she was outside and was immeasurably pleased when he spotted her.

Rob had her where he wanted her, but he was suddenly stricken with the awkwards. He hadn't seriously pursued a woman since before he started his master's degree. Now that it was behind him, Rob was realizing just how much of his life was consumed by his job and academic pursuits. His cousin encouraged him to get out more. He even called last night with the offer of a blind date. Rob declined and hinted that he'd found a girlfriend on his own. When Herb pressed for details, Rob changed the subject. Sometimes he liked keeping stuff to himself until it was a done deal.

"Mind if I sit down?" Rob asked.

"Of course not," Brittan replied. When he sat, she claimed the chair closest to him.

Rob gazed into her eyes and smiled.

She returned a grin and glanced down. At first Rob thought the move was out of shyness, which stirred his interest. But when she lifted her gaze to his, her expression held a forthright edge.

"Did you say you got the fence fixed?"

"Yep. I was just taking Elvis for a walk. He wanted to go south…" Rob allowed the implied message to hang between them.

"Oh." Brittan pressed her lips together, but an impish smile pushed past her resistance.

"Nice evening," Rob mused and gazed across the yard.

"Very," Brittan agreed. "I love the way it smells out here this time of day."

"Me too." He inhaled the aroma of the lake and the foliage while debating whether or not he should give Brittan a hard time for slipping up about knowing his German shepherd. He knew he hadn't mentioned Rocky during their first meeting. She obviously saw him the night they left the rose on his patrol car. Rob was as impressed with the suave way she avoided lying about the slip as he was with the way the Rose placed the clues on his car. While his mischievous side insisted he resurrect the topic, his sensible side suggested he was better off dropping it. The last thing he wanted to do was let her know he knew who the Rose was. Before their relationship went any further, Rob wanted to make sure she was interested in him as a man, not merely as a precinct captain. Her lack of knowledge about *his* knowledge was best for now. This way he could make a healthier assessment of her motives. As sharp as she was, putting her on the spot about her slip of the tongue just might be all she needed to figure out that he knew she was part of the Rose.

Rob stretched his legs and cut her a lazy grin. Her smile verged on flirtatious, and Rob was sorely tempted to reach for her hand. Whatever happened between them, he was ready for the adventure.

He'd be careful but still enjoy the quest. Regardless of her motives, Brittan Shay was exactly the kind of woman who could hold his attention for a long, long time...maybe even a lifetime. She wasn't drop-dead gorgeous, and that was good. Rob never had gone for women like that. Brittan was attractive enough to turn a few heads, but just as important she was smart and witty, with the perfect level of self-assurance.

As the sun sank lower behind the bank of clouds, Rob thought about how much vacation time he'd accrued. He had a good three weeks to use between now and August. *Maybe I should take it earlier in the summer than later,* he mused. He decided he was due some time at his dad's lake house. After all, the place needed a good bit of work.

※ ※ ※

José pulled his Volvo into Brittan's driveway, and the sight of her Jaguar spawned a satisfied warmth in his gut. He'd discreetly asked where she lived before they parted two nights ago, and after a brief hesitation, she told him. José responded by politely asking if he could drop in one evening. She agreed.

He'd called her cell phone 30 minutes ago to ask about coming over this evening. But when she didn't answer or return the call, José decided to swing by her house and see if she was home. She'd mentioned that she spent many evenings enjoying the sunset, and he gambled this was one of those evenings.

With most women he wouldn't have been half as considerate... or archaic in his approach. But Brittan Shay wasn't "most women." And whatever effort he expended would be worth the prize.

He placed the Volvo in park, turned off the engine, and stepped from the car's chill into the balmy evening. Today had been a bit warmer than usual, but this evening held a promise for the perfect romantic encounter by the lake. Chuckling under his breath, José snapped the door shut. The second he did, he recalled the single long-stemmed red rose lying in the passenger seat. He rounded the car, retrieved the rose, and decided to check out the backyard before knocking at the front door. As he rounded the house of many windows, the sound of light conversation peppered with laughter floated from the back.

He stepped into the landscaped garden and, like any predator, absorbed every detail during his approach. Brittan sat in a wooden lawn chair holding a bottled drink. Near her reclined a man whose profile he didn't recognize. A brunette claimed the chair on the other side of the guy. José assumed the two were a couple...maybe a relative and his wife visiting Brittan. Near the shore, a lithe blonde frolicked with a golden retriever.

His gaze settled back on the person beside Brittan. As he neared, José debated the best approach. *Not too bold,* he coached himself and eyed the man. If this male was interested in Brittan and not the other woman, he needed to know Brittan was off-limits—at least for now. Later, when José was done with her, the guy could have her. But for tonight she was still on José's wish list. And while he knew he shouldn't be brash, he also wanted to send a clear message to this potential competition...just in case.

José cruised closer and made his presence known with a subtle cough. Brittan turned to face him. The other two followed suit.

"Oh, hello!" she said with a surprised smile that soon turned edgy. Her quick glance toward the man in the lawn chair was the only clue José needed.

So, the jerk's here for Brittan. José covered his scowl with an ingenuous smile that encompassed them all.

"Hello, beautiful!" José extended the flower to Brittan and let the implication fall where it may. Her grateful smile coupled with the competition's faint frown heightened José's sense of victory. "I called to see if I could drop by, but when you didn't answer I decided to take my chances."

"I left my cell phone in the house," she replied and accepted the rose.

While Brittan inhaled the flower's fragrance, José's attention trailed toward the brunette, whose gaze bordered on a stare. José swallowed a chuckle. Apparently he'd created a situation. José thrived on discord—anything to make life less boring.

Brittan stood and extended her hand toward him. "José, this is my friend Rob Lightly and another friend Lorna Leigh."

"So pleased to meet you," José purred and extended a hand first to Rob and then to Lorna. "A lovely evening," he commented, "but not nearly as lovely as the ladies." He smiled into Lorna's eyes and then focused on Brittan.

She glanced down, adjusted her glasses, and maintained the near-stoic expression José was beginning to suspect masked deep passions. At least he hoped so.

He peered down at Rob, whose scowl couldn't have been more fulfilling. José had debated what to wear this evening and was now thankful he'd chosen the lightweight sport coat and matching slacks. Not only did his natural good looks outshine Rob Lightly's, but he was dressed far nicer than Rob in his stonewashed shorts and a worn T-shirt. José lifted his chin and stopped short of strutting around the yard.

No sense rubbing in the obvious, he admonished.

"Would you like something to drink?" Brittan asked.

"Sure," José agreed.

"I'll get it." Lorna hopped up. "We have any soda you could want and bottled tea and water."

José agreed to water and then motioned toward another wooden lawn chair under an oak tree. "Do you mind if I pull that chair over?" he asked.

"Here. You can have my chair." Rob stood and moved to Brittan's side. "I was about to leave anyway."

"But you don't have to leave," Brittan protested.

He eyed the rose, and José nearly laughed.

"Actually, I've got to be at the station early in the morning," he mumbled.

"Rob's a precinct captain with the Houston Police." Brittan tucked her hair behind her ear and cast Rob a glance of approval.

José fought a glower. But then the serpent within chuckled, and a slow smile relaxed José's features. *So this is one of the idiots I've managed to fool. Maybe this meeting will be more amusing than I imagined.* Like a tiger stalking a naive rabbit, José bathed Rob in an admiring gaze. "I've always had so much respect for police officers." He tilted his head and was careful to keep every feature camouflaged with respect. "I had a brother who was an officer," he lied.

"Oh really?" Rob lifted his brows and gazed into his eyes, apparently buying every word.

"Yes." José nodded and gazed toward the lake. "He was killed in the line of duty. I don't talk about it much." He purposefully made his voice go thick and sensed the silent compassion he'd skillfully extracted from his audience. A strategic glance back at the two revealed that Brittan was the one with most of the compassion. Rob's eyes suddenly held a look of skepticism, although his mouth had softened a bit.

Hmmm, José thought. *Rob Lightly's a little harder around the edges. Not easy. Might not hurt to be on guard.*

Part of José's pleasure was centered on his superior intelligence. He'd outwitted the best. As long as he could keep Brittan enthralled, Rob would be no threat. But in his presence, José reveled in the satisfaction of looking into the eyes of the law that wanted to capture him but couldn't.

"So tell me about your work, Rob." José leaned toward the policeman with feigned interest.

Rob's candid appraisal did nothing to alter José's aura of rapt interest.

"How long have you been a police officer?" he added.

"About 13 years," Rob answered. "I started at 20 while I was still in college. Once I finished my bachelor's degree, I took a few years off from school, and I just wrapped up my master's degree a few months ago."

"What's your master's in?" Brittan enquired.

"Criminal justice. They bumped me to precinct captain when I got halfway through."

"Wow!"

Brittan's focus on Rob would have normally disturbed José, but he was too pleased with the clues that said Brittan and Rob had only met recently. That meant their relationship was still a light flirtation and nothing more.

Rob slipped his hands into his shorts pockets and gazed down at Brittan like a connoisseur of fine art relishing a masterpiece. "I've toyed around a time or two with applying to be chief of police." He shrugged. "Maybe when the time's right."

"Oh, so you're a smart man," José oozed.

Rob's eye twitched. He tossed José a glance and shrugged. "I guess that all depends on what your measuring stick is."

A warm breeze whispered through the trees with a promise of summer in its breath. José didn't verbally press Rob for his meaning, but lifted his brows in silent query.

"If you're comparing me to other human beings..." Rob shrugged. "Well, maybe. You can always find somebody out there who outshines you. That's a given. But if you're comparing me to God, then I'm nothing. And, well, He's the only one who matters, right?"

"But of course," José readily agreed and watched Brittan's Rob-focus warm by the second. "We all are worms compared to Him," José added. "I am daily taken by His creation." He motioned toward the sunset spreading molten gold on the lake. He allowed his gaze to settle on Brittan and willed her to catch his eye. She obeyed. José imagined kissing her and didn't even try to hide his desire.

"Well, I'll take Elvis and go on back to the house," Rob rushed.

"Dad's probably wondering what happened to me." He laid his hand on Brittan's shoulder and looked her in the eyes. "Mind if I call later?" he asked.

"Of course." She shook her head and blinked. "I mean, no. No, I don't mind."

"Okay, great!" he said through an eager smile. After shooting a pointed glance at José, Rob pivoted toward the golden retriever and the blonde. "Come on, Elvis!" he called, and the dog loped toward him.

SEVEN

Rob had only taken one look at José Herrera before pegging him. *The guy's a snake,* he thought as he waved one last time toward Brittan.

She returned the wave, and the viper quickly distracted her. Rob had seen his kind more often than not on the other side of the bars. *José could be a textbook case for a mastermind,* Rob deduced.

He picked up his pace and jogged along the shoreline across the connecting lawns. *Oh get off it,* he scolded. *You're going too far. Just because he's willing to lie to get a chick doesn't mean he belongs behind bars.* Most guys are guilty of trying to impress a woman or two. Rob admitted he was guilty of that in his younger years. But that was before he got serious about Christ.

As he stepped onto his father's lawn, Rob bent to pet Elvis. "Good dog!" he cheered while catching a final glimpse of Brittan and the snake. Elvis licked his hands, and Rob fought the urge to race back to Brittan's yard and lick José—in the old-fashioned, schoolyard sense. He swiped at a trickle of sweat sliding down his forehead.

"Brittan, you're too smart to let somebody like him dupe you," Rob mumbled and straightened. *Any woman who can play the Rose should be able to see through the lines that creep is laying on you.*

He placed his hands on his hips, glared at the A-frame lake house, and pondered the irony of his previous thoughts. He'd decided to take it slow with Brittan in case she was interested in Rob only for his position. But now Brittan appeared as interested in José as she was in him...maybe even more.

"So much for *that* worry," he growled and strode across the yard. The dog bounded forward and barked at the home's back door.

Head bent, Rob moved past the lawn chairs, closed the gate, and rubbed the back of his neck. The sound of the back door opening caught Rob's attention. His dad appeared in the doorway, trying to keep his balance while Elvis barged into the house.

"Whoa there!" Simon protested.

"Elvis!" Rob called, but the dog was too interested in the bowl of Alpo just inside the utility room to heed the reprimand.

"It's his dinnertime, and he knows it," Simon said through a smile.

"Yep," Rob agreed. "I think we need to get him to a trainer. He knocked over the new neighbor," Rob complained while following his father into the home. The screen door clapped shut behind him.

"You look like she tried to slap you for it," Simon replied as he observed his son.

Rob encountered his dad's sharp blue eyes and debated what to say. His dad looked no older than 45, but he was a full 13 years older than that. His tanned skin and thick dark hair radiated health. His trim physique confirmed it. The slight scar on his right cheek and the prosthesis extending from one leg of his shorts were the only signs of physical hardship. Rob knew differently. He also knew that most mature, single women didn't care that the tall man had lost a leg in Vietnam. Women had been throwing themselves at Simon ever since Rob's mother died two years ago. Simon hadn't fallen for any of them, although that 40-something doctor last year had been a close call.

Rob shuddered with the thought. He couldn't imagine having a stepmother that young.

"Well, are you going to answer me?" Simon quipped, "Or just stand there and look at me like a mute martyr?"

"Mute martyr?" Rob echoed and shouldered his way past his father. Ever since his dad started writing a year ago, he came out with terms that sounded downright poetic. But sometimes Rob wasn't in the mood for poetic. Like now. And when those times happened, it got on his nerves. Like now.

Rob opened the fridge and snatched a bottle of water. He downed half of it before he remembered he wasn't even thirsty. He'd already drank a glass of tea with the takeout hamburger he had for dinner, and then he'd downed another tea at Brittan's place.

"What happened?" Simon queried.

"Another guy showed up," Rob explained.

"Ah, a little competition," Simon said through a slow smile.

"Do you have to be so happy about it?" Rob challenged and set the bottle on the counter near the empty Whataburger bag.

Simon laughed outright. "I think it's hilarious!" he crowed. "You went down there thinking you were large and in charge. You were going to go slow and be in control." He glided his hand through the air. "And you come back with your ears down and your tail between your legs. So who's in control *now?*"

Rob stared at the tile and then lifted his gaze to his father. "Do you sit around and think up these things to say," a smile twitched at Rob's lips, "or does it just come spontaneously?"

Simon's grin broadened. "It's all spontaneous!" He gripped Rob's shoulder. "Seriously, does she already have a boyfriend or what?"

"I don't know." The kitchen still smelled of hamburgers, and Rob wished he'd ordered more. He peered inside the bag to see if a stray fry might have gone unnoticed. "I don't think so." His search was rewarded, and he popped the salty fry into his mouth.

"At least nothing official," he muttered between chews. "He's very interested, but I'd wager my best tennis racket that he's a snake." Rob swallowed.

"Hmmm...you don't usually say that unless you mean it."

"Hey, I don't say *anything* I don't mean!"

"Yeah, right!" Simon remarked and rolled his eyes. He opened the refrigerator and extracted his own bottle of water. "Listen, son, if you really like her, don't be so quick to retreat. Comprendé?" He lifted his brows and shut the refrigerator door. "Sometimes the best bones go to the dogs who hang around the longest."

"I know. But that guy was throwing her so many lines that if I hadn't left, I would have beat the stuffing out of him."

"I feel your pain. That's what I wound up doin' to that guy your mom dated before me."

Rob furrowed his brow and waited for his father to continue. Simon didn't talk about Clarice Lightly much, so when he did Rob took the time to listen. He'd loved his mom so much. They'd been as close as Rob was to his dad now. They had an amazingly close relationship. Rob respected both of them, mainly because they'd respected him enough to give him a voice and allow him to be who he was.

"I lived down the road from her, you know," Simon began. "I walked up to her place one night, and she was sitting on the porch with a lecher. Neither of them saw me. When she told him 'No!' and started fighting him, I came to the rescue!" He grinned and shifted his weight off his prosthesis. "Get my drift?"

"Yep." Rob gazed toward the microwave perched over the stovetop, and wished he could stuff José Herrera in it. "I just hope that José creep doesn't try anything like that on Brittan." He doubled his fist. "Good grief!" he huffed. "Who am I kidding? That's exactly what he's after."

"Of course it is."

"I just met her," Rob argued, "and I'm turning into her bodyguard."

Simon nodded. "Doesn't surprise me. I raised you to respect women."

"And to be the neighborhood date police?"

"No, maybe just for her. And if she's the right one, it'll only get worse."

"But I *just met* her!" Rob argued.

"That doesn't mean she's not the right one, does it?"

"No." Rob rubbed his chin.

His dad winced and shifted again.

Rob glanced toward Simon's prosthesis. "I'm guessing today was your day to run?"

"Yep. And the old stump isn't happy. I'm going to have to sit down a while."

"Did you put the chess board up?" Rob glanced toward the dining room where he'd thoroughly thrashed his dad in a game two nights ago.

"I thought you'd never ask," Simon said and sidestepped Elvis who meandered into the kitchen after his evening meal.

"You're a glutton for punishment," Rob teased and passed his father.

"Absolutely not!" Simon playfully shoved his son. "I'm going to beat your socks off and then feed you to Elvis."

"Not on your life!" Rob shot over his shoulder.

Heather gazed out Brittan's window, looking toward her friend and the Don Juan character who showed up 10 minutes ago. Arms crossed, she chewed on her bottom lip. Once Rob Lightly left, José had pulled a chair close to Brittan and snuggled in for a nice cozy chat. Brittan smiled into his face and was as close to blushing as

Heather had ever seen. Brittan mentioned José Herrera a few times over the last couple of days, and Heather had been interested in meeting this man who snared Brittan's attention. Now she wasn't certain she was glad to meet him…and that Brittan had too.

"So what do you think?" Lorna asked.

Heather swiveled to face her friend who was holding two chilled bottles. She reached for the green tea and uncapped it. "Not sure. What do you think?" she asked before sipping the sweet, cold liquid.

"José seems nice, I guess, but I like Rob better."

"Me too. And I'm wondering if José is a little too smooth. Ya know?"

Lorna stepped beside her and gazed outside. "Maybe…"

"It would be really ironic for Brittan to get duped by a smooth talker after she was so worried about us getting snowed."

"Do you really think that could happen to Brittan?" Lorna blotted a dot of moisture off her knit blouse.

"I hope not. Surely she can see that Rob's more genuine," Heather worried and wondered if this was the time to start praying. Her grandmother certainly would have thought so. "I hope Brittan isn't moving too fast because both of us are getting married." Heather twisted the bottle cap back on…only to untwist it again.

"Brittan?" Lorna scoffed. "Mizz Reason and Logic? Are you kidding?"

Heather sighed and cut a side glance toward her friend. "I know. But nobody's omniscient or without any emotions, and that includes 'Brittan the Brain'."

Silence settled between the friends, and a tremor of doubt slowly flickered in Lorna's green eyes. She swiftly shook her head. "But remember, *she's* the one who had the audacity to investigate the mayor of Houston." She lifted her hand. "After all the grief she gave me over Michael, surely she can spot a bad pear."

"Don't you mean a bad *apple*?" Heather corrected.

"What*ever!*" Lorna rolled her eyes and waved aside the faux pas.

After a snicker, Heather stared toward José and Brittan again. The guy looked like he was within an inch of kissing Brittan. In the landscaped splendor, the two could have been lovers on a postcard. Heather shivered, as much from the air conditioner's chill as from her own fears. "Sometimes love is blind," she mumbled and chewed on her lip some more.

"Maybe we should encourage her toward Rob Lightly. He's a police officer. You can't get more reputable than that." Lorna's bare feet padded across the tile floor as she moved toward the doorway.

"Right." *But she might need some supernatural encouragement too.* Following Lorna, Heather stepped from the area rug to the Italian tile that cooled her feet. She cast a glance across the immaculate home decorated in oriental flair. "Let's get out there before José lays one on Brittan that starts a bonfire."

Heather stole a last glimpse out the narrow window beside the door, and what she saw pleased her. Brittan was purposefully leaning away in a move Heather recognized as a silent "back off." But José reached for Brittan's hand and tugged her into his web once more. "Oh boy, here we go again."

"What?" Lorna followed Heather's gaze. "They *are* awfully snug, aren't they?"

"You know, Lorna," Heather breathed, "don't think I'm trying to be over spiritual or anything, but my grandmother would call this a prayer problem."

Lorna and her friend exchanged serious gazes. "Maybe you're right."

"I'm not nearly the prayer expert she was, but I do know that sometimes prayer is the only answer." She picked at the label on her bottle. "This might be one of those times. I feel troubled about José. Something's not right, and Brittan's obviously missing it."

"What do we do?"

Heather scraped her brain for a plan and relived some of those summers she'd spent with her praying grandmother before she passed away. Even though neither of her parents had been much more than social church members, her father's mother had known how to move heaven and had convinced Heather that God really does answer prayers.

"I think my grandmother probably would have just started praying every morning and night that Brittan would wake up and see this guy for what he is," she finally offered.

"Okay, I'm game. Brittan's worth the effort."

"Yep." Heather nodded. "And this time it looks like the situation is out of our control."

EIGHT

The first time he ate at Beynards and spotted the P.C. Mosier painting, José started working toward tonight's goal. He'd recognized quality in the original artwork and investigated the artist. He learned Mosier was an applauded French artist. After gaining recognition in Europe, his work was now popular in Canada and America. According to *Art and Artists* magazine, Mosier was only 40 and predicted to become a legend in time.

The painting in Beynards was dated 1998. That meant it was one of his earlier works. So if the Beynards had bought the painting years ago, they probably had paid very little. They might not even understand its value now—let alone what it might be worth after the artist's death. Once Mosier's death was arranged, the painting could be extremely valuable.

The piece deserves an owner who will appreciate it, José decided as he crawled across the beam that ran the length of the shopping center. The smell of new construction testified that the shopping strip was less than four months old. The tiny flashlight José held in his teeth cast an eerie shaft of light across the top of the drop ceiling that served the restaurant and the other shops. Because his mom's shop was next to the restaurant, there was no wall separating the attics. If there had been a wall, José had planned to cut through it. But that was one less obstacle he had to deal with.

After crawling all the way from his mother's craft shop, he paused, rocked back on his heels, and straightened, allowing his muscles a moment of reprieve. While the knee pads comforted his joints, he had no pads for his hands, save the thin gloves he wore. The palms of his hands burned in protest.

He had carefully planned this evening for weeks, and the adrenaline rush heightened his sense of urgency to complete the job. José breathed evenly and forced himself to remain calm. He would not allow his eagerness to botch the plan. He'd put far too much planning and thought into this theft to make any moves to jeopardize it.

He directed his light toward the platform he'd created out of plywood sheets. Working after hours, José transported the small sheets through his mom's ceiling one at a time. Then he brought up a cordless drill, screwed the boards to one another, and extended them across a row of beams. The platform was strategically placed above the back door. From that vantage, last week José lifted one of the drop ceiling tiles enough to spy on the restaurant manager as he tapped the code into the security system while closing the place. Tonight José planned to work his way over the plywood platform, disarm the security system, and then drop into the restaurant.

The crime took only a month to plan and prepare. Finding an exact copy of the painting and a frame that was a close match to the one in the restaurant were major obstacles. Finally cousin Eduardo discovered a print in an art gallery in Chicago. Fortunately it was one the artist had touched up with paint so at a quick glance it could pass for the original. José discovered the frame at the famous flea market in Canton, Texas. The framed copy now lay next to a black leather bag and a rope ladder on the plywood platform.

José snickered and wondered how long it would take the Beynards to discover their painting was really a print. *They might never notice!* That's what José always banked on—his intellectual superiority in the face of the commoner's low-level thought processes. He learned to count on it as early as junior high, when he shamelessly outsmarted his teachers while charming them into purring kittens.

José resumed crawling. Once he arrived at the plywood platform, he hastened to lift out the drop ceiling panel and slide it aside. Dim light radiated from below, illuminating the attic. He turned off his flashlight and set it aside too. Eagerly he peered into the restaurant, now vacant after a day's worth of cooking and serving and eating. José wiped at a thin rash of perspiration along his hairline and enjoyed the blast of air, as cool as it was fragrant. Just as he'd assumed, the place still held the gourmet aroma that rose on the chilly air to tantalize his senses. Normally the smell would have sent his appetite into a frenzy, but the tension in his gut barred hunger pangs.

He eyed the security system's digital box on the wall near the back door and reached for the leather pool stick bag. He pulled out the pool cue that was in two pieces. After screwing the stick together, he shifted his position to lie on his stomach.

Pressing in the security code was the tricky part. He'd only practiced a couple of times in his mom's shop. Her security code box was located by her back door as well. José easily used the pool cue to punch the buttons without setting off the motion detector. Hopefully the same method would work for Beynards' security system.

José held his breath and extended the pool cue down. As he pressed in the code, his smile grew. The tiny red light near the box's top blinked three times and then went off.

"Like taking candy from a baby," he whispered and lifted the stick back into the attic. He pulled himself to his knees, set the stick aside, and picked up the ladder. After securing the ladder's hooks on the metal beam, José dropped it into the restaurant. He gave the ladder an uncompromising tug. When it proved secure, he scooted the print to the edge of the platform and crawled halfway down the ladder. He pulled the print from the attic, held it closely to his torso, descended the final rungs of the swinging ladder, and dropped to the floor with a faint grunt.

He scanned the restaurant for human occupation. According to the employees' routines, everyone should have left an hour ago. To make sure, José had parked one intersection over and watched them depart. But he never took chances by making assumptions. The silence proved what his investigation had implied. The place was empty. The shadows whispered victory as José silently slinked through the back room that served as the restaurant's pantry. Large boxes and cans lined the shelves, and one whole wall held baskets full of fresh vegetables. He caught the whiff of onions as he stepped through the open doorway leading into the kitchen.

Once he exited the kitchen, he paused just outside the swinging doors and scanned the dimly lit dining area. He realized early in his career that the odds on the presence of a camera were about 50-50. As a restaurant patron, he carefully scoped the place out and found no security cameras. But once again José double-checked—just in case the manager arranged an installation since yesterday. Careful scrutiny revealed no recording devices. He hurried between the tables to the foyer. Once there, he checked for cameras again. He smiled and swiftly performed the painting switch.

With the original under his arm, José stepped away from the wall and laughed out loud. "Perfect!" he proclaimed and took a few seconds to relish success.

As he turned to leave, he reminded himself that taking the painting was the simple part. Now that it was in his possession, the dirty work began. José never planned to make murder part of his career, and even as he climbed the rope ladder back into the attic, he shuddered over the "Do not kill" he'd heard time and again during Mass. Even though he couldn't conjure a scrap of remorse over stealing, taking a life seemed more personal and crossed a line in José's psyche—one that he didn't want to reveal to Eduardo.

Despite the fact that knocking off Mosier was José's idea, he'd reneged after the initial brainstorm. But Eduardo didn't, so José manipulated him into carrying out Mosier's death. Now José wanted to get the killing behind them. Once Mosier was dead, the value of his paintings would skyrocket. And because the earlier pieces were rarer, the one he now possessed might crest half a million…especially if the investor was greedy.

José stretched upward and slid the painting across the plywood platform. The rope ladder writhed as he scurried up and hoisted himself next to the painting. Sighing, he blotted the memories of "Do not not kill" from his conscience. Mosier would undoubtedly go to heaven, so really they were doing him a favor.

Reaching for the pool cue, he allowed logic to settle his thoughts. He then pressed the numbers to reactivate the alarm. With that task complete, he set aside the stick, reached for the lightweight ceiling tile, and clicked it into place, blotting out the light in the attic.

※ ※ ※

Brittan pulled into the Beynards parking lot and put the Jaguar into park. Five days had lapsed since she last heard from José. She was delighted he called yesterday asking for a date tonight. Brittan was much more eager than she'd allowed herself to sound.

Even though she casually chatted with Rob Lightly yesterday afternoon during his jog along the lake, she didn't give him much encouragement, offering only light friendship. She didn't want to hurt him if the relationship with José proved as promising as it seemed. Lorna and Heather insisted they liked Rob better. Although Brittan could see his good qualities, she couldn't stop thinking about the handsome Latino whose dark eyes were as captivating as his sharp mind.

When he'd called, he gave Brittan her choice of restaurant. She'd suggested Beynards again and impishly hinted at another private shopping experience at his mom's place. After a brief hesitation, José agreed and then recommended they go to Salino's for dessert. A high-profile restaurant perched atop the Hyatt Regency in downtown Houston, the place was famous for desserts and fine coffees. Brittan didn't tell him that the skyscraper was right next door to her penthouse. Even though she frequented that restaurant many times, she welcomed the trip with him.

She checked her watch as she stepped into the restaurant and noted that she was 10 minutes early. Brittan recalled José being a couple of minutes late for their last date and figured she had a 10- to 15-minute wait. The smells wafting from the dimly lit restaurant came from heaven, she was sure. Her stomach rumbled as she settled onto one of the padded iron benches near the doorway.

Her cell phone's intermittent ring announced the caller was either Lorna or Heather. Brittan lifted her brows and thought it odd that either of them would call now because they knew she had a date. Wondering if there was an emergency, Brittan checked the caller ID screen, saw Heather's name, and pressed the talk button.

"Hi, Heather! What's going on?" she chirped into the phone.

"Have you heard the news?" Heather blurted.

"No!" Recognizing the urgency in her friend's voice, Brittan straightened and waited for the rest of the story.

"Are you familiar with the artist P.C. Mosier?"

Brittan's gaze shifted to the painting hanging near the hostess station. "Yes. My mom bought one of his pieces last year, and there's another one hanging in the foyer at Beynards. I'm looking at it right now, as a matter of fact."

"Well, he was murdered!" Heather rushed, her voice thick.

Brittan knitted her brows as she tried to make sense of her friend's desperate tone. "Did you know him personally?" she asked.

"No, Brittan, it's not that. He was shot outside his home in Denver—"

"I thought he lived in France." Brittan stood and moved toward the painting.

"He does—did—but he owned a home in the states as well." Heather's voice grew more agitated with every word. "But that's not the point. Brittan, there was *a red rose* left on his body."

Brittan gasped. First the Rose was implicated in a robbery and now a murder? "Oh no!" she rasped as her face went cold. "It must be the same person who stole the Inca necklace. How odd. He sure gets around! What is the deal with this guy? Is he crazy or what?"

The hostess shot a glance toward Brittan and turned away.

"Why would he want to peg us with a *murder?*"

"This is beyond insane," Brittan whispered. "We're going to have to do something!"

"You're telling me? I've repented of any hesitation! I now *totally agree!* This is terrible. You should see the reports. It's all over *Fox News.* Oh my word…just a minute…there's something new. Hang on!"

Brittan strained to hear the news report through the phone but caught nothing except the rise and fall of a female voice.

After their lakeside chat Monday evening about moving in on the rose-dropping criminal, the debutantes were sucked into a social whirlwind. Heather was trapped by her mother who was roping her into myriad pre-wedding rounds. Lorna was obligated to make several public appearances with her fiancé, the mayor. And Brittan had unexpectedly flown to New York with her dad for a round of meetings with his publishing company managers, only arriving back at her lake house yesterday morning.

As of this afternoon, Brittan's main concern was whether or not it was time to transition into the family business. Her father hinted several times about grooming Brittan to take over the family publishing empire one day. During this trip the hint was closer to a whack over the head, leaving her seriously wondering if she should become the next publishing magnate. Her brother, the surgeon, would have none of it, and that left her. She knew if she embraced the family empire it would probably mean closing the door on her participation with the Rose. She wouldn't have the time or freedom.

Heather's call swept aside her concern and consideration about the Shay family business. Whatever her future held in that arena, the Rose must answer these blatant slams on her character.

"Oh my word!" Heather's voice squeaked over the line. "They just recounted all the crimes the Rose solved, and now they're trying to integrate the committed crimes to the solved crimes."

"What? How?"

"Just a minute. I'll have more."

Brittan glanced toward the hostess, now ushering a large party to their table. Only one other group was waiting, and the high school girls were too engrossed in their own conversation to notice her.

She again stepped up to the painting and gazed upon the brilliant work as heavy sadness engulfed her. At this closer vantage, the painting took on a melancholic aura that eliminated its true-to-life effect. Even though Brittan had never met the artist, she hated the thought of such a gifted individual being snuffed out so soon in life. And implicating the Rose nearly blinded her with fury.

We're going to find whoever did this! Brittan thought. Still holding the phone to her ear, Brittan wrinkled her brow and edged closer to the painting. She ran her fingertips across the surface and detected some texturing. At closer vantage she recognized the artwork for what it was—a print that had been touched up. Her mother owned two Thomas Kinkade prints exactly like this.

I thought this was an original piece, she mused and lightly stroked the center of the painting again. *I know it was an original,* she insisted and rested her fingers back on Mosier's signature where it sprang from the print's surface. *This doesn't have the 3-D zing I remember. So what happened?*

"Excuse me! Miss!" The hostess' sharp tone insisted Brittan pay attention.

She snatched her fingers away from the print and gazed at the disapproving hostess. Brittan remembered her name was Liza, but right now her pointed nose reminded Brittan of a lizard.

"Please don't touch that painting," she commanded, gazing at Brittan as if she were the most uncouth woman on the planet. "Or any of the other artwork," she added and pointed toward a row of sculptures recessed in specially designed wall shelves. After a stern stare, the woman gathered up a stack of menus and walked back the way she'd come.

Deciding to steal a photo while she could, Brittan disconnected the call with Heather and aimed her camera phone at the painting. After centering the image, she snapped three shots. The approaching tap of Liza's shoes created a counter rhythm with the ring of Brittan's phone. She noted Heather's name on the ID screen.

"Sorry," Brittan mumbled into the receiver. "I had to take a break."

"O-kay…" Heather's curious voice floated over the phone.

Brittan turned her back on Liza Lizard and strode straight toward the ladies' room. Before she ducked through the dome-shaped door, she caught sight of José entering the foyer. "Just a minute, Heather." She waved and snagged José's attention.

"Hello, beautiful," he greeted as he rushed toward her.

"Excuse me, José," she said and lifted the phone. "I've got an important phone call. Do you mind? It's a friend in distress."

"Take your time." He waved and threw in a smile that would've made Brittan cut the call short were it not so urgent.

NINE

Brittan banged into the bathroom and checked the three stalls to make sure she was alone. A glance at the door indicated there was a lock just waiting to be turned so Brittan twisted it.

"Heather!" she hissed in sequence with the lock's clicking into place. "About the P.C. Mosier painting at this restaurant—it was here last week. Now there's just a touched-up print."

"Are you sure?"

"Dead sure. I just took some pictures with my phone."

"What do you think happened?"

"I don't know. Either the owner removed the original and replaced it with a print or…"

"Or somebody stole the original and replaced it with a print."

"Exactly."

"That's odd, especially since Mosier just died."

"Exactly. I think I'm going to talk to the manager and see what the deal is. Maybe they realized the value of the painting and replaced it with a print. The fact that it coincides with Mosier's murder is probably a coincidence."

"Probably," Heather agreed. "And if that's what they did, it's a good thing because *Fox News* is saying his paintings are going to be worth a mint now."

"Of course. That's the art scene all right. It's almost enough to make somebody murder an artist—especially if they have some of his work."

"Or even just steal one of them—especially if they knew the murder was going down."

"Especially if they were going to *make sure* the murder went down," Brittan deduced. Her mind spun with the implications. "I've *got* to talk to the manager! And somehow I've got to do it without revealing who I am." The last thing any of the friends wanted was a public link to anything the Rose was involved in.

A firm rap on the door was followed by a female voice that was becoming all-too-familiar. "Excuse me!" the hostess called. "Is anyone in there? Excuse me! This door isn't supposed to be locked."

Brittan sighed. "The restaurant lizard is after me," she whispered.

"What?"

"I've got to go," Brittan replied. "See if Lorna can meet tonight."

"Okay."

"Can you bring pizza? I'm starved."

"What about your date with José?"

"He'll have to wait."

"Right. I agree."

Liza Lizard pounded on the door again.

You seriously need a class in how to be nice, Brittan thought. "Gotta go, Heather. I'll call you back shortly."

She snapped shut her thin-line phone, squared her shoulders, unlocked the door, and stared directly into Lizard's eyes.

"You again?" The hostess lifted her brows.

Brittan didn't flinch. "Excuse me," she muttered and sailed past the woman and two young women standing behind her.

José was still waiting in the foyer. As Brittan stepped toward him, he smiled into her eyes and reached for her hands. She extended them and was struck again by how good he looked, especially in a black blazer and matching slacks. She'd worn a black pantsuit too and speculated that with their dark skin and eyes they would look great in a photo together.

Except José could be a model, she noted and hated that she was going to cancel the date.

"You look ravishing!" he said as he wrapped his fingers around hers, tugged her closer, and leaned in with intent in his eyes. Brittan resisted. No matter how attractive and charming José was, she wasn't going to start their second date with a kiss—especially in public.

"I'm sorry, José," she said, "but I'm not going to be able to keep our date."

His grin faded. "Is something wrong? Is it me?" He dropped her hands and rested his fingertips against his chest. "Have I offended you in some way?"

"No—oh, no!" Brittan vehemently shook her head. Then she looked away and thought fast. "My friend…there's been a death," she blurted and peered into his eyes. "I was just on the phone with her. She…she needs me."

"Surely she'd understand if you ate first." He motioned toward the dining area. "Everyone has to eat, no?"

Brittan blinked and was struck with the possibility that José might be pushing some kind of agenda. Not knowing who had died or her relationship with the person, it seemed odd he'd ask her to stay for dinner.

Noting her look, José amended, "But of course not." He shook his head. "What was I thinking?" He touched his temple.

Brittan wondered if he'd read her mind.

"This is surely an emergency," he said. "Is there something I can assist with? Does your friend need…"

"No, but thanks for understanding." Brittan allowed her smile to show the warmth in her soul.

"What if I arrange for takeout and bring it to both of you?"

"It's so sweet of you to suggest." She squeezed his arm. "But I think it's best right now for me to just...be with her. Really, José, you're being far too kind," Brittan insisted and was sorry she'd doubted him. Apparently he was just a true gentleman.

"What about tomorrow night? I was nearly beside myself with excitement over seeing you again and now..." He lifted his hand, and his full lips fell into a disappointed droop.

"I was really looking forward to tonight as well," she breathed and was once again affected by his magnetic charisma. The last time they were together, he'd nearly kissed her. Brittan had resisted because Heather and Lorna were in the house retrieving drinks, and she didn't want to be in a lip-lock when they emerged. Besides, she didn't allow herself to be pulled into such a close relationship so soon. She sternly reminded herself of her commitment to not rush into anything with anyone—no matter how appealing the idea.

"I'm terribly sorry," she added and stepped away. Bending her head, Brittan headed toward the restaurant door with José following close beside her.

"So can we meet tomorrow night?" he questioned again before opening the glass door for her to exit into the cool evening.

Brittan's mind whirled with the possibilities the next 24 hours might hold. A crazy criminal was trying to destroy the Rose's reputation, and they had to catch him. No telling what they'd be up to or where they might be tomorrow night.

"Do you mind if I call you tomorrow?" she asked and pulled her Gucci bag from her shoulder. "I've still got your card in my purse."

"But in your purse is not good enough," José said and took a gold pen from the inside of his jacket. He reached for Brittan's hand and gently pressed her fingers open. "It must be in your heart...or at least in your hand." While he scrawled his cell number on her palm, the pen's fine point tickled her skin. Before Brittan could stop him, he pressed his lips against the number.

"There, beautiful lady." He lifted his head. Only inches from her face, his gaze penetrated her spirit. "You have my number in constant view. Memorize it. Write it on your heart, just as your beauty is written on mine."

Caught off guard, Brittan leaned close before she corrected the impulse. Even though a disappointed wilt tugged at the corners of José's mouth, Brittan slid her hand from his, and he grudgingly released her. Interestingly, she noted that his lips hadn't produced even one tingle in her heart. *Probably because I'm so distracted over what's going on with the Rose,* she reasoned.

Her cell phone's ring reminded her that her friends were expecting to meet. She pulled her phone from the bag's side pocket and noted the caller was Lorna this time.

"José, I'm so sorry. This is another friend. She must have heard from the first friend. We're really in a bad spot. I'm going to have to go. I'll call you, okay?"

"You promise?" he asked, his brow wrinkled in doubt.

"Yes, I promise." Brittan enforced the claim with a smile and flipped open the phone. "Just a minute," she said into the receiver.

"Okay," Lorna responded.

Brittan pulled her keys from her purse's pocket, pressed her car's remote unlock button, and popped open the door. José hovered near. She cast him a distracted smile and wondered if the guy was going to crawl into her backseat.

Once she settled into the driver's seat, he said, "I see you got your bumper fixed."

"Yes, I took it in earlier this week," she absently commented and suppressed the irritation over his insistent chitchat.

"Well, goodbye then," he said and closed the door.

He's just trying to be a gentleman, she decided and started the vehicle before placing the cell phone back against her ear. "Lorna, I guess you've talked to Heather?"

"Yep. She said we're meeting at your lake house."

"Yes. Does that work for you?" Brittan asked.

"Works for me. Heather's bringing pizza. Should I bring a salad?"

"Yes, please do. I just canceled my date with José and I'm starved."

"I'm not so sure about him."

"What do you mean?"

"Well…" Lorna hedged.

Brittan looked in her rearview mirror and began to back up. José now stood on the restaurant sidewalk, hands in pockets, gazing after her like a lovesick lad. Brittan was tempted to whirl the car back into a parking place and postpone the debutante meeting until later. But she hardened her resolve, drove out of the parking lot, and onto the busy street that led to home.

"Well?" Brittan prompted.

Lorna sighed. "I just think Rob's a better choice. I don't know… something about José just, well, bothers Heather and me."

Brittan frowned and then rolled her eyes. "Oh, I see! You're trying to give me grief because of what I did with Michael."

"No," Lorna countered. "Heather thought you might think that."

"Look, I'm not going to get sucked into anything. My eyes are wide open. Don't worry. I'm going slowly with José. As for Rob, he's a really nice guy, but I'm not into dating more than one man at a time. Right now I'm giving José a chance. We'll see what happens."

Lorna sighed. "Whatever you say, Brittan. We just don't want you to get hurt by a schemer."

"You think José's a schemer?" Her brows arched as her tone grew higher.

"He's awfully smooth, if you ask me."

"Since when was smooth bad?" Brittan tapped an index finger against the steering wheel. "Smooth isn't bad as long as it's genuine."

She scowled and pressed the accelerator as she came out of a curve in the tree-lined road.

"I'm speaking from experience," Lorna added. "My trainer was just about as smooth, and you *know* what happened there."

Brittan's grip tightened on the steering wheel, and she pressed her lips together to keep from blurting something she'd later regret. Brittan wasn't half as naive on a bad day as Lorna could be on a good day. Besides that, she considered herself too analytical to be taken in by any man. No way would she be like Lorna and fall for a man who would try to rape her.

"Look," she finally said. "I know José's…polished. But good grief! His mother owns a small chain of craft stores, and he manages them. How much more benign can you get? Do you think he's running a drug-smuggling business in the back alley? Come on, Lorna!"

"Okay, I'm not going to say another word!" Lorna snapped. "But be careful, will ya?"

"I will. *I am!*" Brittan insisted. "You know I always carry my concealed buddy. If José tries something, I'll just shoot him." Brittan glanced into the open folds of her purse where the butt of her Glock 30 protruded. She never went anywhere without her tiny pistol, and Lorna knew it.

"Sounds like a winner to me," Lorna drawled. "Go, girl!"

Brittan snickered and the tension drained from her. She couldn't stay exasperated with either of her friends for very long. Lorna's concern stemmed from the fact that she cared deeply. The three debutantes had been together since junior high, where they met at a blue-blood prep school. Their disdain for upper-crust social restrictions had bonded them, and the three had managed to maintain their independence enough to solve crimes without their families suspecting anything.

Brittan spotted her driveway looming ahead and said, "I'm almost home. I'll see you and Heather soon, right?"

"Right."

TEN

Brittan swept into the house and straight to the phone on the end table. She dropped her purse and keys in the middle of the overstuffed couch, snapped up the phone, and dialed information. Within 30 seconds she was transferred to Beynards' main line. As tempted as Brittan had been to use her cell phone, she knew her identity could be detected with caller ID. Not so with her unlisted home number.

After a couple of rings, Liza Lizard's voice floated over the line. Brittan suppressed a sigh. "I'd like to speak to the manager, please," she said in a no-nonsense voice. "It's urgent."

"I'm the manager," Lizard said.

Brittan slammed her palm against her forehead and collapsed into a nearby chair. "Is Mr. or Mrs. Beynards in?" Brittan asked.

"No," Liza answered. "Is there something I can help you with? I'm their daughter."

Well, great! Brittan thought. *As ornery as she is, she probably won't even listen to me.* Nonetheless, she plowed forward. "There's an original oil painting hanging in your foyer by P.C. Mosier. Or at least, there's supposed to be."

"Well, there's a painting here. I'm not sure who the artist is," Liza said with a tinge of suspicion.

"It's by Mosier," Brittan said. "And it was an original oil last week. But now it's a touched-up print. Did you or your parents replace it?"

"I certainly didn't. I can't imagine that my parents would have," Liza answered. "I'm looking at it now, though, and I don't see—"

"P.C. Mosier was just killed—murdered," Brittan explained. "His paintings were valuable, and now they're probably going to be worth a mint. If your parents didn't replace the painting with a print, who did?"

"I really don't know anything about art, and this piece looks like it did months ago. Who are you? Wait a minute! I recognize your voice. Weren't you just in here?" she asked.

Brittan huffed. "That's immaterial. I'm a concerned customer, and your family may have just been royally ripped off. I wouldn't dismiss it if I were you!" Brittan disconnected the call and squeezed the top of her head. "That woman needs therapy!"

She plunked the phone back onto its cradle and accidentally hit the basket of honeysuckle potpourri she'd purchased at Herrera's shop. The bits of dried flowers and leaves tumbled across the table and to the floor, releasing the sweet fragrance Brittan normally found appealing. But now the smell upped her annoyance. Mumbling under her breath, she bent to pick up the potpourri and place it back into the basket. She was feeling as scattered as the potpourri. An unknown force was trying to wreak havoc with her and her friends' lives. *What if that sicko is planning to leave more roses at more crimes?* Another horrifying thought sent a cold wave of dread through her. *What if the criminal knows who we are and has a personal vendetta against us?*

Brittan slumped to the floor and pulled her knees to her chest. "This can't be happening," she whispered as a wave of fear nearly sucked her under.

The doorbell's ring pierced her terror. Brittan scrambled to her feet and hurried to the door. Fully expecting Lorna or Heather, she flung it open.

Rob Lightly stared down at the cute Chinese gal who was on the brink of driving him to distraction. After only a few times in her presence, he had to admit there was something special about her. Brittan Shay possessed an intangible something like no other woman he'd known. Oh, he'd been attracted to his share of dark-haired females and even been on the verge of getting serious a couple of times. But something always made him end the relationship. Over the last few hours, Rob wondered if Brittan was his "certain someone." She was always looming on the edge of his mind like an invisible promise waiting to be fulfilled. But right now she looked like she could use an embrace. Dressed in a sharp black pantsuit, she appeared to be ready for a night on the town, but her expression said something had disturbed her.

"Brittan? Are you okay?" Rob asked without bothering with a preliminary greeting.

She stared at him. "I...I...Would you like to come in?" she finally offered with a smile that didn't obliterate the raw fear in her eyes.

He stepped into the upscale house that was every bit as gorgeous as he assumed it would be, if the breathtaking flower garden outside was any standard to go by. He first spotted the living room, and he wasn't surprised to see that it was touched with oriental decor. The floor-to-ceiling windows that lined the west wall entertained a wash of evening sunshine, bathing the room in an alluring glow.

He was here because his father insisted he "go after his woman." Rob didn't consider Brittan "his woman" by any means, but his dad was already making assumptions. He seemed unusually interested in Rob's love life and was encouraging him to give Brittan a chance. Rob didn't need a lot of motivating. He was ready and willing to give Brittan any opening she needed.

"Have a seat," Brittan offered, her voice sounding more normal with every word.

"If this isn't a good time…" Rob's voice trailed off as he searched for an indicator of her wishes.

Brittan returned the appraisal with a slight glimmer of desperation in her eyes.

Rob was stricken with masculine awareness that she needed him…or at least a friend. His protective instinct rose to full alert, and his shoulders stiffened. "Is everything okay in here?" He gazed around, wondering if he'd spot some criminal hiding in the shadows.

Her chuckle dashed aside his worries. "Everything's fine," she assured.

Rob relaxed.

"No monsters or lurking robbers or anything." She swept her hand toward the hallway.

"Too bad. I was ready to seriously kick some rear," he drawled and stepped toward one of the chairs.

"Once on duty, always on duty, huh?" she teased.

"Yeah, I guess." Rob shrugged and looped his thumb through his jeans belt loop.

Brittan glanced over his attire—a Houston Police Department T-shirt and a pair of faded jeans he'd worn to the "best comfort" stage.

"Sorry I didn't dress up," he apologized. "Looks like you're about to go out?"

"No." She shook her head. "Actually, I just got home. And you don't have to apologize for how you look. I was just wishing I was in my jeans. I bought a pair a couple of days ago that have tears like yours. That's a first for me. But hey," she shrugged, "maybe even a straight-laced chick can get stylish every now and then."

He laughed and gazed down at his pants. "When my mom was alive, she called this the 'it's time to throw that ratty pair of jeans away' phase. But this is usually just about the time I've got them broken in. I didn't pay big bucks for these, but I've invested a lot of time in them." *And I'd like to invest some time with you,* Rob added to himself. He smiled into her dark eyes and let the flying sparks communicate his thoughts.

She returned the smile, and this time there was no trace of fear. *She's a master at self-control,* he thought and wondered how she might respond if he kissed her. Nothing would please him more than to discover a woman of warmth in the midst of all that logic.

"Want something to drink?" she asked and pointed toward the kitchen.

"Actually, no." Rob stroked his stomach. "Dad just grilled burgers, and I had enough iced tea to drown a fish. I couldn't hold another drop."

"Do you mind if I get myself something? I'm dying of thirst."

"Of course not," Rob agreed and amiably followed her into the kitchen. The floor looked like a black-and-white chess board. The pattern was repeated in the border along the ceiling...and surprisingly in the center of a small table, nestled near a bay window. Rob spotted a sizable marble case on one of the shelves near the window. The chess piece icons carved into the case boldly bespoke the content. Rob's eyes widened.

"You play chess?" he blurted.

A bottle of water in hand, Brittan turned from the refrigerator. "Yes. Do you?" She snapped the door shut.

"You bet!" Rob moved to the shelf and pointed at the case. "Do you mind?" he asked.

"Of course not, but it's heavy. Solid jade." When she untwisted the bottle cap, Rob noticed her fingers were less than steady. He checked her eyes again and was met with a calm appraisal and nothing more.

She's good, he thought and placed the case on the table. *She should become a detective. Wait. She already is one...in a way.*

Rob opened the case and was struck with the intricately carved pieces made from light and dark jade. He stroked a knight. "You play with this set?"

"Yes. It's been in my mother's family for years," she explained.

"I can't believe you actually use it. It's art!"

"Right. But I'm not one to have things you can't use." She adjusted her glasses.

He chuckled. "I can see that," he admitted and didn't mention his collection of Civil War swords. "My dad would *flip* over this set," Rob enthused.

"He likes chess?"

"Loves it. We have a constant battle going. In the last round, he beat me senseless, but that was after I ate his lunch three games in a row. He's really vengeful when that happens." Rob narrowed his eyes, curled his lips, and said, "Go ahead, make my day," in his best Clint Eastwood impersonation.

Brittan sputtered over another sip of water.

"Gotcha!" Rob exclaimed. He pointed at her and mimicked the firing of a gun.

"You did!" she agreed. "But I guess it's good he's got an interest with his," she shrugged, "handicap and all."

"Are you kidding?" Rob exclaimed, lifting his brows. "Did I give you the impression he was handicapped?"

"Well, you said he lost a leg in Vietnam."

"Yes, he did." Rob nodded. "But somebody forgot to tell *him* that. He's a runner and plays racquetball regularly. He has women chasing him all over creation."

Brittan narrowed her eyes. "But what about Elvis keeping him company?"

"He does." Rob's gaze never wavered.

"And you coming over to take Elvis for a walk."

"I do." Rob nodded. "But Dad does too sometimes." Then he

gradually realized that Brittan painted a slightly different picture of his father than he intended to project. "Oh…you thought…"

She grimaced. "Yes."

"Whoops. Sorry." Rob smiled. "That really was an honest mistake."

Brittan crossed her arms. "You seemed so protective."

He sighed. "I *can* go there, I guess. A year ago I found him in a diabetic coma, and I thought *he* was dead." Rob rolled his eyes. "I nearly needed therapy over that. Maybe I still do," he added.

"So what happened? Did he skip his medication, or—"

"No. He just developed it. His mother did the same thing. Runs in the family."

Brittan nodded.

"My parents were like my best friends. Losing mom nearly killed me. If not for our faith, I think it would have killed both of us. Then thinking I was going to lose Dad too…whew!" Rob shook his head. "Now he says I worry too much about him. He runs around like he thinks he's eighteen." Rob barked out a laugh and waved away his worries. "And he royally ignores me and does whatever he wants. So I guess my worrying doesn't do me or him any good!"

"And you're sure you weren't just trying to make me feel sorry for Elvis so I wouldn't—"

"No way!" Rob laid his hand on his chest. "I'd never do that." Despite his desire to project true honesty, his lips twitched.

Her scowl increased. "Why do I get this feeling I was snowed?" If not for her own tiny smirk, her question would have held a sting.

"Seriously," Rob said through a chuckle. "I—"

A phone's intermittent ringing from the living room broke through Rob's claims.

"That's Heather or Lorna," Brittan said, and a tinge of the fear danced across her features again.

Rob continued to gaze at the chess set but couldn't stop himself from straining to catch Brittan's side of the conversation.

He gradually pieced together the clues. Whatever was wrong, it appeared to have something to do with Lorna and Heather as well. That meant it most likely involved the Rose.

"Yes, I'm home now," she said.

Rob stroked a rook.

"No, I haven't. I have company...Rob Lightly."

He peered into the living room. Her back to him, Brittan gazed out the window toward the lake.

"Right," she said, her voice tight. "And how long will it be before you get here?"

Rob debated whether or not he should politely excuse himself, but he just couldn't. After months of following Brittan in the society pages, she miraculously landed in Rob's world. The prospect of watching her and her friends solve a case sent his adrenaline into a spin.

And who knows, he thought, *I may be able to help.* He grinned and wondered how many men in Houston would give their life savings to be in his shoes.

"Right. Okay. I will. Right. Bye." Brittan snapped her phone shut, and while she was turning from the window, Rob made a major issue of holding a pawn up to the light as if examining it.

"I don't want to seem rude," Brittan stated from the edge of the kitchen, "but there's something on TV I really need to watch right now. Some breaking news on Fox," she diverted her gaze, "that Lorna says I need to see."

"Oh, sure, I don't mind." Rob smiled into her eyes. "I'm always up for breaking news. I keep CNN on at the house most the time." Leaving the chess set behind, he walked toward her.

Her blank gaze suggested perhaps he just missed something. His social radar hinted that she would rather he politely leave. But Rob decided to ignore the warning. His voracious desire to see the Rose in action overrode any and all alerts. He would repent later...maybe.

As he neared, Brittan hurried back into the living room toward the TV, nestled in an entertainment center along the south wall.

After a few button pushes, *Fox News* spread across the screen. The beautiful news anchorwoman was discussing issues involving the Rose and the latest implication linking the sleuth to murder. As if that wasn't bad enough, they were paralleling the crime to the murder case the Rose had recently solved—suggesting that the Rose was purposefully committing and solving crimes that coincided. The anchorwoman speculated that perhaps the sleuth had solved the case of who gunned down Houston's mayor two years ago only to gun down a person now. An expert psychologist commented that if the same person who solved the crimes was also committing them, he or she might be schizophrenic.

"Oh no," Brittan groaned.

Rob shot her a glance.

She lowered her gaze. "Just so you know," she admitted, "Lorna and Brittan and I are big fans of the Rose."

"Oh really?" Rob said and rubbed his hands together. "I'm a *huge* fan! Ever since she left a rose on my patrol car, I've been eaten up with the whole deal."

Brittan slowly raised her attention to him, and Rob detected the trace of dread back in her eyes. Her lips opened as if she were about to say something. Rob held his breath, wondering if she would tell him the truth. He swallowed, debating whether he should tell her he already knew.

Then she pressed her lips together, and her focus shifted back to the television. "Yes, I remember reading about that in the paper," she mumbled. "Wasn't it an animal cruelty case?"

"Yes," he admitted and nearly laughed out loud.

"So you were the lucky duck the Rose left the info with that time?" she mused as if it didn't really matter.

"Quack, quack," Rob said.

Her lips twitched.

"You know, I don't believe anything they're saying," he admitted and pointed toward the TV.

"You don't?" Brittan swung her attention back to him, and a spark of appreciation replaced the dread.

"Of course not." He never blinked. "I dismissed the Rose link when the necklace came up missing too. I think there's some guy out there who's mad at the Rose and is trying to get even. That, plus sometimes I think the media just looks for something they can sensationalize. This is no different." He motioned toward the television. "Whoever this criminal is, he's probably banking on the media turning the whole thing into a saga. My guess is he's mad at the Rose because she—if it *is* a she—has hurt his 'business' somehow."

Her eyes widened only a centimeter. If Rob hadn't been the observant sort, he might have missed her reaction.

"That's a thought," she admitted with an expression that suggested she could take it or leave it.

Man, she's good, Rob thought again.

"What are the chances of the Houston Police investigating the murder?" Brittan asked.

"Well…we're looking into that missing necklace business," he admitted. "But this one's way out of our jurisdiction."

"Right. Except they've *got* to be linked."

"Looks that way."

"So maybe the HPD would collaborate with the Denver police?"

"Very likely," Rob admitted. "But it's still out of our jurisdiction, so we're limited in working directly on the case."

"Right. I understand."

"I hope the Rose, whoever she is, will revisit her other cases. Maybe she'll find the link." Rob focused on the anchorwoman, now discussing the latest college shooting.

The doorbell rang. Rob's spine stiffened. He figured it must be Lorna or Heather…or that guy who nearly made Rob lose his religion the last time he was here.

ELEVEN

Rob tuned out the TV and strained for an indication of who was at the door. When he heard a female voice, he relaxed.

"Heather, you remember Rob?" Brittan asked as she stepped back into the living room. Rob pivoted toward the petite blonde who was certainly good-looking enough. But even if she'd been available, he preferred Brittan.

"Of course I remember." She extended her hand and smiled into his eyes. "Elvis' dad, right?"

"Uh…brother," he said through a chuckle. "Elvis belongs to my dad."

"Yes," Brittan drawled and crossed her arms. "His dad—the invalid who has only one leg and runs marathons and plays pro racquetball and chases women."

Heather lifted her brows and shifted her gaze from Brittan to Rob.

"Hey!" Rob exclaimed. "He runs for exercise, plays racquetball at the gym, and does *not* chase women. They chase *him!*"

"Is there something you two would like to tell the whole class?" Heather asked through a broad grin.

"He snowed me." Brittan wrinkled her nose and pointed at Rob.

"Here I was feeling sorry for Elvis' one-legged owner and going light on the garbage-eating beast, and come to find out Rob's dad is really a wild man." The playful spark in her eyes sent a thrill through Rob.

He laughed and lifted both hands. "I'm being *so* falsely accused! I never said—"

"You made me feel sorry for him and Elvis just so I wouldn't call the animal patrol," she said and placed her hands on her hips.

Coming from a woman so composed, Rob took this playful challenge for exactly what it had to be. Brittan Shay was officially flirting with him.

"Did not!" he defended.

"Did too!" she retorted.

"Children, children! It certainly looks like you're getting along well," Heather interjected and eyed each of them.

Brittan bit her bottom lip and glanced away, and Rob no longer had to guess if she was attracted to him...or whether or not a warm, playful woman lay beneath her calm persona. The only issue now lay in figuring out exactly what part José played in her life.

The sooner we can hit the delete button on that guy, the better, he decided.

The doorbell's repeated ringing announced a new guest.

"That's got to be Lorna," Brittan said and hustled back toward the entryway.

The second Brittan got out of earshot, Heather leaned forward and hissed, "She likes you" and gave him a thumbs-up.

Rob lifted a brow.

"We've *got* to get rid of José," she continued. "Lorna and I are praying hard that she'll tell him to hit the trail."

He blinked and widened his eyes.

"I'm dead serious," Heather stressed.

"Okay, I can live with that," Rob admitted.

"We think *he's* snowing her," Heather whispered. "And it blows our minds that she can't see it. We don't trust him—at all."

"So what do you want *me* to do—arrest him?" Rob joked.

"Great idea!" Heather snapped her fingers. "Go for it."

Rob's chuckle mingled with hers.

"Lorna, you remember—" Brittan stopped in mid-sentence.

Rob glanced toward her and a tall brunette at her side. Like Heather, she was dressed as casually as Rob.

Brittan narrowed her eyes and peered at Heather and then him. "What are you two whispering about?" she questioned.

"You, of course," Heather admitted and wiggled her fingertips in a teasing wave.

"Great subject, don't you think?" Rob said through an indulgent grin.

"What's she telling you?" Brittan crossed her arms and scowled.

"Probably your name, rank, and serial number," Lorna drawled and lifted a box of pizza the size of the moon. "Anybody want to eat? I'm about ready to devour the box."

"No," Rob groaned and lifted his hand. "I'm going to pass. I just ate two hamburgers, and the pizza smell alone is making me feel *stuffed!*"

No one protested. The air virtually crackled with the tension he'd sensed earlier in Brittan. No matter how polite and cheerful these three were, they were definitely distracted about the latest news. As much as Rob wanted to ignore the fact that he probably should leave, he couldn't. Despite his fascination for the Rose, he sensed the sleuths really wanted to be alone. They needed time to absorb the latest and plot their strategy. Because Rob wanted to be a regular part of Brittan's life, the last thing he needed to do was aggravate her by inhibiting the process.

The next time he came, he would keep his eyes and ears open and probably be able to figure out their next move. He stepped toward the door. "It looks like you ladies are about to have a slumber party or something. I think I'll scoot."

Silence that lasted a second too long confirmed he'd made the right choice.

"You really don't have to leave," Brittan finally said, and she actually sounded regretful.

Rob weighed her expression and decided she might genuinely be a tad sorry he was leaving. He grinned and clung to every encouragement she offered. "Hey, this rooster knows when a hen party is on, and it looks like you ladies are about to seriously start one. I just hope you don't hurt yourself on that pizza." He motioned toward the box. "It looks like it might be lethal."

"It was the biggest one they had," Lorna bragged and lifted the box.

"Go, girl!" Heather approved. "You put veggies only on one half, right?"

"Right." Lorna tossed a smile toward Rob. "Heather's the vegetarian among us. And, just for the record, I'm the food slob. So the other half is for meat lovers."

"And I'm somewhere in the middle," Brittan admitted. "I eat healthy—as long as I don't see Doritos. Then," she shrugged, "I just lose it."

Heather wagged her index finger back and forth and said, "Naughty, naughty, naughty."

"So the next time I come, I know what I'm wearing." Rob rubbed his hands together. "A giant Doritos bag!"

Lorna's wolf whistle accompanied Brittan's smile, and Rob decided not to miss the opportunity to solidify exactly when that "next time" should be.

"Want to walk me out?" he asked and jerked his head toward the door.

"Sure." Brittan waved to the kitchen. "You guys go ahead. I'll be there soon."

"Don't stay gone too long," Lorna warned. "I think I could eat the whole thing myself."

"I believe it!" Brittan replied and fell in beside Rob.

They stepped out onto the porch and into the final rays of evening's splendor. A chorus of crickets shrieked about the coming night while the cool air, heavy with moisture, warned that spring had yet to surrender to summer. Brittan shut the front door and turned to face him.

The shadows accenting her cheeks made her appear even more exotic than she had in the light. Rob imagined they were ending a date and that it was time for the goodnight kiss. But when Brittan wrinkled her brow and gazed up at him with a worried pinch to her features, Rob suspected she wasn't thinking about a kiss.

With the shroud of indecision cloaking her features, she finally said, "There's something I think I need to tell you. I've been debating whether or not I should mention it, but I've finally decided to just go ahead."

What? That you're fascinated with me? he thought and swept aside the flirtatious retort with *In your dreams, man.*

"Okay," Rob replied, revealing no hint of his wayward wishing.

"I was in Beynards tonight." She pointed up the road. "The Mediterranean restaurant—"

"In the new shopping strip?" he finished.

"Right." Brittan nodded. "Have you been there?"

"Not yet. Want to go with me sometime?" he blurted before he realized he'd even asked.

"Hold that thought." She raised her hand, palm outward, and he caught a glimpse of a row of numbers that resembled a phone number.

Odd, he thought. He didn't peg Brittan for the type who used her palm as a notepad.

"When I was in there last week I noticed they have a P.C. Mosier painting hanging in the foyer," she continued, unruffled.

"The now *dead* P.C. Mosier?"

"Yes. The dead one on *Fox News*." She sliced her hand through the air. "Anyway, I was back in Beynards tonight—earlier—and noticed the painting again. Except this time it's a touched-up print." Brittan paused. "Exact same painting, except now it's a print," she emphasized. "When I got home, I called the manager and asked her if the owner had switched out the real painting for a print. She didn't have a clue about anything and said the owners are her parents."

"So she'd probably know if—"

"Right." Brittan nodded. "I'd just heard about Mosier's death and explained that the artist was dead and that the original they had was going to be worth a mint." After adjusting her glasses, she continued, "And the woman scoffed at me!"

"No way." Rob rested his hands on his hips.

"Yes." She nodded. "She told me the painting looked the same as it did four months ago when they opened the place."

"She couldn't tell the difference?"

"No. To the untrained eye and at a glance, it might not be noticeable. It's in the shadows. The whole place is shadowed. But I can tell the difference." She pressed her index finger against the center of her chest. "My mom's a serious art connoisseur. She owns a Mosier too."

"Right." Rob nodded.

"I'm telling you this because I'm frustrated," Brittan admitted as a puff of a breeze rattled the bamboo wind chime hanging near her front door.

"I knew you were upset when I got here," he said.

"I was. Here's the deal…it looks like the painting was stolen and replaced *before* the murder happened. Well, it has to have been before," she qualified. "News of the murder is just hitting this evening, and the painting was obviously changed out before now."

"So whoever stole the painting might have known the murder was going to happen?"

"Yes, or he might *be* the murderer!"

"That's a logical deduction. There's a reason famous artists have bodyguards. There's always somebody out there who owns their work and would rather have them dead."

"Yes." Brittan crossed her arms and tapped her toes. "And if the same person who stole the painting did plan the murder, maybe he's somebody local. I mean, the necklace was local too."

"Somebody right under our noses?" Rob added.

"Well, at least someone who lives in the Houston area."

"Do you know for sure the painting wasn't legitimately replaced by the Beynards?"

"No—not a hundred percent," Brittan admitted. "That's why I'm telling you. I thought that maybe you'd—"

"Sure. I'll stop in—see what I can find out."

She assessed him through narrowed eyes. "Liza Lizard just might talk to you when she wouldn't give me the time of day."

"Who?" he asked.

"The manager's name is Liza," she said with a sigh. "And I think she looks like a lizard."

He laughed. "Hence the name Liza Lizard?"

"You got it."

"Even a lizard will talk if I show 'er my badge."

"I meant, whether you show your badge or not," she mumbled under her breath and looked away.

Rob searched for her meaning and then said, "Oh, I see. Wow, thanks for the compliment."

She lifted one brow and shot him a glance out of the corner of her eye that made Rob remember that "thought" he was holding. "So...when can we go to Beynards *together?*" he asked.

"Well..." she hedged. "I've been seeing someone..."

"You mean José?"

"Yes, sort of. I mean, we aren't, like, steady or anything. We've just gone out a time or two. Well, actually once. I don't know...I just feel awkward dating more than one man at a time."

"So date *me!*" Rob stated as he laid his hand on his chest.

Brittan solemnly observed him. "I'll think about it."

"Tell you what. Why don't you come down to my dad's place tomorrow night? He's constantly grilling something."

"Is his barbecue the one I keep smelling?"

"Probably. He's a grilling maniac. Tonight it was hamburgers. Tomorrow night I think it's skewered shrimp. If you were to just drop by for a while, that would be..." he slipped his hands into his pockets, "you know, neighborly."

Brittan smiled.

"It would be good for him and for you. He was emphatic about moving away from my neighborhood and out to the lake—even though he had a bunch of neighbors who were more like family. Now I can't get him to even look at any of the neighbors. It never hurts to have a neighbor or two you can depend on—especially these days. You never know, my dad might come in handy—especially if you needed help."

"Or maybe I could be of help to him," she added and crossed her arms.

"There you go!"

"Since he's such an invalid."

"Now she goes and brings that up again." Rob rocked back on his heels and gazed at the darkening sky.

"Okay, okay, what time?" Brittan asked through a laugh.

"Six."

"Do you think you'll have the chance to check out Beynards between now and then?" she asked.

"If you're coming over tomorrow, I'll make a beeline there now."

"It's a deal." Brittan extended her hand and they shook. "Look, you've still got my cell number, right?"

"Yep."

"Send me a text in a few, and I'll send you the photos I took of the print tonight. That way you'll know what you're looking for. Then call me after you talk to them tonight. Do you mind?"

"No, I don't mind a bit," he agreed. "Except you have to understand that once I start asking questions, it becomes official police business and there may be things I can't tell you."

"Right. I just want to know if the Beynards replaced the painting or if it was stolen. I can fill in the blanks from there."

"Sure," he agreed as a tiny voice floated from Rob's belt, "Help! Let me out! I'm stuck in your pocket!"

Her eyes widening, Brittan gazed toward his cell phone.

"That's my ringer," he said. "Like it?"

"It's crazy!" she blurted.

"I've got to do something to keep me laughing," he said as the zany voice began again.

He retrieved the cell. The number indicated it was the dispatcher, and that meant business. Two seconds into the call, Rob knew the little trip to Beynards would have to wait until tomorrow.

"There's a standoff happening down on West Dallas Street," Officer Winston Balstick said. "Hostage situation. Three kids, a mom, and a deranged drug addict. We need the big guns—and that's you."

"Okay!" Rob snapped, his muscles tensing. He hated hostage cases, despite the fact he was considered an expert in the field. Too many times someone ended up dead. Once it had been his partner, Zeb Turner. He glanced toward his dad's driveway, three houses down, where his pickup was parked. He'd had a hunch he should drive his patrol car, but didn't. Now he regretted it.

"I'm coming in my truck. Have someone meet me there with a vest. I've got my gun with me." Rob always carried his gun belt. He kept it under his truck seat when he wasn't on duty. He felt naked without it near.

"Consider it done," Winston replied.

Rob flipped his phone shut and gazed down at Brittan. "Looks like Beynards is going to have to wait. There's a hostage situation on West Dallas. I've got to run. See you tomorrow night, right?"

"Right…I hope." Her forehead wrinkled, and she gazed up at him like she feared she might never see him again. "Be careful."

Rob broke eye contact and stopped himself from thinking about Zeb.

"Call me after you're through and let me know you're okay."

He focused on Brittan again. "I'll be glad to."

Despite the pressure of duty, Rob had the impression that he just might be getting to Brittan. Her gaze looked like she might miss him if he didn't come back.

The lengthening shadows coupled with the fragrant twilight whispered romance, and Rob wished they were strolling hand-in-hand along the moonlit lake. He pictured them pausing while the velvet night wrapped around them like a warm blanket. They were in each other's arms. The kiss that followed rocked the night…and Rob was overcome with a desire to make it happen in real life.

Maybe I should give her something to think about while I'm gone, he decided and then put action to his urge. Without warning he bent and placed his lips on hers. When she gasped, Rob nearly gasped himself. He couldn't believe he followed through on his thought and wondered if she was going to slap him.

As her lips responded to his, Rob's fantasy became real. They held each other close as the kiss lengthened into the breathless zone. Soon breathless merged into a delicious drowning sensation. Even though the sea of amour bade Rob to give into its warm, welcoming waters, Rob feared he was pressing the limits…with himself and her.

Shaken to the core, he miraculously found the strength to loosen his arms and slowly inch away.

She stepped back. Her wide-eyed stare indicated she was every bit as dazzled as he was. A distant whippoorwill serenaded the night while Rob's pulse thumped out a counter-rhythm. *Now what?*

"Well, I guess I'll see you tomorrow night," Rob quipped and instantly wondered if he could have sounded more lame. His gaze traveled to her lips, and he fought the temptation to repeat the kiss.

"Sure. Tomorrow night," she agreed without a blink.

TWELVE

"So you think our prayers are working?" Lorna asked and plopped onto one of the breakfast nook chairs.

"Yes! Yes! Yes!" Heather squeaked out a cheer and raised her fist into the air. "You should have seen her, Lorna. She was flirting with him."

"Brittan? *Flirting?*" Holding a piece of pizza in one hand and a Diet Coke in the other, she raised her brows and focused on Heather.

"I promise! I'm so pumped right now I can't hardly see straight. I don't think I've ever seen such a dramatic answer to prayer."

"Me neither," Lorna admitted. She thoughtfully bit into her pizza and then stared across the room.

Heather rushed to the window that overlooked the driveway. She inched open the blinds and strained to see what might be happening outside. When Lorna's chair scraped against the tile, Heather glanced over her shoulder.

"Don't tell me you're *spying* on them?" she gasped and pulled the other side of the blinds away from the window before gazing out herself.

"Look at you!" Heather scoffed and waved toward her friend. "You make my spying out to be *soooo* scandalous and there you go!"

Lorna snickered. "You are such a bad influence," she accused and brushed her bangs out of her eyes.

Heather turned back to the task but spotted nothing except a blue jay pecking at the earth. Idly she wondered if this was the same bird that terrorized the backyard. "I can't see anything," she finally admitted.

"Nada here," Lorna replied. "We're at the wrong angle."

"Well, we tried." Heather released the blinds and turned back toward the table. Crossing her arms, she ignored the pizza and stared toward a collection of Renaissance crosses covering the wall near the table. "You know, Lorna," she said and stepped toward the crosses, "maybe we aren't praying enough about other things." Heather stroked an ornate cross. She inserted her hands into her jeans hip pockets and pivoted to face her friend, who was chowing down the meat-lover's pizza. Heather resisted a grimace. She knew Lorna was tired of being chided about her diet, but sometimes it was hard to refrain.

Lorna swallowed and nodded. "I was thinking the other day that sometimes we go into investigations without praying at all. We just barge in and hope God will protect us." She reached for a paper napkin and blotted at a dot of tomato sauce on the front of her tank top.

"And then we pray only when we get into trouble."

Lorna placed the pizza on her plate. "Maybe we need to take prayer more seriously."

"That's what I think." Heather nodded. She dropped into the seat across from Lorna. "This new case could get dangerous."

"Yes. I'm thinking we should break into the museum tonight and see if we can download the surveillance camera files. I've gleaned info from my mom, and I think we can pull it off."

"Sounds like we're going to need *a lot* of prayer," Heather acknowledged.

✳ ✸ ✳

As Rob turned toward the road, Brittan stiffened her resolve not to collapse. She'd been shocked motionless when Rob leaned in for a kiss. He'd given her no indication that he was even going to *try*. If he had, she would have kept him at arm's length. But there he was, his lips on hers, and some force Brittan couldn't name urged her to respond rather than push him away. So she responded, like a star-struck teenager.

Rob now strolled along the road toward his father's house as if he didn't have a care. An onlooker would never imagine he was heading into a life-threatening situation. He looked back at Brittan. She would have looked away, but figured it was obvious she was watching him anyway. When he offered a jaunty wave, she waved back and then turned toward her front door.

After stepping into the foyer, she snapped the door shut and locked it. *That will not happen again any time soon,* she admonished. *I refuse to fall prey to impulsive attraction. Good grief!* She snatched off her glasses and rubbed her eyes. *We just met!* Some women might think they were in the first stages of falling in love, but Brittan recognized her strong reaction for exactly what it was: the normal chemistry between the male and female of the species and nothing more. She'd long reasoned that there was a natural spark between a man and a woman, and that was the reason married people needed to be careful about getting too close to someone of the opposite sex...and single people needed to be careful about getting too close to someone who was an inappropriate choice for a mate. Electricity and chemical reactions happened when friendships got too cozy. Rash choices could alter the course of a person's whole life.

No way was she going to get caught up in an emotional whirlwind. She'd vowed long ago to make choices only after she carefully analyzed the consequences. So far that system was working well. She hadn't fallen prey to some of the snares that tripped up her college friends. A few were already divorced, single moms because they'd allowed their senseless attractions to inappropriate men to get in the way of logic.

But you've never responded to another man like you just did, a tiny voice reasoned.

"Good point. But I haven't kissed a man in years," she whispered. Brittan purposefully avoided the college dating game because she didn't want distractions while pursuing her education and she didn't believe she was ready for a permanent relationship. The last time she'd kissed someone, they'd both been adolescents.

My reaction to Rob was just chemistry—a grown woman responding to a man—and nothing more.

She stepped toward the brass-framed mirror hanging near the door. Brittan gave herself a hard stare. "I refuse to get carried away by this," she whispered. After locking her trembling knees, she examined her features to determine if she looked "kissed."

The last thing she wanted to do was encourage Lorna and Heather's questions and speculations. Both friends were shamelessly pushing her toward Rob. She'd already caught Heather whispering with him. It didn't take a brain surgeon to figure out what she was telling him...something about how she and Lorna hoped they would make a couple.

After deciding she didn't look kissed in the least, Brittan turned from her appraisal and spotted someone standing on the edge of the living room. She instinctively jumped, and then realized it was Heather.

"Everything all right?" Heather asked arching her brows.

"How long have you been there?" Brittan replied.

"Long enough to see you whispering to yourself in the mirror," Heather replied with a you-are-acting-really-weird expression. "Everything go okay on the playground?"

Brittan gave her a bland glance and didn't reply. She recognized she was doing exactly what she'd been irritated with Lorna about. Lorna had initially hidden her relationship with Michael

Hayden when they started dating. *Now I'm doing the same thing. How ironic.* But she didn't want to discuss Rob Lightly with them right now. Brittan didn't try to put words to why. Rather, she used her mental energy to keep herself logical, which was the safest course of action.

"Okaaaay," Heather finally said. "I guess it's time for a subject change." She jerked her head toward the kitchen. "Lorna and I decided the best move is to go ahead and access her mom's museum office tonight and get the video files. Lorna has been a busy lady the last few days. She has the alarm system code, the night watchman's schedule, and the key to her mom's office. The surveillance camera's digital files are supposed to be on a computer in her mom's office. Do you agree?"

"Yep. I've been waiting for weeks." Brittan strolled into the living room, and Heather fell in beside her as they moved toward the kitchen. "We've *got* to start moving...and fast. The last thing we need is for this wacko to find out who we are and come after us."

A garbled cough erupted from Heather. "Good grief!" she rasped.

Emerging into the kitchen, Brittan glanced toward her friend's fear-stricken features.

"I didn't even think about that!" Heather admitted, her eyes wide.

"Neither did I...until tonight," Brittan said.

"About what?" Lorna asked.

Brittan pivoted toward her, sitting at the breakfast nook table with the spread of pizza in front of her. She held a mammoth slice of the meat-lovers pizza and waited for Brittan's response.

"Whoever keeps leaving the roses at these crime scenes...what if he's out to hurt us?" Brittan said and eyed the pizza. Even the upheaval with the Rose and the topsy-turvy kiss couldn't stop her appetite. She was famished an hour ago and was even more so now.

Lorna's face slowly drained of color. She dropped her pizza on her plate and shoved it aside. "Good grief!" she moaned. "Why do you think of these things?"

"I don't know," Brittan admitted and settled onto a chair. "I guess somebody has to examine all the angles. I was also thinking it might be good for us to hit the rerun button on the crimes we've solved and see if we can find a link to who might be trying to get us."

"Absolutely!" Heather exclaimed and sat down on her chair. "Lorna and I were just talking about that too."

"Great minds think alike," Brittan said and didn't mention that Rob had given her the idea. "Somebody might have revenge on the brain."

"Right," Lorna said. "So do we examine the people who are behind bars because of the Rose and see what kind of friend and family links they have?"

"Yep," Brittan replied as she tore into a piece of the vegetarian pizza.

Idly she wondered what Rob would think if he knew she and her friends were the Rose. Then she offered up a prayer for his safety. He said he'd call her after the operation was over, and he was supposed to text message her so she could forward him the painting photos. Brittan remembered her cell phone on the end table. She made a mental note to get it and keep it with her until she heard from him. Even though she was *not* falling in love with Rob, Brittan still cared about his safety…in Christian love, of course.

She caught a glimpse of José's phone number scrawled on her palm. For a moment, Brittan couldn't remember why it was there. Then she recalled promising him she'd call to reschedule their date. Hiding a sigh, Brittan wondered how she'd managed to get two eligible men in her life. She was going to have to make a firm choice… and soon. One man was distraction enough.

THIRTEEN

Brittan pressed the light on her watch. The cheap, black timepiece verified that it was four in the morning, exactly the time the security guard took his break. According to the information Lorna had gleaned, he was allowed a 30-minute "lunch break," which he took in the employee lounge on the first floor. Her mother's office was at basement level, along with the museum manager's. The surveillance cameras were not in operation on that level.

"This way," Lorna whispered and motioned the three friends toward the sloped walkway that led to the museum's lowest level back entrance.

Brittan cast a final glance toward the parking lot and Houston's lighted streets. By nine last night, the three friends had gone to bed with plans to arise at three to take care of their "little adventure." The rented Chevrolet was parked in the lot and was easily accessible should they need to make a quick escape. The moist morning held a chill that helped alleviate the perspiration on the back of Brittan's neck. Occasionally a pair of headlights and the hum of a car engine penetrated the streets, testifying to the few people whose jobs demanded their being in transit at this crazy hour.

Brittan scurried down the slope and waited behind Heather and

Lorna near a door marked "Employees Only." All three friends were dressed in black from head to foot. Yesterday evening, while Brittan took care of the car rental and Lorna gleaned the final museum details, Heather went to a sports shop in the mall and purchased black ski masks, which all three wore as caps only.

"Okay," Lorna whispered and took a quick glance over her shoulder. "I'm about to turn the key. Once I do, I have only 60 seconds to enter the security code. Ready?"

"Ready," Brittan whispered. She yanked down her ski mask and maneuvered the knit cap around her glasses.

Heather and Lorna covered their faces as well. "We should have worn these things when we started," Heather whispered.

"We're still learning," Lorna replied. "Okay, here goes." The lock clicked. The door swung inward. Lorna stepped into the darkness, and a series of tiny beeps floated into the night. Soon her covered face appeared around the doorway.

"We're good," she said.

Brittan followed Heather into the hallway. The musty smell reminded Brittan of a library's comforting ambiance. Once they finished this case, she planned to spend an entire weekend in her father's library reading something nice and calming. Her heart beat against her ribs so powerfully that Brittan wondered if she would ever feel calm again. Breaking into her parents' newspaper hadn't ruffled her in the least because she knew that if they got caught, she could talk her way out of trouble. But this was city-owned property, and she didn't think the folks at city hall would be as understanding as her dear ol' dad.

Brittan practiced controlled breathing and told herself to stop the fear nonsense. This stint would be just like every other one they pulled off. They would penetrate the scene, take care of business, and get out before they were detected.

We're the Rose, she reminded herself. *We've been invincible for two years.* Her hammering pulse slowed to mere pounding.

Lorna paused near a doorway with a plaque that read "Board of Directors, Chairman." She inserted a key into the knob and opened the door.

Flexing her perspiring fingers in her thin, cotton gloves, Brittan slipped into the office, followed by Heather and Lorna. Lorna silently closed the door and locked it.

"Whew! We made it!" Lorna whispered. "Now." She snapped on a tiny flashlight and pointed it toward a computer system in the corner. "Copies of the digital archives are supposed to be on that system."

Brittan pulled her own flashlight out of her pocket, clicked it on, and directed it around the room. This nook appeared to be in existence for function only. No frills. Lorna had said her mother only frequented the office as needed—several times a month.

"This is where you come in, Brittan." Lorna glanced toward her friend. The ski mask surrounding Lorna's eyes made her look wicked.

Heather's snicker made Brittan shift her attention toward her other friend. "What?" Brittan asked.

"Your glasses are poking out of the eye holes." Heather let the explanation stand on its own.

Lorna chuckled and Brittan smiled. "Whatever works," Brittan said and moved toward the computer.

Booting it up took less than a minute. The fun part was hacking her way into the system. The only information Lorna didn't have was the password. But given time, Brittan had no doubt she could get in. Most people made the mistake of using common dates and names that were easily remembered.

Brittan pulled out a sheet of paper from her hip pocket and opened it. She'd already asked Lorna for the important dates and other key names that her mom might have used for a password. A possible hang-up was if the password hadn't been set by Lorna's mother. If that was the case, Brittan would be blindly hacking. That would take much longer.

"I'm going to see what I can find on these shelves," Heather whispered and moved toward a row of shelves behind the desk.

The screen's blue glow cast a ghostly aura upon the room, and Heather's dark form looked as devious as Lorna's.

"I'm on the desk," Lorna claimed, and Brittan noticed she'd lifted her ski mask from her face.

Brittan scratched at her own mask and figured she appeared as frightful as her friends. Like Lorna, she pulled the mask up, allowing it to remain atop her head as a cap. The cool air hitting Brittan's face sent a wave of resolve through her being. She *had* to hack into this system. And they didn't have all night.

After 15 minutes, Brittan began to think it just might take the rest of the night. So when she pressed the enter button yet again, she expected the same error message. But this time she met her goal.

"Bingo!" she whispered. "I'm in—*finally*."

Both friends scurried to her side. "I knew you'd do it," Lorna said.

"Me too," Heather added. "You'd make a better criminal than most out there," she whispered through a smile.

"Thanks for the vote of confidence," Brittan drawled and clicked on the icon that read "Video Archives." "Like taking candy from a baby," she purred. Brittan pulled the flash drive from her pocket, inserted it into the USB port, and hit the copy button. "Let the download begin," she mumbled.

"I don't know how long it's been off," a male voice echoed from the hallway.

Brittan's fingers flexed against the mouse and then stiffened. She cast a glance back and up and caught the startled expressions of both her friends.

"I just noticed the light off a few minutes ago. Could be it's some sort of a power failure. I don't see any signs of a break-in. I've just got to check these offices down here, and then it'll be good. Really I don't think anything's up, but thought I should call you and report it—especially with the investigation still on. Having an artifact stolen on my shift made me paranoid."

Silence permeated the hall. Then keys jingled, and the door across the hall creaked open. The male voice spoke again. "Okay. I'll call you if I find anything. Bye."

"We've got to hide!" Lorna hissed.

A tiny window popped up that read, "Download Complete." Her hand trembling, Brittan shut down the computer.

She yanked down her ski mask and glanced over her shoulder.

"Other than beneath the computer desk, there's no place *to* hide," Heather whispered, her panicked gaze darting around the room. "And we all three can't fit under there." She pulled her ski mask down and motioned for Lorna to do the same.

"So what do we do?" Brittan asked. The computer screen went black. She pulled the flash drive from the port and stuffed it into her pocket.

The doorknob rattled. Heather pushed Lorna against the wall, beside the door. Then she grabbed Brittan's arm and shoved her beside Lorna. As Heather crouched in front of the opening door, Brittan didn't need a coach to tell her what was on her friend's agenda. The man's light had barely landed on Heather. He had only a second to let out a garbled, surprised yelp before Heather put her black belt skills to use. She kicked him just below his breastbone.

The security guard fell into a groaning heap and then went silent.

Brittan didn't pause to examine him. She knew a blow to the solar plexus could knock a person out—long enough to ensure their escape if they hurried.

She lunged into the hallway and hit the back door first. The crash bar made exiting a breeze. When the door slammed shut, she glanced over her shoulder to verify that Heather and Lorna were close behind. The sounds of pounding feet and heavy breathing mingled with the distant whirr of early morning traffic as Brittan dashed to the rental vehicle. While she unlocked the door and sprang into the driver's seat, both friends dove into the backseat.

"Stay down!" Brittan admonished and slammed the door. She kept her attention on the museum's back entrance until she pulled into the street. Then she adjusted the rearview mirror to watch the museum until it was out of sight.

"Coast is clear." Brittan removed her ski mask and adjusted her glasses.

Both friends rose. "I hate that I had to do that," Heather said, "but I didn't think I had a choice."

"Are you kidding?" Lorna exclaimed. "You saved our *hides!*"

A clicking seat belt and the car's consistent warning chimes reminded Brittan to put her own seat belt on.

"He won't be out long," Heather assured. "I didn't give him all I had."

Brittan snapped on the right blinker and merged on the freeway.

Giddy with relief, the friends burst into a round of uncontrolled laughter. By the time Brittan steered onto the exit that led toward the downtown penthouse, she was blotting the corners of her eyes.

Brittan slowed and made the final turn that led them into the maze of skyscrapers. "I guess we'll be in the headlines tomorrow," she mused. Now that the laughter had subsided, Brittan wondered about the implications of their little journey.

"The poor security guard," Lorna said through a final chuckle. "He's having all the luck. First the necklace was stolen on his shift, and now he gets kicked into next week."

As the headlights illuminated the city blocks in the distance, Lorna's words sank into Brittan's mind.

"Repeat that, Lorna!" she exclaimed.

"What?"

"What you just said!"

"He was the security guard on duty when the necklace was stolen," Heather interrupted.

"Exactly," Brittan said.

"That's odd," Lorna mused. "The necklace was stolen during business hours."

"Right," Brittan replied.

"Maybe he was moved to the graveyard shift after that," Lorna speculated.

"Who knows? Maybe it was that or be fired," Heather said.

"Can you find out?" Brittan glanced over her shoulder toward Lorna.

"Are you thinking he's involved?" she asked.

Brittan shrugged. "Who knows? But why not at least check him out? It might be a dead end, and then again, it might be a lead." She touched the flash drive in her pocket. "We've got the video files. That's a start. Lorna, would you see what you can find out about the security guard setup tomorrow?"

"Sure. I'll have dinner with Mom and Dad. I'm sure the break-in will be on the news, and she'll be talking about it nonstop. If I ask about the security guard, it won't look suspicious at all."

"Good thinking," Brittan approved and steered the Dodge into the parking garage. The three friends decided to spend the night at the penthouse because the parking garage offered a level of protection unmatched by Heather's suite in the family estate and Brittan's lake house. Parking the car in the garage minimized the chances of it being linked to them. Only a rotating night watchman might find their late night departures odd. Because the departures happened so seldom, Brittan figured the night watchman on duty during one investigation was not the same during the next. She steered the vehicle through the garage and found a spot between Lorna's Jeep and her own Jaguar.

With the museum business behind them, Brittan pondered the other upheaval tonight. Rob had been called out to a hostage situation. He'd promised to call her with news of his safety. But last night when Brittan went to sleep, she'd not heard from him. The evening news had reported the siege was still in progress at ten. Even though Brittan wanted to stay up and wait for his call, she forced the whole thing from her mind and made herself go to sleep. The first thing she checked when she awoke at three was her cell phone, but there was no message from Rob.

Now Brittan was officially worried. And no matter how fiercely she tried to calm her thoughts, they wouldn't be quieted. If Rob didn't call by the time she woke up this morning, hopefully the morning news would report that everything was fine.

FOURTEEN

José Herrera poured a steaming cup of coffee into one of the mugs he took from the row of hooks under the cabinet at the gift shop. His mom's stores were always closed on Sunday, and that was when José took care of most of the bookkeeping. His mother always nagged him about going to church, but he never went. He figured he'd done his time in childhood. No sense flinging himself into a guilt trip over the matter. He preferred taking care of business and never looked back.

He pulled a flask from his briefcase and set it on the table in the center of the cramped break room. José laced his coffee with the alcohol and screwed the lid back on. Last week's "work" had been harder to expunge from his conscience than his normal operations. The drink helped him relax and rid his mind of difficult thoughts. Even though José didn't personally kill the painter in Denver, he was periodically haunted by the thought that he was just as guilty as the murderer.

But I wasn't even there, he reasoned and took a deep swallow of the coffee. *I tried to talk Eduardo out of the whole deal, but he refused.* As the heat spread through his stomach, his nerves calmed. He removed his laptop from its case, placed it on top of the table, and turned it on.

While he waited, José picked up the remote and pressed the power button to turn on the small TV kept in the corner of the room. CNN flashed onto the screen. José never wavered from regularly watching the news, especially when he'd been up to something special. As suspected, they were highlighting the Mosier murder. Shortly after that snippet, a new headline flashed across the bottom of the screen.

He lifted the mug toward his lips.

"More action at the Houston Museum of Art," the spokesman said.

José set the coffee mug back down.

"The priceless Incan necklace stolen three months ago has never been recovered, and now the same night watchman who reported the missing necklace is involved in more action. This time Moe Van Cleave didn't fare so well. He claims someone broke into the museum, shut down the alarm system, and prowled through the offices."

His fingers flexing around the mug, José's eyes widened as a picture of the ruddy-faced fool flashed on the screen.

"No one seems to know the reason for the break-in at this time. Nothing is missing. When the watchman stumbled upon the prowler, who he said was a female dressed in black, he received a blow that knocked him out. She escaped. Authorities aren't saying whether or not this episode is linked to the necklace's disappearance."

José's cell phone buzzed rhythmically from inside the briefcase, and he knew the caller was Eduardo. He downed another swallow of coffee, retrieved the phone, and flipped it open. "Have you been watching the news?" José asked.

"Yes," Eduardo's voice was as calm now as it had been the night Mosier lost his life. He'd simply called José and said "The job's done" in a voice as emotionless as stone. "That idiot!" Eduardo exclaimed. "He let someone into the museum. I just hope this doesn't scare him into talking."

"He knows he'd better not," José purred. "His life depends on it, right?" The only thing José detested about lifting precious artifacts was that sometimes they were required to pay off an accomplice or two. Even though they usually worked around the necessity, they were forced into a payoff three times. So far the collaborators were cooperative. The money that was waved under their noses kept them silent. They also realized that if they leaked any information, they could land in prison at best—or worst, lose their lives. That usually secured their silence. José and Eduardo disguised themselves and never revealed their identities or gave away their locations, but they made sure their threats were believable.

Of all the collaborators, Moe Van Cleave was the most cooperative. He simply unlocked the jewel case and turned his attention elsewhere. Other than getting his wrist slapped and being banned to the graveyard shift, Moe suffered no consequences. Now he'd let his guard down and allowed a prowler into the museum. If he lost his job, José wondered if he might be induced to squeal to save his hide.

He drummed his fingers against the table. Even if he leaked what he knew, Moe had no idea who'd really taken the necklace. José had disguised his appearance with a beard, colored contacts, and a brown wig. Eduardo, posing as a maintenance man, tilted the surveillance camera away from the scene so no footage was taken of the heist.

José always checked and double-checked against the possibility that he left a clue the authorities might pick up. He'd been told he was obsessive-compulsive, and José used the trait to his advantage. So far the process stopped him from leaving any clues. But that didn't stop him from worrying about Moe and what the moron might leak.

"You've gone quiet too long," Eduardo finally said. "What are you thinking?"

"About Van Cleave," José grumped.

"Should we take him out?"

José's throat constricted. "What do you think?"

"Might not hurt," Eduardo commented, as if talking about killing a flea.

José admitted the choice was convenient. He guzzled the rest of the coffee and didn't mind that it burned his gut. When the final drop slid down his throat, a new thought struck him. "On the other hand, maybe this is what we were hoping for." He narrowed his eyes and blindly gazed toward the TV.

"What do you mean?" Eduardo questioned.

"We wanted to flush out the Rose, right?"

"Hmmm."

"Maybe that's exactly what we've done," José prophesied. "You said you thought the murder might be enough to draw her out."

"You're convinced it's a woman, aren't you?" Eduardo asked.

"Yes. I can't get away from it. And the report I just heard said whoever kicked the security guard was a woman—or small enough to be one," he added.

"But do we know she was the Rose?"

"Maybe Moe will help us find out," José mused.

"So we milk him for information, and then we shoot him?" Eduardo asked.

José frowned. He'd heard of dogs getting a taste for blood and turning into killers. Could that happen with people too?

"Let's pump him for information," José agreed. "And then if he needs to die, that's that."

"I'll tell you when I've cornered Moe," Eduardo affirmed. "Stay ready."

"I'm ready now," José said. "The sooner we track down the Rose, the better." He snapped the phone shut. José wouldn't have a second of remorse when he killed the Rose. Juan wouldn't be out of prison for another year. The Rose had stolen years of his cousin's young life...not to mention cutting off Juan's work in the business. He'd smuggled numerous artifacts out of the United States, including Marco Polo's original log of his journeys. After José had stolen that little number from the Rare Book and Manuscript Library at Columbia University, some nut was ready to pay half a million for it. But the Rose had caused Juan's arrest, and when the authorities invaded his place, they confiscated the log. She'd also threatened José and Eduardo's security...and she *would* pay.

Brittan knocked on Rob's dad's front door. The dark brown, A-frame home reminded her of something out of a gingerbread storybook. It only needed a few gumdrops to decorate the windows and the image would be complete. Each house in this stretch of beach was as different from one another as their owners. While Brittan's place was a multiwindowed showplace, two massive log cabins sat between her house and Mr. Lightly's place.

"And this one's the gingerbread house," she said over a yawn.

After sleeping in a bit, she and her friends attended late church, enjoyed lunch together, and went home. Heather took the flash drive home to peruse the video files. Lorna planned to have dinner with her parents and see what she could glean about the night watchman. And Brittan promised to work the Rob Lightly connection. Although she was genuinely interested in getting to know him better, Brittan had every intention of taking advantage of his connections with the Houston Police Force. Even though she might not get access to police files, Brittan could certainly draw out what Rob knew or learned.

I'd be crazy not to, she told herself.

She knocked on the door again and shifted the deli cheesecake to check her watch. It was already two-thirty, and Brittan still hadn't heard from Rob. She watched the local news and heard a report about the hostage situation, but there was no word of any officers being hurt.

Maybe no news is good news, she hoped.

Mr. Lightly's lack of response heightened Brittan's anxiety. *What if Rob's in the hospital, and his dad's with him?* After searching for a doorbell and finding none, Brittan pounded one last time.

The door rattled and an attractive gentleman observed her with a half-annoyed, half-interested expression.

Elvis appeared beside him and offered a friendly "Woof!"

"Mr. Lightly?" Brittan asked. "Rob's dad?"

"Yes." He bent to pat Elvis and eyed the cheesecake. "I'm Simon Lightly."

"I'm Brittan Shay." She shifted the cheesecake to her left hand and extended her right. "I live a few houses down," she said while shaking his hand.

"Of course," Simon said through a grin. "Rob told me about you. You're a bit early though." His gaze trailed toward the road, and Brittan heard a vehicle pulling into the driveway. Hoping it was Rob, she glanced over her shoulder. A black Lexus stopped behind a Ford pickup. The person who got out was tall, blonde, glowing, and appeared to be around 40.

Hmmm, Brittan thought. Simon Lightly was a fine specimen of mature manhood, and Brittan didn't doubt that he attracted a good number of younger women. Tall and broad-shouldered, he reminded her a bit of Sean Connery.

When Brittan turned her gaze back to him, he'd stopped observing her and was smiling at the new arrival. Another discreet peek at the woman revealed she was dressed in scrubs, causing Brittan to deduce she worked in the medical field.

Okay, what's up? Brittan thought. Given Rob's protective attitude toward his father, Brittan wondered if he knew just how much of a social life his dad really had. She conjectured that Rob had no clue.

The newcomer stopped near Brittan and eyed her as if she was a rival. While Brittan had been told she looked more mature than her early twenties, she couldn't imagine anyone thinking she was making a play for a man in his fifties. But the woman's possessive flair suggested she was very much the romantic flame in Mr. Lightly's life, and she very much didn't appreciate another woman bringing him cheesecake.

"Dr. Francis," Lightly said, "this is Rob's friend, Brittan Shay. She lives a few houses down."

"Brittan, this is my doctor, Deloris Francis."

"Hi, Brittan," Deloris said, her features relaxing.

"Hello," Brittan replied and wondered if Mr. Lightly really thought he was fooling her. *As if doctors still made house calls,* she thought but kept her expression innocent. "I just stopped in to see if you've heard from Rob...to see how he is," Brittan said. She lifted the cheesecake. "And I was bringing this by for tonight. That way you'd know I had dessert covered, and you wouldn't worry about it."

"You didn't need to do that," Simon responded.

"I know," Brittan replied, "but I wanted to."

Elvis pranced outside and licked at Dr. Francis' hand like they were the best of friends.

"Is Rob okay?" she added again.

"Sure. He called late last night after he got home. I always make him call when he goes out like that—no matter how late it is. It was late," he added. "After midnight."

Brittan nodded. "I'm glad to hear he's okay. He told me he'd call, but I guess he forgot."

"He probably didn't want to wake you up. And he had to be back at work today. So my bet is he got sucked into something else and hasn't had the chance." Simon winked. "Sometimes he can be a little too work-focused, if you ask me. I'm encouraging him to get out more." He beamed straight at her, and Brittan wondered if she was part of a grand scheme. "Why not give him a buzz? Do you have his number?"

"No." Brittan shook her head. "I gave him mine."

"I'll give you his then." Simon stepped away from the door, and that's when Brittan noticed his prosthesis protruding from his shorts. If not for the stark evidence, Brittan would have never suspected. He carried himself like a man with no thought of disability. When he reappeared, he was scrawling a number on a notepad. "Here's his cell. Go ahead and call him!" he encouraged with a grin the size of Dallas. "He'll be *glad* to hear from you."

She accepted the number and was suddenly immersed in a delicious flashback that involved Rob's lips on hers. She wondered if he'd told his father they kissed. Rob said his dad was his best friend. Brittan broke eye contact and kept her face impassive.

"Well, here's the cheesecake," she said and then darted a polite smile toward the doctor. "Will you be here for dinner as well?" she asked.

"No." Dr. Francis shook her head.

"She's here to check how my new prosthesis is fitting," Simon said, his voice firm. "I lost my leg in Vietnam," he added and glanced down. "I put it somewhere for safe keeping, and I never remembered where I left it." He chuckled.

Brittan smiled. "I see. Well, I'll leave you two to your...I'll just go on back home and call Rob." She pointed toward her house and backed away from the door.

Simon opened the door wider, and as Deloris stepped inside, he stepped outside and said, "Wait a minute, Brittan, if you don't mind."

Brittan halted.

Simon eyed her with a knowing expression. "I know we just met, but I have a favor to ask."

She looked at him and finally gave a slight nod.

"Rob doesn't know about..." He glanced over his shoulder.

"I don't think he's ready for a stepmother, so we just..." He shrugged.

"Okay." Brittan nodded. "So you don't want me to mention her to him?"

"No, please don't. Not right now. I'll tell him when it's time. Just not now."

"All right," she drawled.

"Thanks. And I'm looking forward to tonight."

"Sure. Me too," Brittan affirmed.

"You think I'm being deceptive," Simon noted.

"Oh really?" Brittan lifted her brows.

"Maybe I am," he admitted, "but right now I don't know what else to do. I guess I'm a little protective when it comes to Rob."

"That seems to be going around with you two," Brittan observed.

"Yes, maybe so," Simon said. "When he realized Deloris and I were getting serious, he couldn't believe that I could do that so soon. My wife had only been gone a little more than a year, and he was really bent out of shape. He thought I was rushing and making a mistake, so I just..." He shrugged. "But my wife would want me to be happy." He gazed into her eyes as if needing her approval.

"I'm sure she would," Brittan agreed and wondered how she'd feel if one of her parents passed away and the other started dating again. *It would be really odd,* she thought. Brittan loved her mom and dad and couldn't imagine either one of them with anyone else. "But I can also see that it might be hard for Rob to accept. He said you were really close."

"We were and we still are. That's what makes this so hard." He motioned toward the door. "And I will tell him soon. Deloris and I are both tired of hiding it."

"That is the best option," Brittan concurred.

"If you'll just keep it under your hat until..."

"I will," Brittan assured him. "I'm good at secrets."

FIFTEEN

Brittan strode home and only allowed herself one glance back toward the A-frame home. As she stepped into her foyer and closed the door, she had to laugh out loud.

What a life! she thought. Simon Lightly was acting like a 17-year-old hiding a relationship from his disapproving parents. Except the "parent" was his son.

Brittan hurried toward the south side of her home and into the guest bedroom. Like every other room in this house, it was lined with windows. Brittan stepped around the Chippendale loveseat near the poster bed, inched apart the horizontal blinds, and peered toward Mr. Lightly's yard.

Even though part of her felt like a nosy neighbor of the most annoying proportions, the investigator within would not be suppressed. She was about to release the blinds when Deloris exited Simon's home. Brittan shamelessly watched the woman open her trunk. Then she pulled out a pink striped bag and an overnight case.

Brittan's eyes bugged. She recognized that pink striped bag. She'd brought home one just like it last week. "Victoria's Secret!" she hissed, and her mouth fell open.

When Simon again opened the door for Deloris, he glanced up and down the street and then disappeared inside.

Brittan released the blinds. "I am not believing this," she whispered. *This is beyond a social life...it's downright...active.* Rob had mentioned that he and his father were men of deep faith. A mid-afternoon fling didn't add up to Rob's testimony of his father.

Brittan's eyes narrowed as a fresh realization proved the only explanation. "Either Mr. Lightly's not walking the walk or he's married!" she said and settled on the latter explanation. Simon said Rob wasn't ready for a *stepmother.* He didn't say Rob wasn't ready for his father to start dating. "No." She shook her head. "He said *stepmother.*" Her brows lifted. "That's the reason Simon Lightly wanted to move away from Rob," she deduced. "And the reason he won't connect with his neighbors." *He's hiding this marriage from Rob and doesn't want any neighbor to know either. The fewer people who know, the less likely Rob will find out.*

"Oh my word," she breathed and dropped to the side of the bed. "Rob is in for quite a surprise." She covered her mouth and shook her head. He was *so* certain he and his father were *so* close. This would really be a shocker.

"Oh well." Brittan lifted both hands. "I can't let myself get dragged into it." She traipsed down the hallway and into her living room. *As far as I'm concerned, mum's the word. Rob doesn't need to know I ever knew.*

She flopped onto the couch, switched on *Fox News,* and waited to see if there was any more commentary on last night's museum incident. She'd been following it since she got up this morning. But before she made it through the first round of headlines, her cell phone rang.

Keeping her gaze on the TV, Brittan pulled the phone from her pocket and noted Rob's name. She flipped open the phone and muted the television.

"Hi, Brittan!" Rob's cheerful voice floated over the line.

"Hello," Brittan replied. "I was wondering about you. I never heard—"

"Yes, I'm sorry 'bout that," Rob said. "Dad just called and said you'd been asking about me."

"Wow! He works fast, doesn't he?" *If only you knew just how fast.*

"Yes. He gave me the 'what for' for not calling you. But, honestly, I didn't want to wake you up at two-thirty, and then I had to be back at work this morning. I've been up to my neck in alligators ever since."

Brittan slipped off her sandals, rested her feet on the oriental coffee table, and stifled a yawn. "Up to your neck in alligators?" she echoed.

"Yep, as in too busy to breathe."

"Oh." Brittan chuckled. "That's a new one on me," she said and wondered how Lorna would mix up that phrase if she heard it.

"Did you know the Houston Museum of Art was broken into last night?" Rob asked.

Her muscles tightened. "Yes, it's all over the news," she casually replied.

"My men took the night watchman's report on that," he said.

"Really?" Brittan feigned disinterest. "I guess that affected your day."

"Yep."

"Any leads on who dun it?" she said with a sassy edge to her voice.

"None. If you've seen the news, you know what we know. Looks like it was some woman who knows martial arts. She kicked the stuffing out of him."

"It would appear that way."

"You said you're a big fan of the Rose, right?" he asked.

"Yes." Brittan lowered her feet and sat up.

"This is off the record, okay?"

"Okay," Brittan replied and allowed a smidgen of interest in her voice.

"Think it might have been her?"

"Unless there's any hard evidence, I guess nobody really knows."

"Right. I guess not," Rob replied.

Brittan settled back against the couch.

"Are we still on for tonight?"

"Sure!" Brittan enthused and hoped her relief at the change of subject didn't make her sound overly excited. "I just took a cheesecake down to your dad so he'd know he doesn't have to worry about dessert tonight."

"That was thoughtful," Rob purred. The tone of his voice reminded her of last night...and their electric kiss.

Brittan wondered if he planned to repeat it tonight, and her stomach warmed. Then she stiffened her resolve and forced the kiss from her mind. The last thing she needed was to let her friendship with Rob progress too swiftly or to let her emotions drive her decisions. She was a logical woman and would remain that way—no matter what!

"He seems like a really nice man," she said and kept her voice pleasant yet firm.

"He is," Rob said. "I think tonight will do him good. Even though he's still making contact at the gym and church, he seems to be withdrawing to some degree. It's odd. I can't quite put my finger on it. He doesn't seem depressed. I don't know. It's as if he's limiting his contacts with the outside world. He moved from a neighborhood where people knew and loved him, and now he won't even make friends with any of his neighbors. It's almost like he's...well, maybe...hiding something."

"Oh really?" Brittan said and thought, *You got that one right. If only you knew.*

"Yep." Rob huffed. "He says I worry about him too much."

"Yes, and he seems to worry about you too." Brittan spotted a stray piece of potpourri still on the carpet.

"Think so? What'd he say?"

Brittan stifled a yawn. "Something about you working too much." She bent to pick up the dried flower and tossed it back into the basket.

Rob chuckled. "That doesn't surprise me. He keeps telling me I'll die a lonely old man if I don't stop working so many hours."

"That's encouraging."

"Tell me about it!" Rob replied.

Brittan noticed the faint smudges of José's phone number still on her palm and realized she'd never called him, and she couldn't remember where she'd placed his card. Their banter continuing, she meandered toward the window that overlooked her backyard. Holding her palm up to the sunlight, Brittan strained for a clear view of the phone number but accepted the cause as lost. *Oh well. He'll find me if he wants to talk.*

She snickered over one of Rob's puns and was overcome by a yawn she had no power to stop. The longer they chatted, the heavier her eyes grew. Finally Brittan realized her trip to the museum was catching up with her, and she was seriously considering a Sunday afternoon nap.

"You sound as sleepy as all get out," Rob announced.

"Sorry. I guess I am," Brittan replied.

"What happened? Did you and your two friends go out and have a wild night on the town or something?"

"Right!" Brittan retorted. "We're about as far removed from party animals as you can get."

"So you just hung out together at your place until the wee hours?"

"Something like that," she hedged and tugged the cord that closed her blinds. The long shadows that enveloped the room were as comforting as a warm blanket on a cold winter's night.

"Look, Rob," she said over another yawn, "I'm, like, really sorry, but it looks like I'm going to go into a coma whether I want to or not. I am *so sleepy* I think I'm going to *die!* I…didn't sleep a lot last night. I was up a while, and I think it's getting to me."

"Okay," he said, his voice thick with a smile. "I understand. Listen, before you conk out, don't forget to text me those photos you took of the Mosier print, okay? I'm going to see if I can make that stop when I get off work."

"I'll be glad to."

"I'll be seeing you tonight then."

"Yep," Brittan agreed through another yawn that merged into mutual laughter. After ending the call, she sent Rob the photos. Then she put her cell phone on the end table, wandered to her room, and collapsed onto her bed.

Rob leaned forward in his chair and scrutinized the photos. To his untrained eye, he could see nothing out of the ordinary, but he trusted Brittan's appraisal. With plans to call Beynards soon, Rob inserted his cell phone into the harness on his belt. He leaned back in his chair, and it released the same squeak it had for the last year. Picking up a pencil, he tapped the clutter in the center of his desk.

Without realizing it, Brittan had confirmed what he'd suspected. She and her little friends had a "party" in the museum last night. Idly he wondered what they'd been after. Nothing was missing, according to the report. They'd been really good and left no fingerprints or evidence.

Rob stared at the row of achievement plaques and certificates of merit lining the wall and wondered which of the three had knocked the security guard batty. Sounded like a hard blow to the solar plexus…a martial arts primary move. Rob wasn't trained in martial arts, but he knew the score.

He debated what to do. Arresting Brittan and her buds for

breaking and entering would certainly throw a chink in their relationship. And he had no proof whatsoever that she and her friends
were the ones who broke into the museum. He had no grounds
for a warrant. Not revealing his suspicion to his investigating team
went against everything that had earned all the awards, but he
decided not to mention it.

Whatever the Rose was up to, it was probably for a good cause.
Even though it appeared they sometimes used shady methods, they
got the job done. No telling what rules they broke when they'd
solved the mayor's murder.

"Git 'er dun," he drawled.

He laid aside the pencil and stood. After a hard stretch that
ended in his own yawn, Rob meandered toward the open door
where the smell of stale coffee was as distracting as the hubbub
keeping several officers on their feet. Following his nose to the coffeepot in the break room, Rob picked up the carafe and poured out
something that looked like black maple syrup. The sick thing was
the cops drank the stuff.

He nearly gagged at the thought and prepared a new pot. Rob
was committed to being here until five today. After that, he'd go
home and get ready to be with Brittan again. By the time he was
holding a fresh cup of coffee, he solidified the decision to let the
Rose do her thing. He'd stay close to Brittan though. "Really close,"
he whispered through a smile.

He'd watch and wait, and maybe the Rose would lead him
straight to the person who stole that rare necklace or into the lair
of Mosier's murderer.

SIXTEEN

José walked around the back of Brittan's lake house. When she didn't answer her doorbell, he decided to see if she was in the back. The backyard was only occupied by an ornery blue jay chasing a squirrel through the maze of flora. The shimmering lake caught José's attention, and he strained for any sign of a boat Brittan could be on. All he spotted was a trio of fishermen in a bass boat.

Sighing, José glanced toward the home and wondered if he might be able to spot her through one of the many windows. Her Jaguar was in the driveway, and he suspected she must be home, unless someone had picked her up. He walked near the back door and strained to see through the slits in the closed blinds. Finally José found a gap in a side window. Cupping his hand, he peered into the living room. From this limited vantage, he saw no one. He walked to the next row of windows. The wide open blinds revealed a massive bathroom, replete with a garden tub. His eyebrows flexed as his mind traveled into the next couple of months. By then he should have his prize.

While most of the blinds in the next room were closed tight, one set remained partially open. José gazed through the slits at the woman he'd come to see. Brittan lay on her bed, her back to him. He glanced at his watch and confirmed it was five-forty-five.

Either she's sick or she had a bad night and is taking a late nap, he decided.

A satin coverlet draped across her body, a slinky invitation for José to join her. Her short hair splayed across the pillow, inviting him to run his fingers through the shiny strands. José rubbed his thumb against his fingers and drew in a deep breath. The sweet smell of springtime couldn't compete with the exquisite aroma of her skin. He closed his eyes and was consumed with gnawing desire that worsened as the seconds progressed.

He opened his eyes and stared upon her form once more. Brittan shifted to her back and rested her arm above her head. Her profile was in clear view. Her high cheekbones were as exotic as her full lips that beckoned José to taste their sweetness. His pulse began a hard hammer as he considered climbing through the window...if it was open. José looked down at his blazer and slacks. He'd taken special care with his clothing this evening, determined to outshine that loser from down the road. His attire certainly didn't lend itself to crawling through a chest-high window—even if the window was open. Pride reminded him that sneaking through her window and taking what he wanted belied his original goal of seducing her. He wanted her to willingly acquiesce. *That will be much tastier than anything forced.*

José rested his fingertips upon the windowsill and swallowed the saliva swelling against his tongue. He'd wait...watch until she awoke, and then he'd move to her front door and ring the bell as if he'd just arrived.

Brittan stirred again and turned to face him. Her eyes lazily opened and then widened. Afraid she'd seen him, José ducked. He counted to 10 and then eased up just enough to peer through the bottom of the blinds.

Now wearing her glasses, Brittan stood in front of the dresser, frantically combing her hair. Next she moved toward her closet, flung open the door, and pulled out an outfit. José's pulse leaped anew. She was changing clothes.

When she marched straight into the bathroom and closed the door, he muttered an expletive. Within minutes Brittan emerged wearing a pair of cotton capri pants and a matching beige blouse. The outfit looked like it came from the Caribbean and clung to her petite curves in a mouth-watering way. She stepped back toward the closet, slipped on a pair of sandals, and hurried up the hallway.

Apparently she was going somewhere and was late. When she opened the door, she'd no doubt spot his Volvo in the drive, and he needed to be near it. José trotted around the house and made it to the sidewalk just as the front door opened. He slipped his hand into his pocket and feigned a casual stroll along the curved walkway. When Brittan stepped outside and closed the door, he stopped and faked a surprised stare.

She was on her cell phone and didn't notice him at all. "Okay. Thanks, Heather," she said. "Yes, I'll be glad to take a look later. Just keep trying. Okay...will do...I'll call you later." She snapped the phone shut and looked straight up at José.

"Hello, gorgeous!" he said.

She blankly stared at him.

"What's the matter? Did you forget who I am?"

"No." Brittan shook her head. "Not at all. You just surprised me!"

"Well, you forgot to call me." He faked a pout and moved nearer. In the evening sun, her hair reminded him of iridescent strands of silk.

"Yes, I'm sorry about that." She tugged her purse strap up and onto her shoulder and then lifted the palm of her hand. "I forgot to write it down, and then it was washed off."

"But you have my card."

"I'm afraid I misplaced it," she admitted.

"Should I give you another?" When she hesitated, he rushed, "I came by to see if we could have our date tonight." José extended both hands toward her. "But it looks as if you're already going somewhere."

"Yes, yes, I am." She broke eye contact and gazed toward the road.

A gust of warm wind whipped through the yard and carried the smell of someone grilling. The skin on the back of José's neck crawled, and a sixth sense hinted that she wasn't going out with the girls. He glanced toward the A-frame house, three doors down. José tightened his jaw and wondered if that might be the reason she ended their date last night. She'd said "a friend" had experienced a death and was upset. Perhaps that "friend" was Rob Lightly.

A slow burn started in his gut and spread to his neck. José chose not to crawl through her window, but now he regretted not trying to at least see if it was unlocked. If by some bizarre chance she chose Lightly over him, taking what he wanted would satisfy him and teach her a lesson.

He masked his thoughts with a charming smile and gently took her hand in his. "I guess, then, I will go. I will not outstay my welcome since you have another engagement." He bent over her hand and caressed her knuckles with his lips while savoring the scent of her skin, as enticing as forbidden fruit. Fully expecting her fingers to tremble, he hovered a few seconds before lifting his head and smiling into her eyes.

She observed him with steady eyes that revealed no emotion and her fingers remained firm in his grasp. Fleetingly José questioned if he was losing his edge. At first he was positive he would eventually win her. Now he couldn't deny that she wasn't exactly wilting at his touch.

The sound of footsteps approached from the left. José looked up to see a man nearing with a protective edge to the set of his chin. The guy was dressed this evening as he'd been dressed the last time José saw him—a pair of shorts and a T-shirt that read, "Houston

Police Force." Apparently Rob always wore his badge one way or another.

José's lips twitched, and he worked to stop them from curling into a snarl. *The fool. He and his cronies don't have what it takes to solve who stole the Incan treasure. Yet here he is swaggering from one yard to the next like a know-it-all. Idiot!* José thought while extending his hand toward his rival. "Rob Lightly," he said through his most engaging smile. "Great to see you again."

Rob extended his hand but didn't smile. "I'm sorry, I don't recall your name," he said, and his gaze held an intensity that almost made José look away. He didn't though because the first one to look away was always the loser. *And he never lost.*

"José Herrera," he supplied and marveled at the man's stupidity. José never forgot a name—evidence of his superior intellect.

"Are you ready, Brittan?" Rob asked.

"Yes. I was just stepping out when José was walking up." She offered a polite smile that hinted at an apology.

José lifted both hands, palms outward. "I was just leaving," he said. "I will come by later. Okay, Brittan?" He purposefully ignored Rob.

"Sure," she agreed through an awkward smile as Rob stepped to her side.

Without another word José turned and walked to his vehicle. He settled behind the steering wheel. After snapping the door shut, he cranked the engine and turned the air conditioner on high. The cool blast alleviated the perspiration breaking out along his hair-line. Gritting his teeth, he watched Brittan and the jerk walking toward the A-frame. When Rob rested his arm along her waist, José slammed his fist against the steering wheel. But instead of moving closer to Rob, Brittan stepped away. José's fist relaxed. He leaned toward the window, furrowed his forehead, and examined his woman. Brittan threw Rob a cautious glance, and her expression was as impassive now as it had been when José kissed her hand.

José tapped the steering wheel with his fingertips. Maybe the neighborhood watchdog wasn't gaining any more territory than he was. Brittan was being far from easy with him…and everyone else.

"Good!" José whispered. "Really good." He had no doubt that Rob had tried his moves, but it looked like Brittan was thwarting everyone. That just meant José would have to outwit the watchdog. "And I will," he growled. If it meant he had to watch Brittan's every move and then pounce when the time was right, that's what it meant. He would have her. With her consent or not he would have her. He always got what he wanted.

※ ❀ ※

Brittan strolled from Simon's yard with Rob at her side. After a superb meal with his dad, Rob insisted on walking her home, despite her protest.

"Really," Brittan continued, "you don't have to go to all this trouble. I…" She hesitated and glanced up at him. Moonbeams ignited the lake into what looked like millions of diamonds, highlighting Rob's features and lending his handsome features a chiseled effect.

"Don't tell me," he said through a grin. "You know karate and can take care of yourself."

"Actually no," she replied. "That would be my friend, Heather."

"The fragile blonde?" he asked.

"Yep. She could slice your head off and never blink."

He laughed. "So what about you? Are you packing a pistol?"

"A Glock 30," she answered. "But it's legal. I'm licensed to carry a concealed weapon."

"And let me guess…you're pretty darn good at it."

"Let's just say I'm competent."

"So you don't need a big, strong man to walk you home and protect you from evil monsters that might creep from the depths of the lake, slither into your bathtub, and wait until you're alone to come out and eat you alive?"

"Whoa! Sounds like you've watched one too many horror movies."

Rob joined her laughter. "No…not really. I don't waste my time on that sort of stuff."

"Too busy working?" she questioned and shot him a sideways glance.

He shrugged. "That's what Dad says." He returned her gaze with a warmth that suggested the man had more than walking on the brain. She'd caught him observing her several times this evening with a look that said, "Come hither, sweet thang." A time or two Brittan had been tempted to move a little closer but stopped herself. She absolutely refused to allow herself to be the victim of emotions.

Brittan gazed toward the lake rippling in the moonlight. Rob's growing attraction was as tangible as the pebbles beneath her sandals and as sweet as the smell of the water. After trying to put his arm around her early in the evening, he'd not attempted any more displays of affection. With the moonlight weaving a magic spell on her mind, Brittan wondered if she'd have the strength to step out of his arms if he tried to hold her now.

Speaking of monsters and strange men lurking in the shadows of her home, she wondered who would protect her from herself. Her inner resistance certainly wasn't as strong as it had been at the start of the evening. And as they stepped into her backyard, Brittan's mind wandered to the kiss they'd shared last night…and whether or not Rob would try for a repeat…and whether or not she would stop him.

Her thoughts meandered toward José. When he bent to kiss her hand, she'd received the impression that the man was purposefully trying to charm her. Furthermore, Lorna and Heather had hinted that they didn't trust him. She recalled the frustration of seeing what a no-account jerk Lorna's former trainer had been and encountering Lorna's dismissal of her observations. Reason insisted she consider her friends' observations. Neither of them were dummies, and they'd both said that Rob seemed like a much better choice. Brittan had to admit that Rob's kiss had rocked her world more than any of José's touches or compliments. She hadn't even felt a tingle when he kissed her hand this evening...or yesterday.

As much as José had tried to hide it, Brittan could see that he'd been vexed when she walked off with Rob. She started out thinking she should give José a chance and make Rob wait. But now it was reversed. And after last night and the great dinner tonight, Brittan was leaning more toward Rob. True, José had a brilliant mind and the charm to go with it. However, he'd yet to stir her as Rob did. Even now Rob's glance sent a tremor through her stomach. Brittan went from wondering how she would stop him from moving in for a kiss to wishing he would.

They paused near her back door. Rob slipped his hands into his pockets and smiled down at her.

Brittan swallowed hard and tried not to appreciate his developed biceps too much.

"Do you have an alarm system?" he asked.

"No, not yet. This part of the lake is so peaceful. The realtor told me the crime rate was zilch."

Rob sighed. "And I guess you feel safe with your Glock?"

"Well...I've never had any problems."

"Will you promise me one thing?" he pressed.

"What?"

"That you'll get an alarm system before the summer's over?"

She sighed. "You sound like my dad. But yes, I will. I know it's best to have one. Lorna and I have one at the penthouse we share in town."

"Since you don't have one, do you mind if I go in and check around just to make sure—"

"There are no lake monsters?" she grinned.

"You never know."

Brittan was struck by his desire to defend and protect her. "I guess there's a reason you're precinct captain, huh?"

"I take my job seriously," he affirmed, "and I can't seem to stop. Do you mind indulging me?" His question held an underlying meaning that was punctuated when his gaze trailed to her lips.

Brittan swallowed hard and fought her desire.

"Of course I don't mind," she said crisply. "If you like, we can even set up the chess set, and I can beat you in a game."

"Are you throwing down a gauntlet?"

"I am, I am!" Brittan teased through a giggle that sounded downright girly. She caught her breath and stopped that nonsense before it got out of hand.

After unlocking the door, she allowed him to enter. "I'll just look down your hallway and glance into the rooms, okay?" he asked.

"That's fine," Brittan said through a chuckle.

"And if you don't mind, I'll use your restroom."

"You can't miss it." She waved toward the hall and placed her petite leather handbag on the end table. "Would you drink some decaf if I made it?" she added.

"You bet!" he replied. "Your cheesecake is still with me, and some coffee would be perfect."

His broad shoulders swaying, he moved toward the hallway. Even though he wasn't as snazzy a dresser as José, Rob certainly did make a T-shirt and shorts look good. *Really good.* She'd invited him in for a practical reason though. The chess game would give her an opportunity to subtly pick Rob for clues about the Incan necklace case. She'd looked for any opportunities to open the subject over dinner, but none arose. On the other hand, Rob had told her he'd phoned the owner of Beynards and that he was expecting the man to call his cell phone. Brittan hoped Mr. Beynards called tonight.

Right before she went to Rob's this evening, Brittan called Heather to see if she'd found anything unusual on the video files. So far she'd seen nothing out of the ordinary. Her only comment was that it appeared the camera that should have captured the theft had undergone some maintenance. Brittan planned to call Lorna, who was hopefully gleaning clues from her parents, as soon as Rob left.

Brittan stepped into the kitchen and began making the coffee. The smell wove its magic on her senses, and she wished she could jump in the carafe and swim in the warm liquid. She pulled a pair of crystal mugs from her cabinet and was wondering if Rob wanted cream, sugar, or both when his voice floated from the living room.

"Sure. I'd be glad to. I think that's best, and to tell you the truth, we'll need to take it anyway. There might be some evidence we can glean from it that will lead us to who pulled the switch on you." He stepped into the kitchen and gave Brittan a thumbs-up. "Mr. Beynards," he mouthed.

Brittan's eyes widened as Rob's dialogue now made perfect sense. Apparently Beynards had realized his painting had been stolen.

"If you don't mind, I'll come now," Rob said. "The sooner we can get an investigation started, the better."

Wonderful! Brittan thought and debated about asking if she could come. The Rose always stayed incognito if at all possible, and if she went with Rob to get the painting, she'd blow her cover. However, her desire to scrutinize the Mosier print again nearly outweighed her former decision to remain undetected.

"I'm only five minutes away," Rob said. "I should be there in ten." He shot a glance toward Brittan and snapped the cell phone shut. "Want to go with me?" he asked and slipped his cell back into his belt pouch.

"I'm *dying* to see the print, but I was wondering..." Brittan scrambled for a solution. "Would you mind bringing it back here before you take it to the police station?" She pointed toward the brewing decaf. "I just made coffee. Maybe we could look at it over coffee? My curiosity is going crazy. I guess I've read too many mystery novels." She chuckled and tempered her voice and features for fear she was appearing too eager.

His curious expression took on an unusual intensity that only lasted a second but was enough to make Brittan squirm inside, even though she never blinked.

"Sounds like a good idea." Rob narrowed one eye and gave her another thumbs-up. "You're so observant—you might see something I'd miss."

"Who knows," Brittan replied.

"I'll be back in a few. Keep my coffee hot," he shot over his shoulder as he turned to leave.

"Will do," Brittan affirmed and walked him to the door. When she shut the door after his departure, Brittan wondered again what Rob would think if he knew she was the Rose. She turned to the brass-framed mirror in the entryway and eyed herself.

If he finds out later, it might hurt our relationship, she thought. *He might think I've just been using him to solve the case.* Brittan moved closer to the mirror, peered into her own soul, and got real about her motives. What she saw there brought peace. The truth was, even if there was no Rose and no case, she still liked Rob Lightly. A lot. Even though she was perfectly capable of defending herself, she enjoyed his gentlemanly ways and protective instincts. He made her feel…cherished. And the feeling was a good one. Since she was experiencing such emotions so early in their friendship, she could only imagine how the sentiments would grow.

"Should I go ahead and tell him I'm really the Rose?" she asked her reflection. The answer came when the images of Heather and Lorna barged through her mind. The three of them had a pact of silence. *But Michael and Duke both know we're the Rose,* she reasoned.

Yes, but Michael and Lorna and Heather and Duke are engaged. The guys need to know what their future wives are up to. Rob and I only just met.

Brittan sighed and nodded. "That's my answer," she whispered. "I *can't* tell him. Not yet." *I just hope it doesn't hinder our relationship when he does find out,* she worried.

SEVENTEEN

Clutching the touched-up Mosier print under his arm, Rob knocked on Brittan's front door. The wind had picked up, and the sound of the lake's lapping filled the evening with whispers of a storm brewing. Rob glanced toward the sky and noted a bar of clouds racing in front of the moon.

"It was a dark and stormy night," he was mumbling when the door opened.

Brittan's questioning gaze, illuminated by the porch light, suggested she might be wondering what he was talking to himself about.

He smiled and said, "I was just quoting Snoopy." He lifted his free hand and motioned like a theater pro. "It was a dark and stormy night."

She laughed. "Is there a storm coming?" Stepping beside him, she focused on the sky. "Wow! Clouds. And look at the wind."

"The trees are really getting a beating, aren't they?" Rob asked.

"For *sure*," Brittan stressed, and then her gaze rested on the print Rob was holding.

"Ready to get busy?" he asked.

"Absolutely!"

"After you, m'lady." He smiled into her eyes and motioned for her to enter before him. She returned the grin and stepped back into her home. Even though Brittan seemed as independent as all-get-out, Rob couldn't suppress being the old fashioned gentleman his father had raised him to be, and he was thankful she was lady enough not to resent his expressions of respect.

She hastened through the living room and Rob followed.

"Put it on the kitchen table," she said over her shoulder, "and I'll pour our coffee. How do you like yours?"

"Like I like my women," Rob quipped. "Strong and dark."

As she neared the coffeepot, Brittan shot him a look that was a cross between "Oh really?" and "Oh brother!"

Rob chuckled and placed the print on the table. "What? No protests?" he teased.

"No, I'll just silently put a dose of arsenic in your black coffee," she retorted. "How's that for strong and dark?"

"Yikes!" Rob exclaimed. "Maybe I should have asked for cream and sugar?"

"Oh? So then would you say you like your women blonde and sweet?"

"Ha, ha, ha," he replied. "I've never even had a blonde girlfriend."

"No joke?" she looked up from her task and never blinked.

"Nope. I…" He broke eye contact. "I've always preferred Asian women." Rob sneaked her a peek he hoped flattered her socks off. "Nice, strong-willed Asian women," he repeated and then grinned. "Like I said, *strong and dark*."

"Oh." Brittan concentrated on pouring their coffee, and Rob wondered if she might be hiding a blush.

So…I got to her, he mused and began to seriously get his hopes up for a repeat performance of last night's kiss. Every time he'd tried to move closer to her this evening, Brittan gave him a nudge in the opposite direction. If not for the occasional flicker of interest in her eyes, he would've been discouraged enough to howl at the moon. But the twinkle in her eyes was evidence enough that she too sensed the sparks flying between them.

She approached with two steaming mugs that looked like cut crystal, and Rob made a mental note not to drop his. He glanced at the floor and noted the black-and-white tiles that looked expensive. Rob once dropped one of his mother's china teacups on her Italian tile and knew from experience the carnage that followed.

Once he accepted the brew, Brittan's attention was on the print. She hovered over the piece for several seconds and then peered up at Rob. "Do we need to use latex gloves when handling it?"

"Good question," he said and figured she and her two friends always wore latex gloves when they went on their little excursions. "If I had any hope that we could find a good fingerprint on it, yes. But by the time I picked this up, Mr. Beynards had already taken it down. It was in his office, and he and his wife admitted they'd handled it like crazy. It would be a one-in-a-million chance that there'd be any detectable prints from the thief on it." He shrugged. "Besides, if someone were to go to all the trouble to find a touched-up print to replace the original, my guess is they'd use gloves in the process."

"Yep," Brittan agreed. "Makes sense."

Rob took a deep draw on his coffee. It tasted like a gourmet blend.

"This brew tastes like heaven!" he exclaimed.

"It's the arsenic," she dryly retorted. Before Rob could conjure a reply she said, "Mind if I flip the print over?"

"Not in the least. I examined it at Beynards."

She set her coffee on the edge of the table and turned it over. "Good. The back's not covered," she mumbled. "Did you notice any clues?"

"Not at first scan," he admitted and leaned in beside her for a more serious appraisal. "The Beynards said they couldn't see anything out of the ordinary either."

"Any chance there's an employee involved?" Brittan asked.

"I hinted that they might offer some leads on who had access to the restaurant—especially at night. One of the family members always closes up, and their employees all undergo a background check before they're hired."

"That means they hire people who are either innocent or they've never been caught."

"Right," Rob agreed and watched as she ran her fingertips along the back of the print. The print appeared to have simply been inserted into the frame without the touch of a professional framer.

"Still," Brittan continued, "my gut tells me the missing original has to be linked to Mosier's murder."

"And how often is your gut wrong?" Rob asked.

She lifted her head and stared into his eyes as if she were searching for an underlying meaning. Rob decided he'd better qualify his statement before she suspected he knew her secret.

"I mean," he said, keeping his expression innocent, "in all those mystery novels you say you read…how often are you right about the who-dun-its?"

Brittan went back to the print. "More often than not," she admitted. "Okay, almost never wrong."

While Rob sipped his coffee and studied the print's parameters, he wondered what she would think if she realized what she'd revealed to him tonight. Her admission that Heather knew karate solidified his assumption she and her friends paid a visit to the museum last night. He now debated if he should tell her of his knowledge before they went any further in their relationship. Rob wondered if it might jeopardize their relationship later if she discovered he'd known she was the Rose all along and had used the connection to further his own investigation.

As smart as she is she'll probably remember all the times I mentioned the case or the Rose and might figure I was fishing for information. He gritted his teeth and glanced at her profile. She seemed oblivious to Rob's thoughts and look. *Why does she ever have to know I know?* he reasoned.

Then Rob remembered his concern from their initial meeting. *Maybe she's using the connection with me to glean details to help the Rose solve the case.* His fingers flexed against the cup handle. Those three had broken into the museum for a reason. The logical explanation was that they were on the trail of the criminal who was implicating them in crimes they never committed.

He darted another glance her way. She scanned the back of that print like her life depended on what she found, and a deep realization struck Rob right between the eyes. *Of course she's using her connection with me!*

After a frown rippled his brow, Rob nearly laughed out loud. Brittan Shay was as interested in furthering her own investigation as he was in furthering his. If not for the genuine attraction they shared, Rob would have been furious. Instead he recalled the lyrics of a classic oldie that mentioned something about feeling good being used. Some men might have been offended, but Rob didn't mind the idea of their networking with each other to solve the case. As long as Brittan kept responding to his kisses like she had last night, he was glad to let her use his connections and then follow her right to the crook who'd taken the Incan necklace and murdered Mosier.

The prospect took on an enticing aura that was bigger than life and a long way removed from the normal agenda of his usual operations. Not only would Rob solve the case, he'd hopefully enjoy the chase with an exotic Asian he could dream about at night. His adrenaline began pumping in sequence with his rapid heartbeat, and Rob had never been so glad he talked his dad into buying the house three doors down.

"Look!" she exclaimed and pointed to the lower right corner. "It looks like the loop of a letter coming from under the frame."

Rob bent over her hand and examined the space beside Brittan's finger. "That's exactly what it looks like," he admitted.

"Is it okay if we take the frame off?"

"Of course," he agreed and examined the wooden casing for easy entry.

"On my mom's antique frames, there's usually a way to loosen one side," Brittan explained.

"Right here." Rob pointed to a tiny gap in the frame's upper right corner where the sides came together. He set his coffee mug near hers, picked up the frame, and asked, "What do I do? Just pull on it?"

"Right. Be gentle but firm."

"I can do that." He winked and didn't care if she picked up the double meaning.

Brittan shifted her focus to the frame as Rob separated the corner and revealed three wooden pegs that held the frame together. The bottom corner proved as easy to disconnect, and Brittan reached in to tug the painting from the frame. As the piece slid out, the cursive stamp that became visible read, "Chicago Artworks."

"Ah ha!" she exclaimed. "Looks like we've got a source."

"Maybe!" Rob agreed. "Either that's where the thief bought this piece or where it originally came from. It could have passed several hands before it landed with our crook."

"But what if it didn't?" Brittan reasoned.

"Then it would be a good idea for someone to contact Chicago Artworks and enquire about who might have bought the print."

"Yep," Brittan agreed. "You're very right."

He watched her and was amazed at how she masked her thoughts. At this point he wouldn't be surprised if she were planning to fly to Chicago herself and hunt down the person who sold this print in the first place.

She'll probably have his name, rank, and serial number by sundown tomorrow.

"Will someone from the police department go up there?" she casually asked.

"We'll try to take care of it by phone first."

"Wouldn't it be quicker to just fly up there and not go away until they answer your questions? Seems to me that playing phone tag could take days and days." She broke eye contact and gazed across the room as if she were discussing the price of green beans at the local grocery store.

"Yes, but we don't have the budget or manpower to fly off into the sunset on a whim. Besides, we might be able to network with the Chicago Police Force on this one."

"And, like, they're going to jump right on it?" She covered a yawn.

"Sometimes investigations drag out. This might be one of them." He tapped the side of the frame and smiled. If that didn't send her flying to Chicago, nothing would.

"Want more coffee?" Brittan shifted her focus to him and picked up her cup. The lack of interest in her eyes was so real Rob nearly forgot to answer.

"Oh sure," he said and retrieved his own cup. "Just a warmer upper will be fine," he said and followed her to the coffeemaker.

"So...now what will you do with the print?" she asked.

"I'll take it to the station, file a report, and check it in as evidence. A detective will be assigned to the case. I'm going to ask if I can have part of this one."

"That's not your usual MO, is it?" She gazed up at him as if his life were of the utmost interest to her, and that enforced his assumptions that her interest went beyond the Rose's concern for the case.

"No, but every once in a while I ask to be put on a case," he explained, and his gaze trailed to her lips. Despite himself, Rob couldn't stop thinking about their recent kiss. He'd swooped in and stolen that one. He wondered if he should do the same tonight.

When his gaze trailed back to her eyes, it was obvious that he wasn't the only one remembering the sizzle from last evening.

She jerked her attention to the coffee, reached for the carafe, and topped off his cup and hers. Rob sipped the hot liquid and then decided to go ahead and live dangerously. "Brittan?"

"Hmmm?" She set the carafe back on its hot pad and turned to face him. When she lifted her gaze back up, it stopped just below his eyes. Rob wondered if she was afraid to encounter his full appraisal...afraid of her own weakness.

He nearly smiled but stopped himself. His throat tightened. He plopped his coffee on the counter and then gently pulled Brittan's cup from her grasp. That's when he noticed her fingers were trembling. Rob's pulse went up another notch. Her eyes widened a fraction as her gaze snapped to his. The rush of Rob's pulse mingled with the wind's roar and the first raindrops splatting the window. And all Rob saw in her dark, exotic eyes was the desire to repeat the delicious encounter from last night.

So, Mizz In-Control, you're not doing a very good job of hiding your feelings this time. A thrill zipped through Rob. *I've finally gotten all the way under your skin.*

He held her gaze and slowly lowered his head, savoring every centimeter of the journey until her eyes fluttered shut and his lips encountered hers. The kiss that followed rivaled last night's... and every other kiss Rob had ever experienced. By the time the room was spinning in a confusing whirl, Rob knew he'd met his perfect match.

EIGHTEEN

Brittan's mind swirled with the impact of Rob's kiss. She felt as if she were drowning in a scrumptious, warm sea that pulled her ever deeper and beckoned her to enjoy the satin waters. So Brittan enjoyed—oh, how she enjoyed! She sighed and reached to pull Rob closer but he'd disappeared. With a frustrated groan, she struggled through the darkness in search of him, finding nothing but emptiness.

"Rob!" she called. "Rob! Where are you?" The echo of her lonely cry was her only answer.

Struggling more, she lurched forward and strained to open her eyes…only to stare blankly into her own room. The weak morning light bathed the room in a gray haze. Brittan rubbed her clammy face and sighed.

"It was only a dream," she whispered. The same dream that had awakened her twice in the night. Last night's kiss had rocked her psyche. Even though mere hours had lapsed since she and Rob ended the evening in a clutch, it seemed like days. Already she was hoping to see him today, and her Monday was just getting started. When he left, Rob had seemed as dazed as she was, but he simply said goodnight and took the print with him. He hadn't even asked for another date.

Strange, Brittan thought. In the morning light she debated if he was going to pursue their relationship, but that contradicted the force of his reaction to that kiss...the way he looked at her...the pounding of his heart as he held her close.

Cold sweat assaulted Brittan's neckline. She swung her feet to the floor and stood up. "Get a grip! This is ridiculous...illogical!" she scolded. *Don't let a physical reaction to a man you just met mess with your mind like this!*

She glanced at the digital clock sitting on her nightstand. Her eyes popped open. "Eight o'clock!" she shrieked and picked up the clock. After clicking several buttons, she realized she'd erroneously set it for seven PM.

"Shoot!" she exclaimed. Brittan could surf her way into any computer system she chose, but these digital contraptions were her nemesis. After dropping the clock back onto the nightstand, she bolted toward the shower. She was supposed to meet Lorna and Heather at the Winslow castle at nine, so she barely had time to shower, get dressed, grab a cereal bar, and make the 30-minute drive. Heather had called last night after Rob left and suggested the meeting...designed to help them sort through the clues they'd accumulated and develop a plan for their next move.

Brittan stumbled into the bathroom and gazed at her image in the mirror. The chrome and glass room was as sleek as Brittan's hair was rumpled. She grimaced and wondered how it had gotten so unusually crimped. She'd been blessed with what her dad called "Chinese feathers"—hair as slick as silk that even a night's sleep barely mussed.

Must have been a wild night, she mused, and went into a Rob Lightly instant replay.

"Okay, cut it out!" she admonished and turned for the shower.

By nine-fifteen, Brittan had told herself to cut it out so often that she'd honed her mind strictly to the task at hand: uncovering the criminal who was trying to destroy the Rose's reputation. She followed Heather down the castle's broad hallway and into her wing.

When she stepped into the great room, she spotted Lorna snuggled in the corner of the leather couch with a Diet Coke in one hand and a laptop balanced on her knees.

"Nice you could join us," Lorna said. She downed a swallow of Coke and pointedly checked her watch.

"Yes, I know. I'm 15 minutes late. Sorry." Brittan stepped around a golden feline ready to rub her in greeting. She bent to scratch Lucky's ears, and a striped tabby named Tigger rounded the back of the couch for his share of attention.

Heather scooped a white Persian from one of the overstuffed chairs and walked toward the French doors that opened onto her patio. "What happened? Did you have car trouble or something?" she asked over her shoulder.

"No." Brittan hurried toward the coffee table and nudged aside a vanilla-scented candle merrily flickering in the room's recessed lighting. She plopped her purse and briefcase on the glass-topped table and dropped into a chair that threatened to swallow her whole.

Heather opened the door, placed the Persian outside, and called for her other cats. Lucky and Tigger scurried onto the patio, and Heather snapped the door shut. "Ah ha!" she cheered. "All seven are out now!"

"How in the world are you and Duke going to merge seven cats with a pit bull?" Brittan asked, shaking her head.

"Very carefully," Heather admitted and shrugged. "Actually we're still working on that one. I guess we'll get it figured out once we settle into the house. Did I tell you? The builders start tomorrow!"

"Great!" Lorna enthused and then eyed Brittan anew. "So...you didn't have car trouble?" she asked.

Both friends gazed at Brittan, expecting an explanation for her tardiness.

"I overslept a little," she defended. "What's the deal?" She looked over her left shoulder, and then her right. "Is the president waiting

or something?" she queried, but saw no other guest in the midst
of the palatial decor.

"Nooooo." Heather's lips puckered over the word. "It's just not
like you to be late. As a matter of fact, I don't ever remember you
being late for anything the whole time I've known you."

"Well, there's a first time for everything," Brittan quipped and
popped open her briefcase. She extracted a pad and pen from the
top compartment and also removed her laptop, just in case.

A silent question hovered between the friends until the room
bulged with tension, and Lorna finally blurted, "So, how did it go
with Rob last night? Were you up late?"

Brittan sighed and eyed Lorna and then Heather. Both of them
peered back like two avid movie fans perched on the edge of their
seats during a mystery's climax. They both looked early-morning-
fresh in crisp shorts, freshly styled hair, and dewy makeup, and
Brittan knew she looked like a half-groomed shadow of her usual
self. She'd thrown on the linen capri set she wore last night, but the
beige number was crumpled after one wearing, as all linen was apt
to be. Furthermore, she'd barely had time to dry her hair, let alone
put on much makeup.

She realized there was going to be no getting around talking
about her date with Rob. And once she started reliving their time
together, getting back into the case was going to be a chore. But
she had no choice. Her friends were good to her. They'd stuck with
her even when she'd blown it and secretively investigated Lorna's
fiancé. She owed them at least a brief recounting of her time with
Rob. They asked because they cared—just as she'd asked them
about their men because she'd cared.

"Everything went great," she announced. "His dad's wonderful.
I like him a lot. When Rob walked me back to the house last night,
we had coffee. He left after we figured out the print came from
Chicago Artworks."

"But did he *kiss* you?" Lorna asked, her eyes wide.

"Lorna!" Heather scolded.

"Don't give me that tone!" Lorna scowled up at Heather. "You're dying to know too and you know it!"

"Oh, you two!" Brittan shook her head. "Yes, he kissed me, if you must know. And it's the second time he's kissed me. He laid one on me Saturday night too."

"Ooo-la-la!" Heather enthused.

"And?" Lorna prompted, her face animated.

"And?" Brittan echoed.

"Skyrockets in flight?" Heather prompted.

"I guess you could say that," Brittan admitted, then caught herself gazing across the room at nothing.

Lorna laughed out loud, and Brittan snapped her attention back to her friend.

"What?" she prompted.

"I never thought I'd see you like this," Lorna teased.

"Like what?"

"Dreamy, man." Heather slowly wove her hand through the air and grooved to an unheard rhythm.

"Oh, stop it!" Brittan grabbed a couch pillow and threw it at her friend. "You two aren't any better. Look at you! You've *both* hauled off and gotten engaged."

"Yes, and now we're working on you." Lorna directed an exaggerated wink toward Heather.

"Well, we're a long way from *that*," Brittan admitted. "We're just getting to know each other."

"For whatever it's worth, he's got our vote," Heather said.

"Whatever happened to El-José-O?" Lorna teased.

"Oh *please*." Brittan rolled her eyes. "What is this? Interrogate Brittan about her love life? I thought we were going to be discussing the case." She lifted the tablet.

"We are," Heather admitted without a blink. "But we have to get the *important* stuff out of the way first."

"Besides, you didn't go easy on us. Why should we go easy on you?" Lorna added.

"Now she's bringing up my past mistakes!" Brittan teased.

"Whatever works, girlfriend," Lorna retorted.

"Okay! Okay!" She lifted her hands. "I give up! José stopped by last night when I was leaving with Rob."

"Whoa! I bet that went over like a lead button!" Lorna set her Diet Coke on the coffee table and followed it with her laptop while Brittan and Heather snickered. "What?" Lorna raised her brows and glanced from one to the other.

"It's 'that must have gone over like a lead *balloon*,'" Brittan corrected.

"Yes. What did I say?"

"You said like a lead *button*," Heather explained.

"Oh good grief! You *know* what I mean. You *always know* what I mean. Why do you keep *doing* this to me?"

"You do it to yourself, Mizz Malaprop," Brittan said and adjusted her glasses.

"So anyway, José came up when you were leaving with Rob?" Lorna swiped her bangs out of her eyes.

"Yes. He wasn't all that happy. Oh well." Brittan shrugged. "I think you guys were right about him."

"God is *so cool!*" Heather exclaimed.

"Excuse me?" Brittan adjusted her glasses as her two friends exchanged secretive glances.

"We prayed that you'd swear off of José," Lorna admitted.

Brittan glanced from one to the other. "You prayed?"

"Yep." Heather nodded. "Just like my grandmother used to do, and it worked! Furthermore," she held up her index finger, "I, for one, am convinced we've got to do more of that."

"I think so too," Lorna admitted. "I think we've just been gliding along, assuming God is protecting us."

"Well, so far He has," Brittan insisted.

"Yes...but still...there's something in here," Heather pressed her index finger against her chest, "that keeps whispering that we need to pray more."

"Okay." Brittan shrugged. "That's fine. Whatever." She didn't elaborate, but she had always been of the opinion that God would take care of everything whether they prayed or not. If her two friends wanted to turn into Grandma Moses and decide their prayers were what had swayed her logical thought process in favor of Rob, then let it be. Brittan didn't doubt her relationship with Christ or that God was all-powerful, she'd just always believed that God had given people the ability to make logical decisions, and that He assisted along the way—prayer or no prayer.

Brittan pulled a pen from her case's side pocket. "Let's get busy, okay?"

"Right," Lorna said. "I was just surfing the net, and I've already found out that Mosier released only 36 touched-up prints of each painting."

"Thirty-six each?"

"No, only of his earlier works. He hadn't done his later works."

"And they won't ever be done now." Heather stepped around the couch and sat on the edge. "Want some green tea or something, Brittan?" she asked. "It's a shame for you not to have anything to drink," she emphasized, "while Lorna pours that poison down her throat." Heather pointed toward the Diet Coke.

"Ha, ha, ha," Lorna drawled. "Your tombstone will read, 'Death by green tea,' and I'll be at your funeral with a Diet Coke in one hand and a candy bar in the other."

"Don't count on it," Heather warned, and Brittan knew she was way more serious than Lorna wanted her to be.

"I don't want anything to drink," Brittan said. "I nursed a bottle of water all the way here." She tucked her wayward hair behind her ear and focused back on Lorna. "Okay. So there are only 36 touched-up prints of each of some of his earlier works."

"Right."

"Have you looked up Chicago Artworks?" Brittan asked.

"I did." Heather leaned forward and rested her elbows on her knees. "Downtown Chicago...they call themselves *the* major Mosier source in the United States."

"Ah ha!" Brittan exclaimed.

"I'm already harassing my dad about letting us use the business jet and his pilot to take a trip up there this week," Lorna said.

"If you can't get anywhere, we could charter one. That's my parents' usual MO," Brittan said. "Dad and I just got a great deal when we flew to New York. I'm sure the same guy would work with us. He's a private pilot. Flies business executives all over the place."

"For what it's worth, I already checked on our family jet," Heather added. "My mom's got it tied up for the next several days. She's buying new china for the wedding reception and will be in Boston all week."

"You mean she's not dragging you with her?" Brittan asked.

Heather sighed. "I was tempted but decided to leave this one to her. She's going to go with what *she* likes best anyway. Besides, I can't let you guys go to Chicago without me!"

"Maybe we should do some shopping while we're there," Lorna said.

"Absolutely!" Heather enthused. "I still need a few things for the honeymoon. Twelve weeks and counting," she said and wiggled her eyebrows.

"Oh *please!*" Brittan complained.

"Don't give me that, girlfriend." Heather dismissed Brittan's comment. "You're the Queen of Smooch!"

Lorna shrieked, covered her mouth with her hands, and rocked back and forth while her face turned red through an attack of silent laughter.

"Would you two just give it a *break!*" Brittan said.

"Okay, okay! So Chicago Artworks is the headquarters for Mosier." Heather chuckled. "Now—how do we find out who they sold that print to?"

"Well, we *could* just fly up there and ask them," Lorna suggested.

"You bet!" Brittan tapped the pen against her tablet. "But that would be a rare case of a very cooperative employee. And on top of that, if we get that direct we're going to have to think about some kind of cover."

"I vote we dress waaaaay down, like three high school girls." Heather lifted her hair from both sides of her face. "I could even do dog ears."

"Cute," Brittan said sarcastically and widened her eyes.

"The poorer the better," Lorna added.

"Actually, that just might work," Brittan agreed.

"And if they won't tell us who they sold the print to?" Heather queried.

"We find a place to hide in the gallery until they close the place down and then we tap into their computer system." Lorna rubbed her hands together.

"Agreed," Brittan admitted. "I think that would be way less trouble than trying to get an employee to answer any questions. Unless we can flash a badge—and we can't—I seriously doubt we'll find one who's willing to talk. But...what about the alarm system? I'm sure a place like that will have one that works really well, with a *hot* motion detector on top of that." She thought about Rob saying she needed one herself and mentally placed that on her priority list.

"I guess we could wait until the manager starts to lock up, grab him, gag him, and tie him up until we're through," Heather teased.

Brittan's eyes widened as the possibility took on credence. "We could leave him tied up and then once we've got the files, we could call the police from a pay phone to alert them that he needs to be set free."

"You're serious?" Lorna breathed and picked at the neck of her Princeton T-shirt. "You'd really do that?"

"Wait!" Heather gripped Brittan's arm. "These alarm systems are usually connected to the police station anyway, right?"

"Yes," Lorna affirmed.

"And if Artworks doesn't sign in at its usual time, won't it alert the station that something's wrong?" Brittan quizzed.

"No, I don't think so," Lorna injected. "I don't think they monitor who's logged onto the system and who hasn't. I can check with Dad, but I think it's up to the businesses. The police don't babysit them. If they don't log on and the system is down all night and someone breaks in, then it's their loss."

"Okay, so who's going to take down this innocent person so we can tie them up and get into the computer system?" Heather asked.

Both friends stared at her.

"That's what I thought." She shook her head. "Listen to what we're saying!" Heather insisted. "What if it's some old woman who has a heart attack on us?"

"Okay, okay." Brittan rubbed her temples. "You're right. We're going too far now. Look, all I need is their computer's IP address. Once I get that, I can hack in from my laptop like that!" She snapped her fingers. "And go through any file they have stored. We won't have to tie anybody up."

"Okay, so maybe we just create a diversion while you get the address," Heather hurried.

The three friends nodded. "That worked when we were solving the mayor's murder," Lorna observed.

"Yes, but this one will be *planned*," Brittan added.

"Right," Heather mused. She relaxed against the couch, rested her head on the back, and peered toward the ceiling. "But I'm thinking it might be best to wait until we get there to see what opportunities present themselves."

"Sounds like the smartest move to me," Brittan replied. "And what information did you two get last night?" she continued. "Heather, didn't you say something about the museum's video camera not capturing the theft?"

"Right. It's on the flash drive in Lorna's computer."

"Come on down." Lorna patted the cushion beside her, and Heather scooted to the corner to give room for Brittan to land. "Heather narrowed it down to a few frames, and you'll briefly see that on the day the theft happened, there was some cat working on the cameras."

Brittan settled next to Lorna and gazed at the laptop's screen while Lorna pulled up the clips.

"I've been in the museum with my mom enough," Lorna said, "that I recognize the angles, and *this* camera would have to be the one that was covering the Incan exhibit." She tapped the screen. "But look. Here's some guy operating on it."

"What does your mom say? I mean, does she know the maintenance guys?"

"That's the deal. The cameras are serviced by an outside source, so no one is thinking this is really all that odd."

"Has anyone checked with the security company to see if the cameras were scheduled for maintenance that day?" Brittan asked.

"I don't know," Lorna explained, her green eyes full of speculation. "My mother seems to have limited knowledge. I didn't get a lot out of her last night—other than the museum staff is totally wigged-out over the break-in."

"Lorna says the poor security guard's about to have a nervous breakdown." Heather sighed and shook her head. "I hate it." She pulled a pillow close and hugged it. "I really didn't want to take him down. If he were a criminal, that would be different."

"Yep." Brittan nodded. "But you did what you had to do."

"And I hit him as gently as possible." Heather lifted her dubious gaze toward her friends.

"We know." Brittan patted her shoulder.

"I want to know where he was when the necklace was nabbed," Lorna said, her voice less compassionate than Brittan's. "Mom says he was the one on duty that day."

"I assume the police and staff have questioned him." Brittan sat straighter.

"He says he stepped into the bathroom, and when he came back it was gone." Lorna leaned forward and observed Heather. "Who knows! Maybe you kicked someone who was involved."

"You think he was?" Heather queried.

"Mom says they can't find any reason to implicate him, but I wonder," Lorna admitted. "The museum banished him to the graveyard shift for now. He's fortunate they didn't fire him. A few people on the board are soft."

Brittan focused back on the video clip, narrowed her eyes, and examined the man tinkering with the surveillance camera. "I wonder if Rob knows what they're saying about that camera guy," she mused.

"Humph! Who knows!" Lorna scoffed. "And if he does know anything, will he tell you? We could grow old, get gray, and *die* waiting on info from the police department."

"Amen to that, sister!" Heather mumbled.

"As much as I hate to admit it," Brittan said, "you're probably right. Rob already told me there's stuff he can't tell me."

"You've got to be careful," Heather added. "If you get too nosy, he might suspect you're up to something."

"He doesn't have a clue right now." Brittan waved aside the very idea. "And I'm being very careful not to leak a thing."

"I'm sure you are," Lorna affirmed.

"Now," Heather spoke up and retrieved a notepad from the

coffee table, "we were going to make a list of everyone we've nabbed, remember?"

"Yes." Brittan leaned closer to her.

"I did that last night. Here's what I've got." She brushed the tablet with the back of her fingers and began reading. "Juan Sanchez, the young guy who hacked into the Houston banking system just for fun. He's in prison. My uncle caught embezzling money. In prison."

"The animal cruelty case," Brittan mused, reading the list for herself. "They're all on probation, right?"

"Yep. Which means they're running free," Lorna said.

"But jumping from animal cruelty to murder and international thievery is an odd transition." Heather stared across the room.

"I agree," Brittan said.

"And as money-hungry as my uncle is, I can't see him murdering anyone," Heather added.

Lorna leaned in closer. "We aren't disqualifying anyone yet."

Brittan nodded.

"Then there's the city manager and his mistress cooling their heels in prison for murdering the mayor," Heather continued.

"Hello!" Brittan chirped. "I hear murder!"

"Do we put Herman Soliday and Eve Maloney at the top of our list?"

"Definitely." Heather circled the names.

"And what about Rich Cooper—the associate pastor who framed Trent Devenport for the porn charge?"

"His motive was really personal," Brittan observed. "I'm not seeing him as a suspect."

"Let's not disqualify any of them," Lorna repeated.

"Next I've listed those two who kidnapped Debbie Miller," Heather continued. "Brenda Zapala and Howie Prince."

"Didn't they get a short sentence?" Brittan questioned.

"Not sure…" Heather mused.

"Maybe that's a question we need to answer," Lorna asserted and Heather and Brittan agreed.

"So where do we go from here?" Heather lifted her gaze to both her friends. "This is a long list. We could really get bogged down."

"Let's head to Chicago Artworks as soon as possible, and between now and then, we'll see what we can find out about Herman Soliday and Eve Maloney. If that leads nowhere, then we move on to the next person on the list while we keep turning any and all other stones."

"Okay!" Heather said.

"Meanwhile, I'll see what I can find out about who this is working on the cameras," Lorna said.

"I'll be in charge of researching the city manager and his cronies," Heather stated.

Brittan gave an okay signal while both her friends observed her. "I guess that leaves you free to chase Rob," Lorna teased.

"Would you stop it already!" Brittan begged.

"Absolutely not!" Lorna shot back.

NINETEEN

By nine-thirty Thursday morning Brittan zoomed out her front door with a thermal mug of coffee in one hand and her luggage in the other. She was meeting Lorna and Heather at the airport at ten and was running late for the second time this week. This morning she set the time on the alarm clock right, but forgot to turn it on.

She'd been debating all yesterday evening whether she should call Rob and had been distracted when she set the clock. Brittan's father had monopolized her time most of the week at Shay Publishing headquarters. Brittan hadn't told either of her friends about her father's pressure to step into the family business as vice president, second in command. Brittan sensed her whole life was coming to a crossroad, in more areas than career.

She'd spent every night this week at the lake house with the hope of spotting Rob. She looked for him often but hadn't seen him once. After pining for him to call her all week, Brittan began to consider that the guy might be waiting for *her* to show a little more interest.

"I'll call him when I get in the car," she mumbled. Brittan set aside her luggage, locked the deadbolt, and double-checked the door. She'd scheduled a security system installation for Monday—the first opening on the locksmith's busy schedule.

She grabbed her compact luggage and rolled it toward her Jaguar. Lorna had finally finagled her dad into letting them use his business jet and private pilot for a long weekend. Oliver Leigh grouched about having to rearrange his schedule and cram two flights into the earlier part of the week, but he'd finally relinquished the plane for his daughter's use. Mr. Leigh thought Lorna and her two friends were going shopping. And well they would…after making connection with Chicago Artworks.

There'd been no breaking news about the police tracing the print to Chicago, so Brittan assumed the process was encumbered, as Rob had hinted it might be. He also said he was going to request involvement in the case. That left Brittan expecting a speedier process to the whole thing. With no word from Rob and no indication that anyone in the police department was hot on the Chicago trail, Brittan and her friends were more compelled than ever to fly there themselves.

She was almost to her vehicle when she caught sight of a black Lexus sitting in the driveway three doors down. A tall blonde rolled her overnight bag from Simon's front door.

Brittan lifted her brows. "They sure are busy," she mumbled and wondered when Simon would tell his son he was married. At the rate Simon was going, he wasn't going to be able to hide it from anyone for very long. Brittan once again debated if Rob might be irritated at her for not telling him she knew.

I'll just make sure he never finds out I knew before he did, she thought and scurried toward her car.

She'd barely opened her trunk when Simon's mellow voice floated across the cool morning. Brittan glanced toward the A-frame house and noted the Lexus pulling out of the drive before seeing Rob's dad striding toward her. Dressed in a pair of golfer shorts and a striped shirt with the tail hanging out, he couldn't have looked more relaxed. Brittan was as astounded that he'd kept his secret from Rob as she was that his prosthesis in no way hindered his smooth gait.

She set her coffee on the driveway and plopped her luggage in the trunk. Brittan was snapping her trunk shut as Lightly stepped into her yard.

"Good mornin'!" Uncertainty tinged his neighborly smile.

"Hi!" Brittan returned. After adjusting her bag's shoulder strap, she picked up her coffee and extended her hand to his.

Simon shook her hand, and his blue eyes reminded her of Rob's. Even though Brittan was sorely pressed to immediately ask about Rob, she stopped herself. No sense appearing too eager.

Simon inserted his hand into his shorts pocket and gazed down. "I...uh...it would appear that you keep intersecting my life at the most interesting moments."

Not knowing what to say, Brittan didn't say anything.

"I've managed to dodge every other neighbor we have, but you just keep popping up when I'm trying to be sneaky."

"My mom used to call me a jack-in-the-box," Brittan admitted. "I barged in on her hiding Christmas presents so many times she didn't think it was funny."

Simon's chuckle was as nervous as his smile. "I just wanted to let you know that what you just saw isn't what it looks like."

She lifted her brows and was on the verge of rescuing him from his embarrassment when he blurted, "Dr. Francis and I are married."

"I figured that out."

He stared at her several seconds and then said, "You did? How?"

"Before or after I saw her sneaking into your house last Sunday with an overnight bag?" Brittan allowed the implication to fall where it may.

"I was afraid you might think we were—"

"Having an affair?" she prompted. "No way. Rob told me you two are both men of faith. That worn-out Bible I saw on your end table Sunday night verified it, if nothing else did. Also, when I brought the cheesecake, you spilled the beans."

"I did?"

"Yes. You said Rob wasn't ready for a *stepmother*. At first I thought maybe you and Dr. Francis were just dating or engaged, but when I saw her scooting back inside with that overnight bag, I knew you guys must have gotten married—especially because you used the word *stepmother*."

Simon rubbed his forehead. "You should be a detective," he said.

I am, Brittan thought and then glanced at her gold watch. *Yikes! I've lost five minutes talking to him.*

"Looks like you're trying to leave, and here I am holding you up with *Days of Our Lives*," he drawled.

"I'm sorry," Brittan rushed. "I shouldn't be so edgy, but I *do* have to meet my friends at the airport. We're going out of town to do some shopping," she said.

"Right." Simon shook his head.

"Rob said you run with the big boys...or should I say, the big *girls*."

"Did he?" Brittan asked through a smile and decided to take advantage of Simon bringing up his son. "I haven't seen him around in a few days. Everything okay?" she feigned a casual expression.

"As far as I know." He gestured toward his home and added, "Welcome to my world. Sometimes he gets sucked into something at work, and I don't hear from him for days."

"I guess that fits your lifestyle, huh?" Brittan teased.

"Well, yes, as a matter of fact it does." His eyes twinkled, and the bright morning sunshine enhanced his healthy tan.

"Marriage seems to agree with you, Simon Lightly," Brittan observed through a sly smile.

"It does indeed," he admitted and then sobered. "If you have any good pointers on how I can tell Rob, please let me know. I've *got* to tell him. My ability to keep this hidden is wearing thin, in case you haven't noticed."

"Yes."

"You two seem to be getting along well, and I was thinking maybe you might help me." He leaned toward Brittan, as if beseeching her for any scrap of input.

The lightweight pantsuit Brittan had donned now felt as heavy as wool, despite the spring breeze. She swallowed hard. "Simon, I'm afraid that if Rob found out I knew about this before he did and that I hid it from him, it might harm our—our friendship."

"Yes…." Lightly gazed toward the rustling trees lining the east side of the road. "I can see that."

"I really wish you'd go ahead and tell him before he knows I know," Brittan continued.

"You really like him, don't you?" Simon's keen gaze suggested he didn't need any confirmation.

Brittan maintained her impassive stance and decided it was best not to tell Rob's father something she hadn't even told Rob, although Rob would be daft if he missed the message in their last kiss. The guy was outstanding! He exuded confidence, thoughtfulness, and strength. And she'd missed him the last few days.

"Just tell Rob I said 'hi' if you talk to him before I do," she hedged and moved toward the driver's door.

"Why don't you call him?" Simon pressed. "I gave you his number."

She shrugged and didn't reveal that she planned to do exactly that before boarding the plane. But there was no guarantee she'd get him.

"Deloris certainly didn't mind calling me." He laid his hand on his chest. "And she *nabbed* me too. 'Go and do likewise,'" Simon encouraged, quoting Scripture with a mischievous grin.

"You certainly are the king of subtle, aren't you?" she drawled and cut him an upward glance.

"I try," he said.

Brittan pressed the unlock button, and the car chirped as the lock released.

"I won't keep you any longer." He lifted both hands.

"I'm sorry to be in such a rush," Brittan admitted and checked her watch again. "But I'm supposed to meet my friends in 20 minutes, and it takes me 30 to get there. I'm seldom late, so they're probably already wondering where I am."

"Enough said." Simon shifted his weight and, with a wave, turned toward his yard.

Brittan noticed that he carried himself like an athlete with two good legs. If he were wearing slacks, no one would ever suspect this healthy specimen of manhood was missing a limb and was a diabetic.

"Oh...Simon!" Brittan called on a whim. "Would you do me a favor while I'm gone?"

He pivoted to face her. "Sure, dear. Anything." His agreement was muffled by the sound of the lawn mower next door. Brittan focused on the woman perched atop the mower for a second. *I should probably be more conscientious about alerting my neighbors when I'm gone,* she decided. She'd been slack in getting to know them, and Simon was really the only one she felt comfortable asking for any kind of support.

"I won't be back until Sunday," she explained. "Would you keep an eye on my place? Rob was worried that I don't have an alarm system yet, and now I'm starting to think I've dragged my feet on that deal. The real estate agent was so adamant about there being no crime here. I just—"

"Humph!" He scowled toward the noisy lawn mower and stepped closer. "She was right too!" he said, his voice elevated. "Last week I accidentally left my back door wide open, and I was gone all day." He motioned toward his home. "When I came back, nothing had been touched."

"I believe you." Brittan nodded. "I have a penthouse in downtown Houston, and it's so much more relaxed here. It's unreal!" The smell of freshly cut grass now wafting from next door intensified the cozy neighborhood ambiance.

"Well, don't fret none, darlin'," he drawled with a clever smile. "This ol' army man will keep an eye on your place."

"Good," Brittan said with a sigh. "I'm having an alarm system installed Monday. They couldn't get to me until then."

"Sounds great," he said, "but don't let Rob get you scared. He sees crime all the time and can be a little paranoid."

"Yeah, I gathered that," Brittan admitted. "The other night when he walked me home, he asked to check my house for a lake monster."

Simon crossed his arms and turned down the sides of his mouth. "Now *that* sounds more like an excuse to get inside to me," he said.

Brittan chuckled and jingled her keys. "Maybe it was."

"Well, I've kept you long enough. I need to hush before I give away all Rob's secrets." With a wink, Simon waved and turned toward home. "Have a safe trip," he called over his shoulder.

"Thanks!" Brittan responded and decided she liked Simon Lightly.

As he entered his yard, his shoulders swayed much like Rob's did when he walked. Brittan wondered if Rob might be this attractive and appealing in his late fifties, and she fleetingly hoped she'd be around to find out.

TWENTY

José stepped into Beynards and was enveloped by the gourmet smells that made his stomach growl and demand immediate fulfillment. Liza glanced up from her station and smiled at him as if she were as ravenous as he. José would've been daft to miss her clues, but he'd yet to take Liza up on her offer. Her pointed features stopped her from being beautiful, and her mind wasn't sharp enough to hold his attention long. But José was feeling restless this afternoon. Even though he'd stopped in to relieve his hunger, for the first time he was tempted to linger with Liza…or invite her to linger elsewhere.

He strolled forward and idly thought of Brittan. He hadn't seen her since Sunday, although he'd tried to intersect with her a few times. The latest attempt had been an hour ago. Even though her car was gone when he went by her house, José rang her doorbell on the off chance she was having her Jaguar serviced or detailed. She wasn't home, and José wondered if she was with Rob Lightly somewhere.

It's time to stop playing games, he thought and offered Liza a handshake. When she responded, he wrapped his fingers around hers and didn't release them. He wanted Brittan. And he would have her. But today Liza was available. And even though he wasn't stirred by her, the thrill of dallying with a woman whose family he'd just ripped off was very inviting. Part of the fun was gaining the trust of those he'd outsmarted.

"You're lovelier than ever today, Liza," he enthused and shot a discreet glance toward the Mosier print. It was no longer hanging on the wall. A landscape was in its place. José swung his gaze back to Liza, who was so busy simpering over his touch she never noticed his surprise. The print's absence ensured an afternoon with Liza. José had to know what was going on. Perhaps they were redecorating and were too dense to notice their original was now a print. He bent over Liza's hand and brushed his lips against her knuckles. Her fingers trembled. As José lifted his head, he took a chance on her not detecting his quick scan of the entryway. No sign of the print. José grinned into Liza's dark eyes.

"I'll have the seat closest to you today," he purred.

Liza bit down on her bottom lip and swallowed hard. "Of course," she replied, her voice husky.

José followed the slim-skirted woman toward the first table past the entryway. When he settled in his chair, he said, "It doesn't seem that you're all that busy this afternoon."

"No, it's after the lunch rush." Her come-as-close-as-you-like expression, along with her tone, made José feel like a lunch entree himself. He was disgusted but he faked enough interest to reap a flush under her olive skin. He gambled that she was now flustered enough to tell him what he needed to know without realizing what was up.

"Do you have time to join me for a glass of wine while I eat?" he questioned and threw in a wink. "My treat."

"Well, I *am* due a break," she admitted. "I'll just have to tell Callie to watch the front."

"You do that, babe," José encouraged.

He'd barely had time to peruse his menu when she was back with an uncorked bottle of wine and two glasses. "I've been saving this for a special occasion." She settled into the chair across from him.

"Well, this *is* special," José said. He watched the dark liquid splash into the glass like thin blood. Liza's fingernails, tipped in scarlet, also brought blood to mind—Mosier's blood...now on his hands. José rubbed his palm on the tablecloth. He shoved the murder to the back of his mind and concentrated on the confirmed bid of nearly a million dollars for the painting. That helped. Eduardo was delivering the item tonight. The money would be transferred to a Swiss account by midnight. The thrill of another successful venture almost obliterated the "Do not murder" from his conscience.

José ignored Liza's scarlet fingernails, picked up his wine goblet, and downed a third of the liquid. "So tell me, Liza, your parents own the restaurant, right? Isn't that what you told me?"

"Yes, it's a family business. We all work together." She sipped the wine and ran her finger around the rim of the glass.

The woman was sending enough hints to make a eunuch sweat, but José remained cool. "I assume with your stylistic flair, you're the one who decorated the place?"

"I helped."

A waiter arrived with a basket of bread and some pesto. He was several inches taller than Liza, a few years younger, and possessed her prominent nose. When the waiter threw him a proprietorial glare, José assumed he was related to Liza.

The second the waiter left, Liza leaned forward and giggled. "That's my younger brother," she explained. "He's very protective of my sister and me."

"Ah...so he must think I'm making a move on you," José teased. "What would ever give him *that* idea?"

Her eyelids drooped. "I have no idea," she returned coyly.

José slowly slipped out of his sport coat. He spent enough time at the gym to ensure a trim physique and sculptured biceps. Most women noticed. Liza was no exception. Her gaze trailed toward his arms and then back to his eyes. The warmth in her expression said she was in such a drooling fit she'd gladly tell him anything he wanted to know.

He broke off a piece of bread and dipped it into the pesto. Before placing the bite into his mouth, he asked, "So what did you contribute to the decor?" He ate the bread and his stomach rumbled its approval. "Let me guess," he continued before she could answer. "That sculpture, right?" He pointed toward an icon of a Greek maiden whose provocative dress implied sensuality.

"How did you guess?"

"It fits you," he said and slightly arched one brow, "or at least my perception of you."

She blushed. "I was in charge of the sculptures and the art—all except the one painting that used to be in the foyer—my dad had that one a while. And now—" She stopped and looked directly into his eyes. "Can you keep a secret?"

"Of course." José laid his hand on his chest. "Is there something wrong?" he questioned and leaned forward.

"Yes, there is!" Liza whispered. "Just a few days ago that painting was *stolen!*"

José widened his eyes. "No!" he whispered. "Are you sure?"

"Yes!" She darted a glance across the sparsely populated restaurant and lowered her voice more. "A customer filed a report with the police department, and an officer called my father. I think it was a woman who was in here over the weekend. I saw her touching the painting. Later someone called, asking questions." Her eyes widened and she stared at José as if he'd sprouted horns.

"Yes, I remember now!" she exclaimed. "I think it was that woman who was with *you* the other night."

"What?" José wrinkled his brow.

"I saw her leave with you that night—the same night she touched the painting and I told her to stop. And then later a customer called and said she thought it was a touched-up print. I didn't believe her, but someone had a police officer call my dad. He checked it out and confirmed it. The policeman took the print for evidence."

"And you're sure it was Brittan?" José questioned.

Liza's shoulders stiffened. "Is that her name?"

"Yes. Brittan Shay. A small Asian woman?"

She waved her hand as if brushing aside the very thought of her rival. "Well, I'm sure enough to *assume.*"

José picked up his wine glass and drank the last swallow. As the aromatic liquid swept a warm path to his stomach, he retrieved the bottle and refilled his glass. "This is very interesting," he said as if he couldn't care less, yet an uneasy sweat broke out along his spine.

I guess Brittan's got an eye for art I don't know about, he thought, recalling the way she'd broken their date that night. She *said* a friend needed her due to a death, but now José doubted her claim. Did running out on him have something to do with the print? That was the night Mosier's death hit the media too. But he couldn't imagine that the painter's death in any way influenced Brittan's noticing the print or rushing from the restaurant.

As José sorted through the issues, his mind stumbled onto another question: *What police officer investigated the stolen painting?*

He swirled the wine in the goblet and smiled into Liza's eyes. "I just met someone from the Houston Police Department," he stated as if discussing a laundry list. "I believe he and Brittan are friends. I wonder if he was the one who called your dad."

"What's his name?" Liza asked.

"Lightly. Rob Lightly." He hid a grimace.

She placed her elbow on the table and rested her chin in her hand. "That sounds a bit familiar. I'm not that great with names."

"He's tall, broad shoulders, blue eyes."

"Yes, that sounds like him. But if you want to know the name for sure, I can ask Dad."

"Oh, that's okay," José said and allowed his gaze to trail past her in a dull scan of the shadowed room. "Don't ask on my behalf. I was just curious." He smiled into Liza's eyes and wondered if he'd made a dreadful mistake by bringing Brittan here. Even though he'd recognized her intellect, he'd underestimated her. She was almost as observant as he was—and that shook him.

He eyed the toasted bread. Perhaps desire blinded him to something about Brittan. After all, she was running around with a police officer…the same police officer who was investigating the missing painting. *Maybe I need to stay away from her,* he wondered. *Or move in to make sure she doesn't know too much.* José frowned. She certainly deserved a closer look—and not for the reasons he'd originally pursued her. He drummed his fingers against the table. If she wasn't home tonight, perhaps he'd rummage through her lake house. He always made it a top priority to thoroughly understand anyone who might hinder his plans. The detection of the Mosier swap happened too soon. Maybe Brittan was simply an observant heiress who ignorantly foiled his plans, but maybe there was more to it. Whatever the case, it was time for José to know more.

He observed Liza with no feelings and even less desire. He never went for women who threw themselves at him. And given the recent plate of information he was just served, José wasn't in the mood. But he'd never let Liza know. The last thing José wanted her to suspect was that he'd pumped her for information. So he reached across the table and rested his hand on hers. He'd enjoy his lunch and follow through with whatever Liza expected. That was the only way to cover his tracks. He wouldn't worry about her hurt feelings once the date was over, and he'd avoid the restaurant—and her—from then on. In light of the print being discovered, that was probably the smartest move anyway.

TWENTY-ONE

🌹 "Excuse me!" Brittan called toward the long-nosed clerk sitting behind an antique desk that resembled an ancient organ.

Lifting his head, he gazed over narrow-rimmed glasses and scanned the three friends from top to bottom like a prune-faced mortician sizing up a corpse to see if it would fit a coffin.

Heather's discreet snicker was echoed in Lorna's under-the-breath chuckle. Brittan kept her face impassive.

As planned, they'd flown to Chicago that morning. They checked into the Hilton, dined in the restaurant on the top floor, and took their time perfecting their high school kids disguises. As eager as they were to rush directly to Chicago Artworks, the three waited until early evening. The Artworks website indicated they were featuring a guest artist from six to eight o'clock. The three friends decided to wait until that reception was on so the employees would be distracted, giving the debutantes' diversion a greater chance of success.

They arrived at the gallery wearing no makeup and cheap department-store clothing.

"Is there something I can help you with?" the man said in an affected voice.

Oh please, Brittan thought.

He rose from his desk, and his dark suit hung loosely from his lanky frame.

"P.C. Mosier," Brittan said and didn't bother to sound polite. "Know him?"

"Yes, of course," he said like they were idiots to even ask.

"We just, like, heard he died," Heather chimed in a squeaky voice that was new to Brittan.

"Yes, and we were, like, totally blown away since we, like, were just introduced to him." Lorna emphasized her valley-girl tone by smacking a wad of gum and blowing a bubble.

Brittan glanced at her and thought *Great job,* just as the bubble popped on her nose. The "mortician" would never guess they could each buy the gallery if they so chose, and that was exactly the impression they were going for.

"You'll find Mosier in the east alcove." He carelessly motioned to his right. "But *please* don't touch anything. Even prints of his paintings are going for top dollar this week."

You'd get along well with Liza Lizard, Brittan thought. *No touchy! No touchy!*

"Like, thanks so much," Heather squeaked out, and Brittan wondered if her two friends could have acted any more air-headed. She thought they both deserved Oscars. Heather's dog ear pony tails were as effective as Lorna's mammoth wad of Bazooka bubble gum.

Brittan had opted for the thick-framed geek glasses she'd ordered especially for such occasions. The three turned toward the east wall and ambled in the direction the man had pointed. As they drew closer to the Mosier alcove, the scent of oil paint became more pungent. Only when they reached the Mosier section did Brittan notice another alcove on the west side of the building. A group of onlookers hovered at a distance behind an artist who stroked paint onto a canvas.

"Pssst," Brittan said. "Looks like that's the guest artist." She jutted her head toward the west.

"Yep, and he's certainly got his paint odor on," Heather commented.

Brittan noticed several in the crowd holding cups and the faint aroma of coffee mingling with paint. Her gaze landed on a table that held silver-plated urns and gourmet treats.

That's when the mortician stepped into their line of vision, perused the goodies, and then gazed around the gallery. When his gaze met Brittan's, he lifted his nose and turned his back.

"How funny!" Lorna whispered. "I think he's guarding the food."

"He thinks we're here to filch the freebies," Heather drawled.

"That means we're doing a good job," Brittan affirmed. "We've convinced him we're poor kids."

The three friends snickered and ducked into the east alcove. The walls were dotted with P.C. Mosier paintings. His marked style was easily detected and stood out against less brilliant works.

"Poor guy," Lorna mumbled. "He was so gifted. It's awful that someone killed him."

"Yes. Ironic, isn't it?" Brittan adjusted her purse strap on her shoulder. "The gift that made him famous is probably what led to his death."

"Ah man, would you look at this?" Heather worried. "They've got a wall full of his touched up prints. How in the world will we ever trace the one in Houston when there's no telling how many they've sold?"

Brittan stepped to Heather's side. Lorna followed suit. Even though there was a good selection from Mosier, a number of vacant places along the wall validated the artist's popularity.

"I don't see a print like the one at Beynards," Brittan observed.

"Good point," Lorna admitted and toyed with the hem of her floppy T-shirt. "Maybe they only sold a few."

"There's a limited number of each released." Heather twisted one of her dog ears around her finger.

Brittan gazed into Heather's eyes and tried to recall how she already knew that. Then it clicked. "Right. I remember you mentioned that a few days ago."

"Yep. Looked it up on the Internet on Monday, remember?" She nodded, and her dog ears bobbed with the motion.

Lorna's gum snapped and Brittan glanced her way.

"You aren't doing so hot lately, are ya?" Lorna teased.

"What's that supposed to mean?" Brittan adjusted her glasses.

"I mean you're slipping," Lorna replied.

"Slipping?"

"Yes. You were late to our meeting Monday. You were late this morning, and you didn't look like you'd slept worth a hoot! Been out with the Smooch King again?"

"Don't rag her," Heather said. "You were way worse with Michael."

Brittan focused back on Mosier's works and didn't respond. Truth was, she knew she'd been slipping all week, and she wasn't in any kind of a mood to be teased about it. *She* was always the one who came up with pertinent information and details, but this week her info side was turned off. And whether she admitted it or not, her dreamy side had taken over. Not only was she having recurring dreams about Rob, but her father had caught her daydreaming numerous times as well.

She'd called Rob this morning on the way to the airport but reached his voice mail. Now Brittan wondered if she should call him again or continue to wait. She could almost hear Simon Lightly say, *Call him again!* She was beginning to clearly see Simon's motives. The sooner his son found a wife, the more free Simon would be to openly enjoy his marriage. Those two had pulled together after Rob's mother's death and were still trying to hold each other up like two grounded eagles with broken wings. Brittan sensed they were both ready to fly but were afraid to leave the other. Ironically, fear was keeping them both grounded.

"Don't you think, Brittan?" Heather's meaningful whisper pierced her thoughts.

"What?" she asked and stared blankly at her friend.

Lorna hummed the theme song from *The Twilight Zone*, and Brittan leveled a pointed glare at her. "Just stop it already!" she admonished.

"I was *saying*," Heather cleared her throat, "I don't think that clerk is going to answer any questions. We need to divert to your plan."

"Yes." Brittan crossed her arms and peered in the direction they'd come from. "I think the mortician is going to be as cooperative as a corpse. Best thing to do is figure out how to get him discombobu-lated so I can slip to the computer and get the IP address."

Heather giggled. "He reminded you of a mortician too?"

"Remember that get-well card we saw a few months ago that read, 'Ben Sic Morgue and Funeral Parlor'?" Lorna recalled. "He looks just like that wrinkled guy on the front."

Brittan snickered. "You're *right!*"

Heather sobered and lowered her voice. "Whatever we decide," she breathed, "we need to pray first." She glanced over her shoulder and then looked Brittan squarely in the eyes. "We never did, you know."

"What's the deal with you and all this praying?" Brittan replied. "It's like you've turned into Mother Teresa."

"Brittan, I can't get away from it," Heather replied. "I keep getting this awful feeling that if we don't do some serious praying this time, we could really mess up."

"I'm all for prayer," Lorna chimed in. "Hey! It worked on getting you hooked up with Rob." She pointed at Brittan and wrinkled her nose.

"Well, it's not that I'm *against* praying." Brittan rested a hand on her hip. "It's just that I can't see us dropping to our knees and praying every 10 minutes."

Sighing, Heather rolled her eyes. "Oh pullleeeezzze," she drawled. "I'm not even going to go there, but I do think a quick prayer in the ladies' room before we do anything could go a long way. The last thing I want is to get thrown into a Chicago jail. We came close at the museum, you know."

"I feel your pain on that one," Lorna said.

Brittan nodded and decided to go along. "If you want a prayer session in the ladies' room, let's go for it. But next time, if we're going to turn into prayer mavens, maybe we need to think about it *before* we leave the hotel."

"I totally agree," Heather replied. "But like I said, I didn't think of it until now. And really, all that does is drive home my point. We're just surfing along like a bunch of daredevils, and—"

"And so far God has protected us." Brittan lifted her finger.

"Yes, He has. But He's been telling me that we've got to get serious about the prayer thing."

Brittan caught a glimpse of a middle-aged couple stepping into the alcove. Discreetly she jutted her thumb toward them. "Meet me in the restroom in five," she admonished and pretended to lock her lips. Both Lorna and Heather nodded and walked in opposite directions while admiring the art.

Faking intense interest in a landscape print on an easel, Brittan looked toward the man and woman who were far too engrossed in the artwork to acknowledge three students. Brittan was meandering back toward the front desk to determine what kind of diversion they could create when the memory of the coffee setup posed the perfect option. If Lorna and Heather created a topsy-turvy-table fiasco with spilled coffee and scattered cookies, she was certain the mortician and any other staff on the loose would be so upset they'd never suspect someone was hacking into the computer.

If they managed to knock the artist's palette out of his hands and spill any extra paint, I could probably do the deed in slow motion. She nodded to herself and strolled through a display of decorative urns, hand-painted in elaborate motifs. According to the sign, they'd been handcrafted by Beatrice Donaldson. Her photo accompanied the one-of-a-kind masterpieces. Unlike her artwork, the wiry-haired woman looked like she could use a bit of image sculpting.

Each to her own, Brittan thought. Narrowing her eyes, she gazed over the display toward the front desk and calculated the distance between the computer and the urns. Only 10 feet separated the two. The computer system was presently unattended and a perfect target.

If the coffee thing doesn't work, we can always shatter an urn or two, she thought. Brittan noticed the price in front of one and winced: Ten thousand bucks. *Oh well,* she thought, *if we have to pay for a couple of these babies, it'll be worth it to get the IP address.*

She turned a furtive glance back to the alcove and caught Lorna's eye. Still chomping that gum, Lorna's attention was drawn to the urns. Her eyes widened a fraction, and she looked back at Brittan. She jerked her head toward the coffee service and then strolled toward another center display that featured marble sculptures. One scuplture of an Asian beauty reminded Brittan of the crystal statuette her mother had given her for Christmas. Fully expecting one or both friends to appear at her side or move toward the ladies' room, Brittan waited.

Her phone vibrated and hummed from her purse's side pocket. Brittan had set it on vibrate before entering because a sign on the door came close to threatening death, dismemberment, or three years in "artist prison," if any customer allowed a cell phone to ring inside the gallery.

It's as bad as the library, she grouched and pulled the phone from her purse. Expecting a call from her mom, Brittan's eyes widened when she saw Rob's name on the screen. She scanned the far wall, where she'd spotted the restrooms, and darted straight toward the door marked "Women."

Once inside Brittan flipped open the phone and breathed a hello.

"Hey, Brittan," he said. "I got your message. Sorry I didn't call you right back. I was on an airplane when you called."

"Really?" she said and walked through the furnished lounge, toward the row of stalls. After a quick check underneath, she confirmed she was alone.

"Yes. It's been a hectic week. I had today and tomorrow off, so I decided to go out of town. I'm in Chicago."

"Chicago!" Brittan echoed. Her brow wrinkling, she stepped back toward the lounge and collapsed on a floral settee.

"Yep. I'll let you figure out why."

"Because of what we talked about the other—other night?" She gulped as her mind raced with the implications of Rob catching sight of her in Chicago.

"You got it. Like I told you, the department is dragging its feet. They wouldn't approve my trip because of budget restrictions. So I was condemned to finding out what I could by phone. The Chicago PD put me on their call-back list, and you know what that means."

"No, what?" Brittan sounded as calm as possible.

"It could drag on *forever.* So I decided to use my days off and come to Chicago. I'm standing outside Chicago Artworks now."

"Now?" Brittan croaked and stood.

"Yep. Anytime a policeman flashes his badge and acts really charming he can get access to all sorts of information. Such a police officer would have to be careful, or he'd cross jurisdiction lines."

"Isn't he already?" She balled her hand and paced toward the doorway.

"Well…a little. The worst that could happen is that I'll get my wrist slapped. But it's worth the risk for the *best* that could happen."

"That you'd find out who bought the Mosier print that landed in Houston?" Brittan asked and scrambled for a plan.

"Right. I'm going on your gut instincts, by the way."

"Mine?"

"Yes. You said you think the missing painting is linked to the murder, and your gut instincts are almost never wrong. So I figured it was worth some quick, serious digging to see what I could uncover."

The bathroom door opened. Her nerves taut, Brittan jumped. The second she realized the entrants were Heather and Lorna, her shoulders relaxed. Their timing couldn't have been more perfect.

"Who are you talking to?" Lorna mouthed.

"It's Rob!" Brittan mouthed back. Then she pointed toward the building's entrance and mouthed, "He's outside."

"Outside Chicago Artworks?" Heather whispered.

Brittan's desperate nod accompanied Rob asking, "Brittan? Did I lose you?"

"No. Sorry," she replied. "I just got distracted. I was wondering... if you find out who bought the Mosier print, can you tell me? Or is that classified info?" She held her breath.

"Who wants to know?" he teased.

"Me, of course! I'm just very curious. After all, I was the one who spotted the print. Enquiring minds want to know," she added mischievously.

Rob chuckled. "Well, this *isn't* official police business, is it?" he asked. "I'm on my own time, right?"

"Right." She extended a thumbs-up to both her friends.

"And since I *am* on my own time, maybe what I learn on my own belongs to me...sort of...for now anyway."

"Exactly."

"Hmmm...yes. I'll tell you all about it when I see you."

TWENTY-TWO

Rob gazed through the glass windows that were sand-blasted with the words "Chicago Artworks." A big poster hung beside the brass-trimmed door announcing the presence of an artist working inside. Rob wasn't the least bit interested in the guest artist. He was here because of the three student chicks who'd entered the place about 20 minutes ago.

When his dad called him this morning and told him he saw Brittan and that she was flying somewhere to shop, Rob's inner warning system had squawked, "Does not compute!" Even though he was just getting to know Brittan personally, she seemed far too practical to fly anywhere without a definite motive...and flying somewhere for leisure shopping didn't fit her personality. The longer Rob thought about it, the more convinced he was that Brittan and her two buddies were going to Chicago. And if so, it was to visit Chicago Artworks.

The three had that close call at the museum last weekend, and Rob was eaten up with what might happen at Chicago Artworks. At the rate they were going, they would get themselves thrown into jail before this was over. And who'd be there to protect Brittan if she flubbed the operation? Sure, they were gutsy women. Sure, they could defend themselves. But they were still amateurs. They weren't invincible. If Rob's trained partner could get himself killed, so could Brittan and her friends...and without half the effort. As much as Rob told himself he should stay in Houston and mind his own business, he realized he simply couldn't.

Instead of driving to his father's place and hanging out until he saw Brittan like he'd planned, Rob drove to the airport and waited on standby until he got a flight to Chicago. He was en route by noon. By five, he'd procured the name of the person who purchased the touched-up Mosier print. Upon close scrutiny at the police lab, a faint number under Mosier's signature—35—was found. The prints were numbered, which made tracing the purchase much simpler.

The brisk city wind whipped at his jacket and reminded him this wasn't balmy Houston by a long shot. Rob glanced toward the sun, oozing between skyscrapers as it chased the horizon. The after-hours traffic sporadically hummed along the street. Night would be falling soon, and the whole landscape would change. Brittan and her friends needed to get out of there before they did who knew what.

Rob decided the best thing was to flush them out.

"Rob?" Brittan said.

"Still here. Listen, I'm heading into the art gallery so I need to go. Are you going to be home this weekend? If so, I'd like us to get together."

"Sure!" she answered, and her enthusiastic tone made him smile.

"Great!" he replied and, as an afterthought, decided to ask one more question. "Brittan? Remember I've mentioned that my dad is being sort of...reclusive...for lack of a better word?"

She hesitated. "Yes."

"I'm not asking you to spy on him or anything, but if you see anything out of the ordinary with him, would you let me know? I'm worried about him."

"He seemed fine when I talked to him this morning. I really

don't think you should worry about him. He worries about you too. You guys are like two mother hens."

"I know." Rob rubbed his forehead. "We had to hold each other up when Mom died, and I guess it's a habit now." He rested his hand on the door's brass bar. "Look, I won't keep you any longer. This isn't the time or place. It's just been on my mind," he added and pulled open the glass door. "I'm heading into the gallery now. I'll be in touch."

"Okay, bye," she rasped and ended the call.

Rob sighed and admitted what his subconscious had been insisting on for months: *Dad might be seeing somebody behind my back.* The possibility struck him as less odd than it had several weeks ago. He wanted to settle down and get married some day, why shouldn't his dad want the same?

He paused on the edge of the entryway and scanned the gallery. The smell of oil paints and coffee permeated the place. He strained for a sign of Brittan. Imagining the three friends hiding from his view, he nearly laughed out loud. Even though they were probably vexed, Rob had gleaned the necessary info without their having to put themselves on the line. He ambled toward a display of marble sculptures and walked behind it. Through a gap between two pillars, he eyed the front doorway. Sure enough, the three women exited the ladies' room and slithered through the front door. Rob had to stop himself from laughing again when he saw Heather's dog ears.

Before she left, Brittan gazed across the room. Even though her thick-framed glasses blocked a good view of her eyes, Rob could have sworn she looked straight through the gap in the marble pillars and smack into his eyes. He held his breath. When she turned back toward the door with no expression whatsoever, he assumed she'd not seen him. He released his breath, counted to 100, and meandered toward the front door. A hard stare out the window revealed no sign of them. Once on the sidewalk, Rob scrutinized the street and spotted them trotting toward the Hilton, one block over.

He ducked his head, walked in the opposite direction, and wished he could spend the evening with Brittan. But that would have to wait until they both got back to Houston.

Only when he stepped on the next block did he realize he'd just chased a woman all the way to Chicago for the sole purpose of protecting her. Granted, he was protecting her from *herself,* but still protecting her.

She's really getting to me, he thought, and that was the reason he'd kept his distance for a few days. After that Sunday night kiss stunned him senseless, Rob decided he'd better get some space and gain equilibrium. But now he recognized his symptoms for what they were. "I'm falling in love with her!" he whispered and stepped into a shaft of sunlight that illuminated the sidewalk with a final caress. Rob understood that he was in the beginning stages of love, and it would take time to develop. He also realized he'd never felt this strongly about any woman—and certainly never plunked down a credit card for a last-minute, unbudgeted flight that nearly cost a week's salary.

When he caught sight of the Holiday Inn towering a block away, Rob broke into a sprint. Like his dad, he enjoyed running several times a week and had missed it this morning. By the time he entered the small lobby, his heart was thumping in sequence with his heavy, controlled breathing. Spotting the stairs entrance, he decided to continue the workout. The physical exertion did nothing to ease the haunting awareness of his budding love and the fact that he might need to tell Brittan what he knew. What started as covering his tracks was now beginning to feel like deception. He'd reasoned there was no harm in hiding his knowledge until she chose to reveal herself, but now he was falling in love. If their relationship was going to deepen, it must be built upon honesty.

By the time he hit the second flight of steps, Rob realized he didn't have much of a choice. He *had* to come clean, and the longer he waited the more betrayed she'd feel if she found out he'd known all along. At the top of the third flight, he imagined telling her and dreaded the potential mess.

A very annoying Scripture floated through his mind: "In everything, do to others what you would have them do to you." He scowled. Rob decided to tell her, no matter how difficult the conversation might be.

He approached the third floor doorway and pounded the crash bar. The door whipped open and banged into the wall. A young blonde carrying an ice bucket down the hall jumped, and thin slivers of ice toppled to the floor in all directions. She stopped and stared at him in terror.

"Sorry." Rob held up both hands. "I'm a police officer," he continued in an effort to soothe her fear.

Her dubious look testified she was struggling to believe him.

"Let me help you. Maybe we should call housekeeping," he offered. As he neared, he became aware that his breathing was heavy enough to disturb her if she didn't understand he'd started running a city block away and come up three flights of stairs.

Yelping, she stumbled back and ran toward what Rob hoped was her own room. Shaking his head, Rob scooted the spilled ice toward the wall with a Reebok-clad foot and hurried to his room.

As the door closed behind him, Rob knew the conversation with Brittan would have to happen soon. But understanding that he needed to tell her and that he *would* tell her didn't erase the *dread* of telling her. Depending on how exasperated she got, it might jeopardize their relationship. He opened the fridge and yanked out a bottle of water he'd placed there earlier. As he unscrewed the lid, Rob decided that if it was going to end their relationship, he needed to know now, before he totally lost his head—and heart.

✳ ✳ ✳

José waited until darkness settled upon the streets like thick fog. The Texas air was pregnant with humidity that threatened suffocation. The day had grown warmer each hour and, like a barometric pressure cooker, a thick wall of clouds crept across the sky. They hung low and promised to wreak havoc should someone sneeze wrong. The weatherman announced a tornado watch. Even the crickets were in silent hiding. The lack of wind added to the ominous threat.

The lithe Latino crept through the pine trees that lined the east side of Brittan's road. Dressed in black, José chose to walk the mile to her house rather than drive and risk being spotted. His Volvo was parked at his mother's shop, where he'd left it after going to Brittan's house to make sure she wasn't home. Even though her Jaguar wasn't in the drive, he'd stopped and rang her doorbell. When no one answered, he cruised back to the shop and waited until night fell. Now he carefully placed one foot in front of the other to keep his progress as soundless as possible.

"Great night for a murder," José mumbled, and he wondered how Eduardo had fared. His assignment had been to intercept the museum security guard before the guy left for work. Eduardo had watched him long enough to know he lived on a corner lot in a quiet Houston neighborhood. He was to remind Moe Van Cleave that his life depended on not leaking any information to the press or police. José stressed to Eduardo that murder wasn't necessary at this point. Roughing the guard up would suffice to let Van Cleave know he was dealing with people who took his silence seriously. However, Eduardo's parting comment involved doing whatever he had to do.

"Do not murder" reverberated in José's brain despite his many attempts to stop it. When he spotted Brittan's lake house, José blocked the refrain.

He crept to the edge of the trees, searched up and down the road, and then ducked across the street like a panther. He darted straight for the side of her house but only got halfway up the driveway before a motion light switched on. José sucked in his breath and dove toward the house.

Pressing his back against the wall, he waited to see if any neighbors stirred. With midnight swiftly approaching, José hoped none of them were awake or looking outside. After several minutes of listening to his heart pounding, he scrutinized the roof's back point. As he suspected, another motion light hung from the eaves. Navigating around motion lights was easy once you spotted them. It involved staying close to the house so the sensors didn't detect you. José did exactly that and remained in darkness.

He reached Brittan's bedroom window. He'd chosen this entry because he'd been here once and knew what options were available. Plus if she had an alarm system, there was a chance the windows weren't wired to it, only the doors. He would start with the window and see how far he got. If the alarm went off, he'd race across the road, run to the shop, quietly get into his car, and drive home. If the alarm didn't go off, José had a step-by-step plan for what to do next.

He pulled off his black backpack, unzipped it, and extracted a pair of thin plastic gloves. He slipped them on for a tight fit. Then he found the gap between the upper and lower windows and pressed his fingers into the crevice. The window didn't move.

José shifted to his next step and retrieved the glass cutter from the pack. He planted the cutter firmly on the pane. Clamping his teeth, he pressed the apparatus against the glass and waited for any action from an alarm system. When no siren sounded, José dragged the cutter inside the frame until he'd completed a square. Then he tapped the fault with the back of the glass cutter. The initial crack was far from the neat line he'd anticipated. Nevertheless, it enabled him to break away the rest by hand. He carefully placed the pieces on the ground, dropped the glass cutter into the backpack, and removed a penlight. The beam illuminated the window lock.

Before reaching inside and turning the lock, he took a leather pouch from the pack. José clamped the flashlight between his teeth and unzipped the pouch, which held six tiny receptors that would allow him to monitor every conversation Brittan had in her home. The first one he'd plant under this windowsill. Even if opening the window set off an alarm, José would achieve part of his goal. In most cases people never thought to look for bugs when they discovered their houses had been broken into. Burglary was always the assumed motive. He would ensure that assumption by taking a few things of value and creating havoc here and there.

After fumbling with the first receptor, he removed the waxed paper slip that protected the adhesive he'd smeared on the back. Pressing the bug underneath the windowsill was as easy as shoving his hand past the blinds and finding a smooth surface.

José zipped the bag, stuffed it into his shirt pocket, and palmed the flashlight. "Now for the rest," he whispered through a satisfied snicker.

Unlocking the window was as simple as planting the bug. "Now, baby, let's see you open without yelling at me," he purred.

The window slid up with minimal effort and no noise, save a slight rasp of wood. José smiled. No alarm sounded. There was still the possibility that the house was fully armed, replete with motion detectors. To test for that annoyance, he removed a tennis ball from his backpack. After raising the blinds, he tossed the ball high into the bedroom. The only sound was its plopping on the floor.

You silly, silly little girl, he thought. He picked up his backpack and dropped it into the room. Hoisting himself into the opening, José crawled through head first and slithered to his feet. He found the tennis ball and shoved it into an outer pocket of the pack.

The flashlight beam trailed across the room as José fanned it from one wall to the next. The bed was neatly made. The decorations were the latest style. A diamond shimmer erupted when the light scanned the dresser. José hurried closer and spotted a carved crystal statuette of an Asian beauty carrying a basket. The piece looked expensive and unique. He picked it up, slipped it into his backpack, and pulled the leather pouch from his pocket.

Surveillance of the bathroom indicated a prime spot for one of his devices—right under the sink ledge near the wall. He exited the restroom just as a wicked gust of wind whipped at the blinds and sent the curtains into a frenzied billow. The low rumble of thunder implied that the tornado threat should be taken seriously. José imagined fighting the wind and rain and dodging lightning all the way back to his car. He decided to make short work of the rest of the job.

Within five minutes, he'd emptied some drawers, tossed sofa pillows, spilled a plant, and strategically placed bugs in every room. No matter where Brittan went, she wouldn't be out of his hearing unless she hid in a closet and whispered. And why would she do that? Within a few days, José Herrera would know exactly what Brittan Shay was up to and why a young woman of such considerable fortune had bothered about a stolen painting.

On his way out, he opened her jewelry chest and grabbed a handful of baubles. Unless his flashlight was deceiving him, she didn't go for elaborate stones…just gold. That was okay. Gold could be easily pawned, and the shops he used for smaller jobs never questioned the source. He shoved the pieces into his backpack. They clinked against the last item he'd stolen—a high-dollar CD player, as powerful as it was small.

TWENTY-THREE

Heather gazed around the shadowed room and struggled to orient herself to her surroundings. The place didn't look familiar in the least, and she grappled with why she wasn't in her own bed at home. She rubbed at her eyes, stroked her temple, and then remembered.

We're at the Hilton in Chicago, she told herself. Even though the curtains darkened the room, the glow of morning's first light oozed around the edges. Heather gazed toward the bed near hers. Brittan lay on her back with her arm over her head. A gauzy haze clung to her, enhancing her olive skin and full lips.

No wonder you've got two men on your trail, Heather thought and marveled at how Brittan had managed to keep suitors at arm's length until now. Perhaps she'd mastered the art of snubbing to the point that men accepted defeat before the chase ever started. Whatever the case, Brittan seemed to have snared Rob Lightly. Hopefully he'd snared Brittan as well.

"Go, girl!" Heather whispered and tossed aside the covers. After a routine trip to the bathroom, she slipped on her satin robe. She went into the suite's entertainment area, decorated with Renaissance replicas and rich tapestries. After a yawn, she paused by the window, dug her toes into the thick carpet, and pulled on the curtain cord. The drapes whispered open and unveiled the waking city.

Heather gazed down at the early morning traffic and wondered what Duke was doing right now. She checked her watch and remembered that it was five-thirty in Texas. "He's probably still asleep."

Extending her left hand, Heather wiggled her fingers. Her ruby engagement ring delightfully shimmered as if it, too, was waking with the morning light. She hugged herself and dreamed of her approaching wedding.

Just 12 weeks and counting, she thought and giggled under her breath.

Her laughter ceased as her recent dream swooshed through her mind. "An omen of doom." Heather pressed her fingertips against her temple. "That's why I woke up so early. It was that awful dream."

She and Lorna and Brittan had all been running from the mortician manager in Chicago Artworks. He'd chased them from the gallery and down a dark alley. Once the shadows closed in on him, he'd turned into a Dracula figure wielding a knife. His first target had been Brittan, and no matter how much Heather screamed, he didn't stop the attack. Just as Brittan had been about to die, Heather cried out to God and the attacker vanished.

Heather stood at the window, blindly staring at the skyscraper across the street. Dread crept up her spine and seeped into her soul. She'd told Brittan yesterday that God had been impressing her to pray more, and she was beginning to think there was a very good reason. She settled into one of the wingback chairs and rested her forearms on her knees. Staring at the carpet, she recalled their pastor saying that prayer was the oil that helped the cogs of God's kingdom turn. Even though Brittan seemed to have trouble grasping this right now, Heather knew she got it. She sensed this concern about prayer was somehow related to Brittan's safety.

"Something is wrong," she whispered. "I know it." This case and investigation felt different than the others they'd worked. Darker. More threatening. *Someone out there has a vendetta against the Rose. Whoever it is killed a famous artist. What would stop him from killing Brittan, Lorna, and me if he got half a chance?*

A chill gripped her and then released. Rubbing her face, Heather considered Rob Lightly's presence in Chicago. It was so odd that he flew all the way here just to find out who bought the print...and even odder that he was here at the same time as they were.

Maybe God planned this to protect us from a total fiasco, she thought and considered what kind of havoc they would have created if they'd followed through with Brittan's plan to overturn the coffee table and disconcert the artist. She imagined her dog ears cocked sideways, Lorna with a streak of paint on her face, and the manager wearing a coffee urn. She snickered and then sobered when she envisioned a swat team swarming the place and carting them off.

Heather propped her elbows on her knees and cradled her forehead in her hands. "Okay, Lord," she whispered, "please protect us from ourselves. Stop us from doing anything that would really risk our lives. Even though we've had a good bit of success, we're still not exactly experts at this. We take chances. You know that. Please give us wisdom. I have a hunch we're going to need it."

Heather lifted her head, leaned back in the chair, and stretched her legs. She rested her elbows on the armrests and made a tent of her fingers. Brittan said Rob was after the name of the person who bought the Mosier print. Before they left Chicago, they had to know who it was and if they needed to follow up here.

"We came all the way here for that information," Heather whispered. "We can't leave without it." Despite her sense of caution, Heather also knew the Rose couldn't passively bow out of this investigation. There was too much at stake.

✳ ✳ ✳

Brittan fumbled with the coffeemaker sitting on the service bar in the bedroom. Her mouth felt like paste, and she was more than ready for a hot blast of coffee to baptize her tongue and jolt her brain. After blindly maneuvering through the process, she pressed the start button and then went for her glasses on the nightstand. That's when she realized the swirl of sheets in the bed next to hers didn't have Heather beneath them.

Covering a yawn, she tightened her pj's drawstring and padded toward the entertainment room. On the way she glanced into the other bedroom where Lorna slept. Still no Heather. A brief journey across the short entryway led into the main room and straight to Heather. Her friend sat in the chair near the window. Hunched over, she stared at the floor as if she were considering life's greatest dilemmas.

The sound of the coffeemaker's faint gurgling filled the room, and Heather glanced toward the doorway. "Hey there, you," she said through a smile. Without her makeup, Heather looked like a pale angel sitting in the morning haze.

"Hi." Brittan strode to the chair opposite Heather and plopped down. "I'm making coffee if you want some."

"I usually hold out for hot green tea," Heather said, "but I think I'll live dangerously today."

Brittan extended a thumbs-up. "Go ahead! Live life on the edge," she mocked with a faint smile.

Heather playfully stuck out her tongue.

"What are you doing up so early?" Brittan covered another yawn.

"A dream woke me up—a nightmare. I was dreaming the mortician receptionist guy had morphed into a vampire and was chasing us down an alley. He was about to stab you when I woke up."

Brittan winced. "Why do you have to be so violent? And why me?"

"You tell me," Heather replied. "Seriously, I've got this strange feeling that we're really not safe—and you especially." Heather's blue eyes grew round like a night owl's.

"Don't look at me like that." Brittan rubbed her upper arms. "You're giving me the creeps."

"I'm not trying to," Heather assured. "Have you heard from Rob?"

"Not unless he responded to my text already." Brittan had sent Rob a message yesterday evening, asking him to call her. Maybe she could get him to tell her the name of the person who bought the Mosier print over the phone. "Let me check my cell." Brittan rose and retraced her steps to the nightstand where she'd plugged in her phone to charge overnight. A quick check of her message icon indicated no return messages, and Brittan was beginning to wonder if Rob received her request. She was of the opinion that they shouldn't leave Chicago until they had that name.

The coffeemaker burped out a final blast of steam and was silent. Brittan poured herself and Heather mugs, picked up a couple of creamer and sugar packages, and returned to the sitting area.

"No word from Rob," she grumbled and extended Heather the cup, followed by the condiment packages.

"I vote you call him before too much longer," Heather said. "I don't want to leave Chicago until we have that name."

Brittan raised her brows. "Oh really? The way you were acting, I was thinking you were ready to pull out and forget the whole thing."

"Nope." Heather shook her head. "I don't see how we can. We've got to get the criminal who's dropping those roses. We've *got* to."

"I agree," Brittan said. She enjoyed her black coffee and remembered what Rob had said about liking his women strong and dark. Smiling, she also recalled the kiss that happened after his audacious comment. "I think I'll call him in an hour or so and see what I can find out," she said and wished she could tell him she too was in Chicago.

"That'll be seven-thirty." Heather sipped her coffee. "Think he'll be up?"

"If he's not, he needs to be." Brittan wiggled her brows.

"And you didn't join the army—why?" Heather mocked.

Brittan rolled her eyes and stood. "I'm hitting the shower. Why don't you pray that I won't get washed down the drain?" she teased and walked toward the bathroom.

"Don't knock it, girlfriend," Heather said. "It could save your life."

"I know," Brittan replied over her shoulder and wondered what had made her take such an irreverent shot at Heather. She *did* respect Heather's desire to pray and figured she'd probably interrupted her friend this morning. But still, she was having trouble swallowing the constant focus. Up until now Sunday prayers had worked well enough. In her estimation God was a practical being who worked logically and succinctly within the framework of the laws of science and nature that He'd created. Other than that, He did what He wanted when He wanted. As for protection, Brittan fully believed God expected her to exercise her common sense in protecting herself. That philosophy had succeeded for many years, and she had no doubt that it would continue to work.

TWENTY-FOUR

"Help! Let me out! I'm stuck in your pocket!" the shrill voice floated from Rob's pants, lying where he'd dropped them last night when he turned off the TV and crawled into bed. "Help! Let me out! I'm stuck in your pocket!"

With a groan he tossed aside the covers and fumbled for the phone. Without looking at the ID screen, he mumbled, "Hello," into the receiver, fully expecting his dad or a colleague. When Brittan's voice floated over the line, Rob sat straighter.

"Good morning, Rob Lightly," she said, her tone friendly yet firm.

"Hi!" he responded and hoped he didn't sound as drowsy to her as he did to himself.

"Did I wake you up?"

"Uh…"

"Sorry," she said. "It's just that my curiosity is raging, and I figured you were an early riser."

"Usually I am," Rob admitted. "But I stayed up late last night watching an old western."

She laughed. "Complete with damsels in distress who find lake monsters lurking under their beds?"

"Yes, as a matter of fact," he drawled. "How'd you guess?"

"Just a wild coincidence."

Brittan's laughter wove its way around his psyche and made Rob wish she were with him now...and they were married. He rubbed his face hard and stood. The coffeepot called, and he marched toward it with purpose.

The last thing he remembered before falling asleep was a fleeting prayer that if God wanted him to tell Brittan he knew she was part of the Rose, He'd arrange a conversation where the admission flowed naturally. While Rob had meant the prayer, he hadn't expected a call from her first thing this morning. His groggy mind still wanted to put off the admission a while longer.

"What do you need?" he asked and realized he sounded abrupt. "I'm assuming you didn't call to talk about lake monsters," he added and made a special point of putting a smile in his voice.

"Actually, I called to talk about *paint* monsters," she responded. "Did you get the name of the person who bought the touched-up print?"

He grabbed the carafe and meandered toward the bathroom sink. This conversation was already showing signs of lining up for a perfect opportunity for telling the truth. Once in the bathroom, he flipped on the light and gazed toward the ceiling. *I'm really not ready for this, Lord. It could get awkward, and I'm too sleepy for awkward.*

"I sent you a text message last night," Brittan finally continued, "but I was beginning to think you didn't get it."

"I got it," he admitted and didn't bother to explain that the reason he hadn't responded was because of his struggle over the Rose. Before he went to bed, Rob was still resisting the inevitable. His prayer for God to open up a conversation wasn't from a heart that wanted to admit he'd been deceptive—it was more a desperate heart requesting that God make the confession easy *or* let him off the hook altogether. Now he silently argued that telling her in person was probably best. However, a thought he didn't expect barged into his mind and would not abate. *Tell her now!*

"Are you okay, Rob?" Brittan asked.

"Uh, yes. Sorry I didn't call back last night. I was just…"

"Is this a bad time? I can call later."

"No," he replied and didn't expound. Rob set aside the carafe, turned on the water, and shoved the container under the faucet. "Listen, I did get the name," he finally said.

"Oh?" she replied, and Rob had never heard so much caution in one word. Apparently the woman knew something was up. No telling *what* she was thinking.

With the carafe full, he plunked it on the counter, switched off the water, and stomped back into the bedroom. When he reached the window, Rob yanked on the curtain cord and glared down at the traffic.

"Look, Brittan," he finally blurted, "there's something you need to know."

"You're seeing someone else, right?" she hedged.

He barked out a laugh, but as soon as the spontaneous reaction erupted he realized she probably didn't appreciate it. "Sorry," he said. "It's not that *at all!* And it never occurred to me you'd even think that. For what it's worth, Brittan, you've got me where a few women have wanted but never managed." The smile in his voice underscored his meaning.

"Oh," she said, her voice laced with relief and curiosity.

"I'm assuming *you* want me there," he added.

"Oh yes! And…while we're on the subject, in case you've wondered, I've decided the man I want to date is you."

"I gathered that after Sunday night," he drawled and wondered how they'd gotten here. "I didn't figure you were the kind of woman who'd level that kind of a kiss on one man while dating another." Rob relived their warm embrace while the charged silence came close to making him sweat.

"You're right. I'm not."

Sighing, Rob finally admitted he *had* to tell her—*now*. The further they progressed in their relationship, the more betrayed she'd feel if she learned the truth. Rob moved toward the rumpled bed and kicked his shorts out of the way before dropping onto the edge. He rested his fist upon his knee and gazed at his plaid pajama bottoms until the design blurred. Let the chips fall where they may. The time had come.

"There is something you wanted to tell me?" Brittan prompted.

"Yes," he admitted. "But first let me answer your question— the reason you called. I *did* get the name of the guy who bought the print. As things turned out, the prints are numbered. That one was number 35. The man who bought the print paid cash and didn't leave an address. However, the manager remembered the sale because it happened only a few weeks ago. He said the man was a tall Latino."

"That narrows it down to about a million men," Brittan scoffed.

"Right...except..." Rob paused and imagined Brittan leaning forward, waiting for every syllable.

"Except?" she echoed.

"The tall Latino hit on a female employee while he was there."

"Oh really?"

"Yep. They went to a bar. And she is not happy with him at all. I don't know what happened, but she was ready to tell any representative of the law everything she could about him. His name is Eduardo Sanchez. And he lives in Texas—Palestine, to be exact."

"Great!" Brittan exclaimed.

"Want to meet up Saturday night and see if we can find him?" Rob asked.

Tension and silence filled the air.

"Brittan?"

"That might be taking it a little far, don't you think?"

"It depends on what *you* think," Rob replied, "and how bad the Rose wants to get to the bottom of this case."

More silence.

"Yes, I know your secret," he said, his voice soft and powerful. The words rolled off his tongue in an astonishing way. Weight lifted from his spirit. "I've known since the night you and your friends left the rose on my patrol car last year."

A garbled gasp preceded her bewildered response, "All this time?"

"Yes."

"And you didn't tell me?"

"I didn't know what to do," he admitted.

"How did you find out?"

"I followed you home last summer and did my homework. I was fascinated by you. I read about you in the society pages. When Dad was looking for a lake house and couldn't make up his mind between the A-frame and another one across the lake, I realized you had a place three doors down from the A-frame and I talked him into it. The places were equally good, except the A-frame had a bonus—Brittan Shay a few doors down." He hoped his honesty would create some magic.

"The whole time you—you've known we're the Rose?" she repeated.

"Yes, and I know you're in Chicago now. When my dad told me you were going out of town to shop, I figured this is where you were heading. I got the guy's name before you and your friends could get yourselves into more trouble than you could get out of."

Stony silence indicated his admission wasn't going over all that well.

"Brittan?"

"So you've been lying to me?" she said, her voice rising.

"No—it's not like that at all!" Rob defended. "I didn't know any of this was going to happen this way. I only hoped that you'd—that we'd—and when we did, I realized it was turning into way more for me way faster than I thought. I knew I had to tell you and the longer I waited, the higher the chances you'd feel betrayed."

"I feel betrayed *now*," she growled. "I feel like a…a mouse that's been played with by a cat."

"I'm not a cat by a long shot," Rob said in earnest. "And I'm not playing games." He stood and scrubbed his hand across his face. The phone went strangely silent. He pulled the cell away from his ear and gazed at the screen. "Call ended."

"Well, that went over like a ton of bricks," he said toward the ceiling. "Now what?"

Brittan snapped her phone shut and gazed at Lorna and Heather. Both were staring at her with widened eyes.

"He knows who we are?" Lorna whispered and brushed her rumpled hair from her eyes. Still in her nightshirt, she'd only been up a few minutes when Brittan called Rob. What had started as sleepy-eyed appraisal had morphed into intense staring.

Brittan nodded and dropped her phone onto the carved coffee table. "He knows," she ground out. "And he *has known* since the night we left the rose on his patrol car." She narrowed her eyes and rested her hands on her hips.

"Oh man," Heather groaned. Still dressed in her satin robe, she'd been planning to take a shower when Brittan decided the time had come to call Rob. "He's played us for fools," she said. "I remember that day he first met me in your garden." She narrowed her eyes. "He asked me if I remembered the animal cruelty case the Rose had left him evidence on." She lifted her hand. "And the whole time he knew I was up to my eyeballs in it."

"Well, don't feel like the Lone Ranger." Brittan whipped off her glasses and pressed her fingers against her eyes. "That same night he asked me how I knew he had a German shepherd when I thoughtlessly blurted out something about his dog. But he *knew* how I already knew and didn't tell me!"

Brittan plunked her glasses beside her phone. "I don't believe this!" She groaned as her mind whirled with the implications and the myriad questions that went with them.

Has Rob keep our secret safe?

Will he tell anyone now?

Is this the only reason he met me...dated me?

"I guess we didn't do such a hot job of covering our tracks that night," Lorna admitted.

Brittan lowered her hands and shared a meaningful gaze with her friends.

"What'll we do now?" Lorna asked.

"Who knows," Brittan muttered. "He did give us the name of the guy who bought the painting—Eduardo Sanchez. Rob found out he's a lecher if nothing else. He lives in Palestine, Texas. I think that's a few hours north of Houston."

"That's a lead," Lorna observed.

"Yes and he's not that far from the Houston area," Heather mused.

"Or that's what he told the woman he made a pass at," Brittan explained. "Whatever happened, it didn't go well, and she was mad enough to tell Rob everything she knew about him."

"I say we forget the shopping and head back to Houston today," Heather suggested. "The sooner we can turn over this new stone, the better."

"I agree," Lorna said. "I'll call our pilot and tell him we're outta here."

"Okay," Brittan agreed. Slipping her hands into the pockets of her shorts, she moved toward the window. Her shoulders drooped as her spirit sank. She recalled other times when Rob could have told her the truth but, for whatever reason, hadn't—such as the evening he'd kissed her the first time. Earlier that night Brittan had flipped on the TV and told him she was a big fan of the Rose. Looking back she recalled a trace of humor in his eyes, but she hadn't questioned why. Now she knew.

He was probably laughing at me, she fumed. *Of course I told him we were just big fans of the Rose,* she thought, *which was only a half-truth.* Brittan grimaced. *But we have a vow of secrecy, and Heather and Lorna's men didn't learn they were the Rose until their relationships turned serious. Rob and I weren't "there" yet,* she reasoned.

When someone stepped beside her, Brittan glanced up to see Heather, a compassionate set to her mouth. "I'm sorry. I know you were really starting to like him."

"Yes." Brittan stared hard at a pigeon on a skyscraper's ledge. Not in the mood for laying open her breaking heart, she decided to open another subject. "Did you ever get that email you were waiting on—the one about the city manager and Eve Maloney? What's his name again?"

"Herman Soliday," Heather supplied.

"Yes. You said on the plane you were expecting info about his family from that genealogy expert."

"Yep. I checked it when you were in the shower. Soliday is an only child. Both parents are deceased. It doesn't look like there's any family on the outside who'd want revenge."

"That doesn't eliminate friends."

"Right. I'm carefully exploring those angles, but I haven't come up with much."

"What about Eve Maloney?"

"The vote's still out on her."

"Lorna said she still hasn't heard back from the security company to see if the cameras were scheduled for maintenance that day," Brittan stated, knowing she was repeating information Heather already knew, but anything was better than talking about Rob.

"Like Lorna said on the plane," Heather softly said, "she can't get them to return any calls or emails. She's thinking about going in person but in disguise."

Brittan lifted her gaze to Heather's. That latest tidbit was new to Brittan. "She needs to be careful."

"I know." Heather's eyes clouded.

"I'd like to look at that video clip again," Brittan said. "I'm wondering if we're missing something that's right under our noses."

"Be my guest." Heather motioned toward a computer lying on the coffee table. "The files are saved on Lorna's laptop."

TWENTY-FIVE

Saturday morning Rob pulled into his father's driveway and placed his Dodge truck in park. The ten o'clock sunshine was blasting from the blue May sky and beckoning the world to enjoy the lake. Apparently his dad had spring fever. He'd called Rob at seven to ask him to come over for brunch, of all things.

Rob opened his door, slid to the driveway, and squinted against the sun while he tried to piece together his father's logic. Even though Simon was the king of dinner grilling, this was the first brunch. Thankfully Rob wasn't scheduled to work until mid afternoon and was free.

His motivation for coming over involved more than the quiche and biscuits his father promised. Rob hoped to see Brittan. He glanced toward her place, but the Jag wasn't in her driveway. She'd mentioned that she and Lorna also shared a penthouse in downtown Houston and maybe she was there—unless they were still in Chicago. But Rob didn't think so. He figured they'd hopped the plane pronto and come home to see if they could find Eduardo Sanchez. Rob could already tell them there was no Eduardo Sanchez listed in the Palestine phone book or in the multiple directories the police were privy to. There were numerous listings nationally, but that didn't help. Rob believed whoever bought the print had used a pseudonym with that woman.

"So much for that trip," he mumbled and then turned for his father's home. Rob hadn't heard a peep out of Brittan since she'd hung up on him. He'd debated about calling her several times but had yet to scrounge up the courage. He knew her well enough by now to understand that she was probably analyzing this situation from 40 angles and mulling over details, such as whether he'd kept their secret to himself. He had—and he'd be glad to tell her if she gave him the chance.

He eyed the sparkling lake visible between the houses and figured the water was as cool as the morning was warm. Rob had thrown on a T-shirt and swim trunks and hadn't bothered with anything else except sandals. He planned to take a dip off the pier when his brunch settled. Then he'd laze around in a lawn chair until his trunks dried and it was time to go home and get ready for work.

Ringing the doorbell, Rob cast a final glance toward Brittan's place. He sure wanted to see her...or at least hear her voice on the phone. When his dad opened the door, he looked at Rob and said, "You look about as cheerful as a pancake. What's the matter? Love life crashing?" He waved toward Brittan's place.

"How'd you guess?" Rob mumbled. He hadn't told his dad a thing, but the guy had a way of sizing up Rob's existence in one glance.

His father opened the door wider, and Rob stepped inside. The place was neat as usual, and void of anything except masculine necessities. The delightful smell of food wafted into the living room. His dad always had been able to cook better than his mother, and she'd constantly raved about his culinary masterpieces. Rob missed her most when he and his dad got together for meals. He sure could use motherly encouragement today.

He glanced toward the table where her photo always sat and

saw nothing but a lamp. He frowned and tried to remember the last time he'd seen her picture but drew a blank.

"Unless you've all of a sudden gone fancy on me," Simon said, "the quiche is on the stove, and you can help yourself. If you like, we can eat on the deck out back."

"Works for me," Rob agreed. Shoulders hunched, he let his nose lead him to the kitchen. Simon followed close behind.

When they made it to the stove where two quiches awaited his attention, Simon gripped Rob's shoulder and asked, "So what happened?"

"Well…" Rob gave his dad a glance, opened a cabinet, and grabbed a plate. He hadn't even told his father what he knew about Brittan…and debated whether he should reveal that now. Finally he just dug into the quiche, added a homemade biscuit to his plate, and decided to gloss over the problem as best he could.

"We just had a misunderstanding, I guess. It'll blow over… maybe."

"Oh," Simon said and went for the coffee. He poured a couple of cups, extended one to Rob, and didn't bother to fill a plate for himself.

That's when Rob saw past his own angst and noticed the dark circles under his father's eyes.

"You okay?" he queried.

"Who, me?" Simon lowered the cup from his mouth.

"No, that mouse on your shoulder," Rob chided. "Yes, you. You look like you haven't slept in a week."

"I know," he admitted and stared past Rob.

"So whazzup with *you?*"

Simon rubbed at his ear and then said, "Let's go on outside. We'll talk out there."

"Sure, Dad," Rob said and set aside his own problems.

By the time they settled at the wooden lawn table, Elvis had begged for his own helping of quiche, and Simon set it on the deck in a paper plate. "There—you spoiled rotten mutt," he groused. "You eat better than I do."

"Did you ever call that trainer I found?" Rob asked.

"No, not yet," Simon admitted. "It's on my to-do list."

"You know he's going to get fat if you keep feeding him extras."

"You mean like you?"

"What? I'm not fat!" Rob patted his belly and chomped on the quiche. It tasted like it came straight from heaven.

"No, but I'm always feeding you extras—like now." Simon lifted his brows, and Rob realized for the first time his dad was dressed in Dockers and a sport shirt—not his usual Saturday morning fishing attire.

"Are you going to a funeral or something?" Rob asked.

"No." Simon shook his head and sighed. "I'm going to a wedding—or rather—I've been to a wedding."

"So early?" Rob asked and popped a piece of biscuit in his mouth.

"Actually it was a few months back." Simon peered into his son's eyes, and Rob slowly stopped chewing.

"What are you trying to say?" he croaked.

"Remember Deloris Francis?" Simon asked.

"Yes."

"She and I got married."

Rob swallowed and reached for his coffee. "What?"

"Even though you weren't ready for a stepmother, I was ready for a wife, Rob, and well…" He shrugged and continued, "I finally decided to take the plunge."

"But I'm nearly old enough to date her." He downed as much of the scalding liquid as his throat would tolerate.

"She does look young, I admit," Simon said. "But she's 44—only 14 years younger than me."

"Only? You're almost old enough to be her father!"

"Not quite."

Rob sighed, leaned back in his chair, and gazed toward the cloudless sky. The lake lapping at the shoreline whispered the clues Rob had begun to piece together but had yet to see the final picture. "I get it now," he said. "This explains everything."

"Like what?"

"I was telling Brittan that it seemed like you were turning into a recluse or that you were hiding something." He laughed and lifted his hand. "Now I see! You were having an affair."

"Yes…but with my *wife*," Simon stressed.

Narrowing his eyes, Rob observed his father. "Why didn't you just come out and tell me, Dad?" he asked. "I thought we were close."

"We are, but when you saw how close Deloris and I were getting, you gave me a lot of grief, and I just decided to—"

"Do what you wanted to do anyway and hide it?"

Simon's mouth turned down as he nodded. "Pretty much. I hate to tell you this, Rob, but it's really time for both of us to…well… let go."

"Have you been watching Dr. Phil again?" Rob accused.

"No. Your mother's death did a number on both of us, and for a while we turned into two hermits. We had to hold each other up or go down, but now the holding time needs to end so we can get on with our lives."

"I had a double whammy," Rob admitted and gazed across the lake. "I watched my partner Zeb get shot the year before I watched Mom die in her hospital bed."

"I know." Simon's quiet admission revealed deep understanding. "I know," he repeated and briefly gripped Rob's shoulder.

"Funny thing," Rob said over a dry chuckle, "when we were assigned as partners, I wondered how in the world we'd overcome the age gap. And then we wound up nearly as close as you and I." His voice thickening, he stared at a patch of clover near a pine tree.

Finally Rob looked at his dad, who observed him with man-to-man understanding.

"You had a bad couple of years. But I think it's going to be better from now on." Simon waved at his son. "Look at you! You're chasing a woman yourself!"

"And you're not dead by a long shot," Rob said and shook his head.

"No, I'm not." Simon leaned back in his chair. "Deloris is going to be here soon."

"Why does that not surprise me?" Rob grumbled and tried to talk himself into accepting the inevitable.

"Will you at least give her a chance?"

"She'll never replace Mother. I can't even *view* her as a mother." Rob lifted his hand and strangely felt more alone than ever.

"Of course not," Simon agreed. "And she isn't and doesn't want to replace your mom. All I ask is that you treat her as my wife— nothing more. And, well, I'm not sure she can wrap her mind around being a mother to someone your age either." He grinned. "But maybe the two of you can try to be friends. She's willing if you are."

TWENTY-SIX

When Brittan flipped on her living room light, the first thing she noticed was the upset fichus tree near the window. It was turned on its side with dirt spilled in all directions. Her eyes wide, she scanned the rest of the room…the disheveled couch cushions, the scattered potpourri, the empty space in the entertainment center where her CD player had been.

"Oh my word! I've been robbed!"

Brittan dropped her handbag and released the handle on her luggage. Both plopped to the tile with a click and thud. She gripped her forehead as her mind whirled and offered several immediate options.

Call the police.

Go through the rest of the house to see what else is missing.

Run back outside—in case the burglar is still in the house.

The last option seemed the safest. She snatched up her purse, bolted back through the front door, and fumbled for her cell phone. That's when she noticed Rob's truck parked three doors down, between a black Lexus and a Ford pickup. Instead of dialing 911, she raced across her neighbors' yards and stopped when she reached Simon's front door. After pounding on the door, Brittan figured they must be outside. She darted around the house and spotted three people sitting on the deck.

Brittan bounded up the steps and Rob, his father, and Mrs. Lightly turned to look at her as if she were an alien who'd dropped from the sky. Even in her frenzied state, Brittan had the presence of mind to realize she'd intruded upon something more than a routine conversation. As of a few days ago, she knew Rob still didn't know his father was married. Now he was sitting with Simon and his wife. For her life, Brittan couldn't remember the woman's name. The image of her disheveled house blotted out everything but dismay.

"Brittan?" Mrs. Lightly said. "Are you okay?"

"I'm so sorry to interrupt, Mrs. Lightly," she panted, "but—" She looked at Rob who had stood up. "My house was broken into while I was gone!"

"You're kidding!" Simon exclaimed.

"No. I just got home and—it's a wreck."

Rob lunged off the deck, and Brittan raced after him. "Just a minute!" he called over his shoulder while trotting toward his pickup. Gasping, Brittan wondered what he was doing until he slammed the truck's door. That's when she spotted his handgun.

"Just in case the guy's still in there," he explained.

Brittan pulled her pistol from her purse, fell in beside him, and looped her long purse strap over her head.

As they approached Brittan's house, Rob eyed her Glock 30 and started to speak, but stopped. "Whatever floats your boat, I guess," he said. "But I'd rather you stay outside while I scout the house." They paused near the front door, and Rob looked down at her with a hard glint in his eyes that dared her to argue.

"I'll check the kitchen," she replied.

"*No!*" he demanded.

"Yes!" Brittan shoved past him and stumbled into the entryway. While she *had* run for help rather than risk facing the thief alone, her bravado had increased now that she had backup.

"Good grief, woman!" Rob erupted and followed while Brittan

rushed toward the kitchen. The fluorescent lights illuminated the room. No sign of the intruder. Brittan whipped open the storage closet and spotted nothing but cleaning paraphernalia and a vacuum.

Frantically she glanced toward the shelf that still held her keepsake chess set. She swallowed against the lump in her throat and turned toward the living room.

"Stay here!" Rob demanded. "I'm going to check the rest of the house."

Brittan ignored him and followed him into every room, checking every closet. Once in her bedroom, they spotted the raised window with the pane cut out.

"That's how he got in," Rob stated and lowered his gun.

"Great!" Brittan put her gun on her dresser and immediately missed the crystal statuette her mother had given her last Christmas. "And he took my lady too!" she huffed.

Rob swiveled to face her, and Brittan was struck with how blue his eyes were and how his tan had deepened since she last saw him. His swim trunks and sandals hinted that he'd been spending his share of time in the sun.

He started to speak and then stopped as awareness sparked between them.

The combination of attraction and feeling vulnerable culminated in Brittan wanting to fling herself into his big, safe arms. Never the clinging vine sort, she stiffened her spine and refused the impulse. Despite her recent aggravation with him, Brittan couldn't deny that Rob had something that snared her as no other man had.

Rob's expression softened.

Brittan didn't know *what* he was going to say.

But all he said was, "What lady?"

"Excuse me?" Brittan squinted.

"You said he took your lady."

"Oh. It was an original crystal statuette Mom gave me for Christmas. Her voice broke as she pointed toward her dresser. Brittan refused to give in to the sting in her eyes. "You were right," she croaked. "I really dragged my feet on getting an alarm system. I have a security firm scheduled to be here Monday. But—" Brittan spotted her open jewelry chest and groaned. She didn't have a lot of jewelry here, only some gold pieces. She hated the thought of having even one item taken.

"I feel so violated," she whispered and hurried to the chest. A quick perusal validated the intruder had snatched only a handful. Fortunately her heirloom pieces were in a safe at the penthouse.

Only when she turned from the chest did Brittan realize Rob had grown strangely silent. On his knees, he examined the space under her windowsill.

"What are you doing?" Brittan questioned and stepped toward him.

He held up his hand and looked up at her. Placing his index finger against his lips, he motioned for her to be silent and then pointed outside. He stood, grabbed her hand, and tugged her down the hallway.

Wrinkling her brow, Brittan offered no protest as he led her outside and didn't stop walking until they were close to the road. After releasing her hand, he peered up the street one way and then the other.

"What is it?" Brittan asked.

"The motive for the break-in wasn't robbery," he said, shoving his gun in his pocket. "Your house has been bugged. I spotted something protruding from beneath the window ledge. It's definitely some kind of receptor. Where there's one, there's probably more."

Brittan's face grew cold despite the sun's warmth. Heather's haunting admonitions echoed through her mind. She'd insisted that she was praying for protection—especially for Brittan. From the start of their careers as the Rose, Brittan had felt invincible. No matter what they did, they always came out unscathed, undetected, undaunted. They'd taken many chances and never once been caught or harmed.

Heather said she felt this case was different—as if there were some sort of threat hanging over them. Up until now the Rose had always been on the chase. Now Brittan sensed the force of someone hunting the Rose. Perhaps that someone suspected who they were and bugged her place to confirm their identities. Maybe it was the same person who murdered Mosier and stole the Incan necklace.

"I know what you're thinking," Rob said. "And it might or might not be related to the Rose. There's no way of knowing right now. Do you have an ex-boyfriend who might want to know what you're up to? Like, if you're seeing someone else?" His all-business persona didn't waver.

She opened her mouth to speak, but he held up his hand.

"I've seen this sort of thing over and over again. Sometimes men become obsessive about ex-girlfriends."

"No, no, no." Brittan shook her head. "I haven't dated since high school. Well, until recently," she added and looked away.

"Okay," he said and Brittan detected a satisfied nuance to his voice. When she glanced back his way, his just-the-facts-ma'am expression hadn't changed.

"Then my next guess is that it has to do with who you are publicly more than with the Rose. After all, you *are* Leon Shay's daughter. I'm surprised your family doesn't make you have a bodyguard."

"They would like that, but not me. I agreed to be licensed to carry a pistol rather than be chained to Butch."

"Butch?"

Brittan shrugged. "You know, a beefy he-man who wouldn't even let me go to the restroom by myself." She faked a shiver. "*Deliver* me!"

"I'd like to see someone try to keep you cornered," Rob drawled.

"What's that supposed to mean?"

"You've got a mind of your own." One corner of his mouth lifted.

"And you don't?" she challenged.

"Nope. I share mine with three other people."

Brittan didn't let herself smile. The spark in his eyes suggested his attraction for her was as strong as ever. Even though Brittan experienced a moment of weakness in the house, she had yet to fully recover from his deception. And the longer she thought about it, the more the aggravation returned.

"So it looks like I've got a stalker," she stated. "I mean—other than you."

"I'm not a stalker!" Rob protested.

Brittan rolled her eyes and tapped her toes. "You've been watching me for months, you talked your dad into buying a house next to mine, and you followed me to Chicago. How do *you* define 'stalker'? And how do I know you didn't bug my house?"

"Ah come on, Brittan!" Rob lifted his hand. "Give me a break! I'm a police officer. I don't break the law."

She balled her hand and slipped it into the pocket of her linen jacket. "That's not logical anyway," she said with a sigh. Tension settled on them. Brittan locked her knees and eyed the trees across the road. When she looked back at Rob, he was glaring at the world. Brittan realized that in her impudence she had royally insulted him.

"Sorry," she mumbled. "I'm rattled. This isn't something you'd do."

"Yeah, no problem," he replied. "Some women might be flattered that a guy went to all that trouble just to get to know them."

She thoroughly perused the lake house and debated whether

or not to let his words make inroads. Deciding to sort it out later, she said, "Now what?"

"Wait a minute!" Rob exclaimed and turned toward his dad's place. "Wait just a darn minute!"

"What is it?"

"When you ran up on my father's deck, Deloris knew your name." He pivoted back to her. "And you called her Mrs. Lightly. I just found out they were married today, but you already knew, didn't you? You've already met her."

Brittan looked at Rob's face and then glanced past him. "Yes, I've known a while."

"Why didn't you tell me?" he demanded.

"I guess for the same reason you didn't tell me you knew I was part of the Rose," she challenged.

Again silence settled between them. Rob's face grew a shade darker. "I can't believe you let me...I even asked you to tell me if you noticed anything unusual!"

"Yes, and your dad was struggling with how to tell you. I thought it was his place, not mine." She crossed her arms.

"But if you and I..." He pointed to her and then himself. "If a relationship is going to work, it's got to be based on trust and honesty."

Brittan's laugh held no mirth. "That's ironic coming from you!"

"That's different!" he fumed.

"Different?" Brittan shot back.

"I specifically gave you an opportunity to tell me and you didn't!" Rob rested his hand on his hip and glared down at her.

"Oh *please!* This is absolutely ridiculous!"

"Maybe it is! But it's still *very annoying!* And I'm as hacked off at you as I was at Dad."

"Why? Because you couldn't keep him under your thumb?"

"Noooo!" Rob exploded as he wagged his head from side to side. "Because he didn't give me the respect of telling me in the first place. I'm a big boy!" He crammed his fingertips against his chest. "I would have dealt with it! It's the deception that's the deal!"

"So we're back to that topic—the one you know so well."

He worked his mouth, glared at her a while longer, and then shook his head. "We're getting nowhere. I'm *through*." He sliced his hands through the air like an umpire making a call.

Brittan wasn't about to let him know she'd hoped for so much more. Obviously this relationship was hitting a dead end. Part of the reason she'd avoided dating in college was to save herself from the headaches of the man-woman tangle. Hashing out issues in a relationship could zap a person's strength, and she'd rather spend her mental energy on something that lasted. Apparently it wasn't Rob Lightly.

"Look!" she asserted. "My house has been broken into. I've got bugs. Who knows where and who knows why! Can't we talk about this other business later? What do I need to do? Should I call the police to file a report?" She stared at him and hoped he would never suspect how glad she'd been to see him.

"I can do it," he growled and turned back toward the house. "I shouldn't have gotten off task. It's been a bad morning. I'm going to call in backup, and we'll go over the house. We've got a device that detects bugs. We'll get rid of any we find. But I recommend you not stay here until a security system is installed."

"Don't worry, I won't," Brittan affirmed. She turned toward her house and stopped halfway up the walkway. When she turned around, Rob was inches behind her. His halt was as abrupt as her words, "I hope you don't tell anyone what you know," she said.

"Brittan, I haven't leaked a word to anyone since the night you left the rose on my car. What makes you think I'll all of a sudden turn into a blabber mouth?" His lips twisted in a sarcastic smirk.

"Why didn't you tell anyone?" she bit out.

"Because I respected your wishes. I knew you didn't want to

be known." He shrugged and his defensive edge diminished. "So I didn't."

Brittan sighed and examined the chip in her toenail polish that was exposed by her leather sandals. Everything was falling apart today—right down to her pedicure. "Well, thanks. We were worried you might have told someone. Or you might tell someone now."

"Now that we're breaking up?" he asked.

"Yes, I guess," she mumbled under her breath and continued walking. This time she couldn't fight back the watery eye syndrome.

"Oh, and Brittan?"

She stopped and didn't turn around. Otherwise, he'd see she'd gone misty.

"I ran a check on Eduardo Sanchez. No deal. I think that might have been an alias."

"We spent last night hitting that wall too," she admitted. Her back still to him, she added, "And now the museum security guard is missing. I wonder if he's okay." The news had been all over Houston when the debutantes arrived home yesterday afternoon.

"Me too."

"You guys were at the museum the other night, right?"

Brittan turned to face him and sized up his expression. Surely he didn't think the Rose had gotten rid of the security guard.

"I don't think his missing is linked to whoever broke into the museum," he supplied, "if that's what you're wondering."

"Even though some of the media is going there?" she asked, feeling like she was suffocating.

"Yes."

"Good." Brittan pivoted back toward the yard. "I'll be waiting out back," she said over her shoulder and rounded the house. This didn't seem like the ideal time to be sitting in Eden, but Brittan didn't have much of a choice. The last thing she wanted was to go back into the house where her every breath could be heard by whoever planted those bugs.

She shivered and decided it might be best to stay at the Shay Building penthouse. Even though the flat was in downtown Houston, the security was tops. Too much was happening to not employ utmost caution. The security guard was missing, and Brittan feared the worst for the poor guy. The time had come to lie low—really low—for her safety, her friends' safety, and the Rose's image. Brittan didn't want to be the next murder victim, and she didn't want the Rose to be implicated for crimes they hadn't committed.

The farther Brittan strolled into the backyard garden, the more credence Heather's warnings held. She settled into a lawn chair and gazed on the lake that was blissfully shimmering as if the world were trouble free. Before she realized what she was doing, Brittan breathed a prayer and hoped God was more responsive to pleas for protection than she'd thought.

TWENTY-SEVEN

Heather sat at the red light and tapped her index finger against the steering wheel. The second Brittan called and reported the break-in, Heather was out the door and on the way to support her friend. She waited for the light at the intersection near Beynards restaurant. She scanned the shopping strip, and her attention was immediately drawn to a killer pantsuit in the window of the dress shop called Pizzazz. Brittan had bought a to-die-for dress there, so Heather had made a mental note to frequent the place.

A movement down the strip snared her focus. Heather noticed José Herrera leaving a shop called Herrera Crafts and Gifts. Brittan had mentioned that José's mother and aunt owned the shop and several more like it. Heather narrowed her eyes and wondered what the man was up to these days. He held a phone to his ear and a briefcase in his other hand. He looked like he was barking orders into the receiver like an army sergeant chewing out his troops. The ugly scowl was the antithesis of the Prince Charming persona he projected around Brittan. Heather decided her initial assumptions about him were correct.

The guy's a fake with one thing on the brain, Heather thought. When someone blasted a horn behind her, she noticed the light had changed to green and a long line of traffic waited on her to roll.

She gassed her Mercedes and directed another stare toward José as she passed the shopping strip. He snapped his phone shut before stepping toward a silver Volvo.

Bad day at the farm, huh? Heather thought.

By the time she approached the next bend in the road, gut instinct suggested José was up to something he was trying to hide. If the guy really was a fake, no telling what he was involved in.

He seemed obsessed with Brittan, Heather thought. Now that Brittan and Rob weren't exactly an item, Heather and Lorna hoped she wouldn't gravitate back to José. Heather chewed her bottom lip and mentally debated how best to stop that from happening. If José had a woman in every port, and Heather thought he might, then Brittan wouldn't go near him.

She knit her brows and slowed the car down. *Follow him!* The thought bore upon her like a missile from heaven. *But I need to support Brittan right now,* she argued. The command bombarded her mind even more strongly.

A driveway into a vacant plot of land on the west side of the road proved the perfect place to turn around. Heather swung her Mercedes into the drive and stared straight ahead. Taking time to think about Brittan's plight conflicted with José's inevitable progression from the parking lot. If Heather was going to follow him today, the opportunity would be lost if she waited.

I could call Brittan and explain that I'm running late, she mused. *I don't have to tell her why.* She shook her head. *She's too perceptive. She'll know something's up. If she figures it out, she won't appreciate it.*

Closing her eyes, she pressed her fingertips between her brows and said, "Think, think, think."

Heather's eyes popped open. *I'll call Lorna,* she decided. *She's on her way too. Lorna can tell Brittan I'm on my way. She's good at that sort of thing. Maybe Brittan won't suspect anything if Lorna handles it right.*

Without further debate, Heather reached for her cell phone and whipped her car back onto the road. Pressing the accelerator, she zoomed in the direction she'd come from. Once she rounded the final curve, the craft store intersection came into view. A silver Volvo pulled through it as the light changed to yellow.

Heather's first instinct was to stop for the light, now 20 feet away. Fearing she'd lose José, she darted a glance in all directions. When she didn't spot a policeman or cross traffic, Heather pressed the accelerator and zipped in front of a white coupe. A long, angry honk made her peer into her rearview mirror. Two vehicles swerved to miss each other, and Heather figured the white coupe had veered into the path of the SUV to miss her. She winced.

"At least they didn't crash." She kept going. She stayed two cars behind José, tagging him all the way to the interstate.

That's when she pressed Lorna's speed dial number.

"Whazzup?" Lorna answered.

"Are you with Brittan yet?" Heather asked.

"Pulling into her driveway now. Ooo…two cop cars are here."

"Good—I mean good that you're there. I'm going to be late. I spotted José Herrera, and I'm following him."

"What for?"

"I don't know. I just had this urge to follow him, and I couldn't get away from it so I'm doing it. I'm also afraid that because Rob and Brittan are on the outs, she might gravitate back toward José. I'm hoping he has a woman in every port, so to speak. I'm going to track him a while and see if it leads to one of his ports. If so, I'll somehow let Brittan know. Then she'll zap him if he shows up and that will be that. Presto, he's gone! And we don't have to worry about it anymore."

"Sounds like a plan to me," Lorna approved. "I'll hold down the fort here."

"You do that, and tell Brittan I'm running late. It's the truth. Maybe she'll be so distracted she won't suspect anything. I was worried that if I called her, she'd hear something in my voice no matter how I tried to cover it."

"Right. Good idea. I've got it covered."

"Go, girl!" Heather encouraged as an 18-wheeler whizzed past her. Keeping an eye on the silver Volvo still two cars ahead, she gripped her steering wheel and braced herself for the inevitable wake of wind that followed.

"Oh!" Lorna blurted.

"Now what?"

"Brittan just walked out of her house. Rob is beside her. Yikes! They don't look happy with each other."

Heather sighed. "We might lose him," she admitted.

"We can't!" Lorna exclaimed. "He knows too much. It's the rule of the Rose. The man who finds out who we are has to marry one of us."

"Right. But this one pulled the wool over our eyes."

"We're going to have to get over it," Lorna stated. "I was exasperated at first myself, but really, I'm beginning to think he didn't quite know how to handle it."

"Whatever you say." Heather sighed.

"She's *got* to follow through with him!" Lorna insisted.

"And you think Brittan's going to get in line like a good little girl?" Heather laughed. "You know she's too strong-willed for that!"

"Desperate times call for desperate measures," Lorna threatened.

"So hold them at gunpoint and call a preacher."

"I might!" Lorna declared before the two friends bid adieu.

Chuckling, Heather laid the phone in the top of her purse. She concentrated on the Volvo. After a few more road signs clipped by, José slowed for an exit. Heather slowed even more and allowed another car to wedge between them. Taking the exit was a breeze.

When he turned right on a country road that led through several small intersections, Heather missed the mark on making it through. José moved ahead of her. She momentarily lost sight of him when the road turned to the left but soon spotted him slowing for another turn. Heather veered after him and noted the street sign on the rural residential road, Ivy Lane. José pulled into the driveway of a sprawling stucco house. "Herrera" was written on the mailbox.

Heather's shoulders drooped. "This is just his house," she mumbled, but noted the house number on the mailbox anyway: 637. *Six-thirty-seven Ivy Lane*, she rehearsed. Even though she didn't think she'd need the information, Heather absorbed every detail… just in case.

Once the address was carved into her memory, she idly wondered what José did to earn the dough to afford such a place. "Manage his mom's shops?" she scoffed. "I don't *think* so!"

She continued to roll by the estate at a reasonable pace, darting occasional glances to monitor what was happening. José scrambled from his vehicle, slammed the door, and trotted up the sidewalk. He was halfway to the door when a man wearing jeans and no shirt burst out. Heather barely caught a glimpse of José shoving the guy while a scrap of a dog hopped around them like some jumping bean. Then her view was blocked.

Frowning, Heather realized she might have stumbled onto something she hadn't been looking for. While other women had been her motive, maybe a different type of drama was going on. She halted at the next intersection marked with a stop sign. Tapping her index finger against the steering wheel, Heather debated her options. A country road, disappearing through a shroud of trees, posed itself as a definite possibility.

She drove her vehicle forward and whipped down the lane. As she'd hoped, a swath on the side of the road offered a perfect place to leave her car. Heather pulled in and stopped. While she wasn't totally out of sight, and this wasn't the perfect place to hide a car in broad daylight, Heather decided it would have to do.

Retrieving her cell phone and keys, she slipped from the vehicle and locked it. Thankful she hadn't taken the time to change from her workout gear, Heather entered a field and made good time in her running shoes. Within three minutes she was behind José's house. The dense trees there provided perfect cover. Resting for a moment, she watched the house and then darted across the backyard toward the home's north side.

Panting, Heather pressed against the house and waited as sweat trickled down her spine. The only sound that pierced the peaceful May afternoon was the muffled arguing of two men. Heather doubled over and crept along the side of the house until she came to a row of windows. Straightening, she leaned forward just enough to take a peek inside.

She peered into an empty kitchen. The immaculate room, decorated in the latest fashion, lacked clutter. *He must have a full-time maid,* she decided and added another financial burden to his list. Heather glanced toward the manicured lawn and placed a gardener's salary on the list as well. Either José Herrera's wealthy family had supplied him with a trust fund the size of Arabia or the man was doing something that generated a hefty salary.

The arguing ceased. A door slammed. Heather succumbed to a reflexive duck and then scolded herself. The slamming door had been inside. There was no reason to duck.

She eased back up just as José Herrera backed into the kitchen. Heather's eyes widened. Hunched forward, José appeared to be carrying something heavy. He progressed a couple more steps when Heather realized his hands were wedged beneath the arms of a limp body whose head lolled toward the window. A trickle of dried blood marred his temple. Eyes closed, the pallid man appeared to have seen better days.

Heather caught her breath, and her mouth fell open. "The museum security guard!" she whispered, recognizing his features from the nightly news. He'd been missing for several days now. Her mind spun with possibilities. Either the security guard was dead or severely injured.

The farther José backed into the kitchen, the more obvious it became that someone else carried the guard's legs. Soon a tall, thin man emerged into the kitchen. Heather recognized him as the guy from the front yard. Even though he bore a mild resemblance to José, he lacked the dashing good looks. Neither his skin nor hair were as dark as José's, suggesting he might be part Anglo. Both were struggling to carry the hefty security guard.

The pint-sized Chihuahua Heather had seen in the front yard darted between the partner's legs, and he stumbled. José lost his grip, dropped his burden, and broke into a scalding round of Spanish directed at his partner. The man's face grew red, he clamped his jaw, and then fired a long line of words back.

José grabbed the man by the front of his shirt and snarled another round of what had to be threats. Despite the dog's excited yelps, their voices were so loud Heather detected the enunciation, although she didn't understand a syllable...until the last word—"Eduardo!"

Heather swallowed a surprised yelp while José slowly released Eduardo's shirt. With a firm command, he pointed at the security guard. Eduardo grudgingly picked up his load again, José grabbed the guard's arms, and they progressed toward an area out of Heather's range.

Driven by her need to see, she hunkered down and scurried under the row of windows. Now on the other side, she raised up and watched in horror as José opened a stainless steel chest freezer. He barked out another command, and the two hoisted the security guard into the freezer.

He's dead! Heather gasped. *They're putting him on ice until they can figure out what to do with the body.*

Her stomach clenched. A wave of nausea sent a clammy rush up her face. *José Herrera isn't just a con man. He's a murderer!* And on the heels of this realization came questions, all linked to his motive for ending the security guard's life.

Maybe the guy knew too much, she reasoned and balled her fists until her fingernails ate into her palms. *They were the ones who took the necklace. And don't tell me this isn't the same Eduardo! They took the painting too...and murdered Mosier!*

Her skin prickling, Heather pressed herself against the house and blindly stared across the yard as the implications bombarded her. She'd felt so strongly that Brittan was in danger, and now she knew why. Forget worrying about José's other women. He was a thief and murderer!

In the midst of Heather's realizations, she fleetingly wondered what would happen if the men discovered her. The pristine yard came into sharp focus. The grass was as green as a golf course in bright afternoon sunshine. The sun's stark rays illuminated all it touched—including her. She gazed down at her attire: a pair of pale gray running shorts and a white T-shirt that read "Princeton."

I'm a clear target, she fretted. *If they spot me, they'll be putting me on ice.* Instinct insisted that she bolt from the house and run for the woods, but Heather forced herself to think logically. *No one has spotted me. If I make a run for it, they might see me. I'll text Lorna and have her call the police.*

Heather closed her eyes and forced herself to breathe slowly and deeply. The smells of earth and flora calmed her nerves as she directed a desperate plea toward heaven. Finally she opened her eyes and scanned the area for cover. Her gaze fell on a row of dense bushes near the front of the house. If she wedged herself between the home and the bushes, she'd be shielded from view unless someone was straining to see her. Without delay, Heather hunched down and darted for cover.

TWENTY-EIGHT

Brittan stepped from the kitchen into her living room. She scrutinized every inch, wondering if Rob and the crew had really discovered all the bugs. While one officer took her report, another helped Rob thoroughly scour the house with an electronic device he vowed was fail-proof. At last count, there'd been six. Rob declared they found them all. Now both police cars were pulling from her driveway, and Rob was walking to his dad's. Once everyone left, Lorna, of all people, had suggested she make herbal tea for both of them. She shooed Brittan from the kitchen and insisted she go sit down.

"Heather must finally be getting to her," Brittan mumbled under her breath. Even though Lorna's suggestion seemed unusual, Brittan didn't argue. She could use a gallon of warm, raspberry tea right now. Having her home broken into shook her to the bone. She felt violated and in need of comfort.

Glancing toward the empty spot where her CD player had been, Brittan strolled toward her couch and slumped down. After some time passed, the doorbell rang. Sighing, she got up, walked to the door, and peered through the peephole. Rob stood outside, gazing straight at the door.

Brittan swallowed hard and decided she had to answer. He'd just been here and knew she was home. They'd barely shared a civil word while he was here, and Brittan didn't have a clue why he'd come back. As for their relationship, she'd already hit the cancel button and didn't want to contemplate the disappointment now setting in. She'd gotten her hopes up with Rob Lightly, and she had even begun to suspect he might be "the one."

She opened the door and looked at him in silent query.

"Are you going to ask me in?"

Brittan swung the door wider and allowed him to step inside. He swiveled toward her and said, "I've been talking to Dad, and he says I need to talk to you."

"Oh?" She raised her brows and closed the door.

"Yes."

"That was quick. You've only been gone a few minutes."

"Well, he and I were already talking with Deloris before you came and got me. It didn't take very long for us to finish up."

"Okaaaaay," Brittan drawled.

"Do you mind?" He motioned toward the couch.

"No, go ahead," she said with a nod.

He walked toward the living room.

Slipping her hands into her pockets, Brittan followed. Despite their issues, she couldn't deny that the man was made for shorts and T-shirts. Even in a pair of swimming trunks and a worn shirt, he looked good. *Very* good.

The second Rob settled on the couch, he started talking. "First I want to tell you that I see your side of things."

"Really?" Brittan claimed an armchair and adjusted her glasses. Even though she was still numb from the break-in, she willed her mind to full-alert status.

"Yes, really." He rested his elbows on the tops of his knees, hunched forward, and stared at the floor. "I was a little hard on you earlier today."

Brittan gazed past him and stopped herself from caving in too easily. After all, the man had been deceiving her and baiting her for weeks. How could she trust anything he said now?

He lifted his gaze and peered at her.

Brittan felt he was seeing into her soul with a sincerity that was a silent answer to her unspoken thoughts. Recalling that she'd deceived him too, she squirmed inside and broke eye contact.

"Losing Mom a year after losing my partner threw me into a control spasm, for lack of a better word. It was like life was totally out of control. Two of the people I loved the most were ripped from me, and nobody asked me if it was okay. I went into survival mode, needing to do whatever I could to make sure my dad didn't leave me too. Finding him in a diabetic coma didn't help me at all."

Despite logic demanding she not get sucked into his story, Brittan's focus remained fixed on Rob's sincere eyes, as blue as the sea.

"Anyway," he continued, "I think you were right earlier today when you said something about me trying to keep Dad under my thumb. I'm not happy about admitting it, but maybe it's true." He shrugged. "It was a shock to find out he's married and has been hiding it from me. But—"

"I didn't want to hide anything from you, Rob," Brittan broke in. "I found out accidentally and encouraged him to tell you. I didn't think it was my place."

"I know." Rob nodded. "He told me. I shouldn't have blown up at you like I did. And really, that's all I came over to say." He straightened and silently observed her.

Brittan didn't move or give any indication of her emotions. She wasn't certain what she felt or where she wanted this to go.

"Look, Brittan, I really like you *a lot*. For cryin' out loud! I've been fascinated with you for months!"

She rested her hand on the armrest and slowly gripped the end.

"I talked my dad into buying his house because of you."

"And then you kept dangling the Rose in front of me like an ornery boy tormenting a cat."

"But we were *both* hiding stuff from each other, weren't we?" His quiet question held no condemnation, only the ring of truth.

Brittan looked down. "Guess I've been kind of hard on you too," she admitted.

"Brittan!" Lorna erupted into the room. Cell phone in hand, she lifted her attention from the phone to the room's occupants. "Rob!" she exclaimed. "I didn't realize you were here!" Her face ashen, she hurried toward them. "But thank God you are!"

Brittan jumped up. "What's the matter?" she demanded.

"It's Heather!"

"Heather? Is she all right? Where is she?"

"She says she's fine. She was following José Herrera," she added as if the information were common knowledge.

"What!" Brittan pressed her fingertips against her temple.

Lorna nodded. "I didn't tell you because—" She shook her head and focused on the phone. "She just sent me a text message. José is the thief. He's with Eduardo right now. They also murdered the security guard."

Rob jumped to his feet. "I knew that guy was criminal material! I just *knew* it!"

"There's more," Lorna said. "Heather is at José's house. They just put the dead guard in a freezer." Lorna read some more. "José lives at 637 Ivy Lane, a subdivision east of Houston. Heather is outside the house hiding in the bushes. She says to send the police!"

"Six-thirty-seven Ivy Lane!" Rob repeated and darted for the door. Hand on the knob, he turned to Lorna. "Tell Heather to get out of there!"

Lorna's cell phone dinged. "Wait! Here's another message."

Brittan gripped her throat and debated whether to follow Rob or stay home. At the same time, she felt as if she were drowning in a river of despair. She, who'd always trusted her logic, had made a terrible mistake in judgment. *I've been with a murderer and never even knew it!*

And on top of that, it sounded as if José and Eduardo might be the ones who'd been leaving roses at crime scenes. They had to have a reason to kill the security guard. If he was threatening to tell all about the necklace heist, that might be motive enough.

She worriedly gazed around her home. *He might have even bugged my house!* she thought and swallowed a groan. *I've entertained the devil himself! How could I have been so dumb?*

Lorna's voice floated into her self-incrimination. "'Someone's coming near,'" she read. "'Pray he won't see me!'"

"I'm outta here!" Rob barked. "You two stay put!"

The last text message was all Brittan needed to make a decision. "I'm coming with you!" she exclaimed.

"No, you're not!" Rob commanded.

But that didn't stop her. She grabbed her purse, ran down the hallway to reclaim her Glock, and dashed back up the hallway.

Rob was barricading the front door.

"We're going, Rob!" Brittan insisted. "Don't try to stop us! The Rose stays together!"

Lorna snatched up her purse and hurried to Brittan's side.

"No way! This time, you might get *killed!*" Rob pulled his phone from his pocket and pressed one button. "I'm calling the station and having them dispatch a team to that address."

Brittan growled as she stuffed her gun into her purse and ran to the back door. "Hurry, Lorna!" she hollered over her shoulder and banged open the door.

Brittan raced outside. Rob ran after her while dictating the details of Heather's situation.

Glancing over her shoulder, Brittan first spotted Lorna's wide-eyed expression and then glimpsed Rob close behind her.

He flipped his phone shut and bellowed, "Brittan Shay! You're *not* getting away!"

She upped her speed and dashed straight to her driveway. Lorna's Jeep was parked behind her Jaguar. "Oh no! You're blocking me!" Brittan yelled.

"We'll go in my Jeep!" Lorna directed. Even in a skirt and sandals, her long-legged strides ensured her arrival at the Jeep before Brittan.

Rob was close, but Brittan didn't know how close until his breath tickled her neck and his strong arms clamped her in an unyielding vise.

"Let me go, you idiot!" Brittan shrieked.

"I *won't!* I've already lost two people I love, and I'm not going to lose you because of your own stupidity!"

"I'm not stupid!" she argued and crammed her elbow against his ribs in a self-defense move that worked on her ornery brother when they were kids.

Rob's surprised grunt was followed by his loosening arms. Brittan rammed her foot onto the top of his, and he yowled.

"Let her go now!" Lorna demanded.

Brittan glimpsed her friend whacking him with her purse while twisting one of his ears.

Rob released Brittan.

She stumbled forward and then whipped around.

"Do you two have to get so violent?" Rob broke away from Lorna and gripped his ear.

Panting, Brittan glared at him. "You can't control me any more than you can control your dad. I'm going to help Heather whether you like it or not." She raised her chin. "If you want to ride with us, fine! Otherwise go in your own vehicle."

His glower took on a tinge of respect. Rob lifted his hand, palm outward. "Okay, but if you get yourself killed, don't come cryin' to me!"

Brittan shouldered her purse. "Don't worry. I don't cry to anyone—dead or alive."

"So what's the plan? Are you two just going to drive up to José's house, knock on the door, and see what you find?"

Brittan and Lorna exchanged glances.

"It's worked before!" Brittan exclaimed.

"There's a squad of police heading over there now. You'll get in the way and mess up the operation," Rob reasoned as he rested his hands on his hips and watched Brittan.

She exchanged another glance with Lorna as common sense blanketed her initial reaction. As much as she hated to admit it, Rob was right. In every other mystery they'd solved, this was when they backed out and let the police do their job. But they'd never had a situation where one of their lives was so directly in danger. They had no idea whether José had spotted Heather and no clue if she was still alive. The thought of losing Heather, coupled with the stress of the break-in, had sent Brittan into reactionary mode, which was not her normal MO.

"I don't know what to say," Brittan admitted and closed her eyes.

Lorna moved to Brittan's side as she slumped against the Jaguar. "I think we lost it there for a few minutes," Lorna admitted.

"Hell-o!" Rob chimed. "And you both made *me* lose it! I promise! You women are nuts! First you go traipsing off to Chicago, planning to do who-knows-what in a multimillion-dollar art gallery, and now you were going to march headlong into a murderer's den. What's next? Taking on the mafia?"

"If they need taking on, then so be it." Brittan opened her eyes. "We aren't afraid."

"I gathered that much," Rob ruefully admitted and rubbed at his ear.

"And anyone—any man in my life—will just have to deal with that because I have no plans to stop," she challenged.

Rob narrowed his eyes.

"You can't go chasing after me and intercepting my every move," Brittan continued.

"And you think I shouldn't have now? Go ahead!" He waved toward the Jeep. "Botch the job and put Heather's life in more jeopardy."

"I'm not saying that," Brittan admitted. "By the time we got out there, we'd have figured out not to interfere and stay out of the way. You didn't have to act like an ape!" She rubbed her arm. "And we'd have been fine in Chicago. We've been fine from the start. We aren't inept, even though you seem to be convinced—"

"Would you two stop it! Look!" Lorna held up her cell. "Heather's in trouble. If we aren't going over there, we need to at least pray that she'll come out alive and safe! There's no telling what's going down!"

Brittan eyed the phone and had never felt so helpless. In most situations she was in control, she had a plan, she understood the logistics. But now everything was spiraling out of control. She couldn't even trust her own judgment anymore. She'd been flirting with the devil without knowing it and had been about to run ahead of the police to rescue Heather.

Brittan's confusion mounted to mammoth proportions until at last she understood that prayer was their best offense. "Yes," she finally croaked, "we've *got* to pray."

TWENTY-NINE

Heather wrapped her arms around her knees and hunkered into a tight ball behind a wall of lattice. She'd taken a gamble that the combination of the dense bushes and the lattice would hide her, especially because the house was white, and her shirt would blend with that background. But the test was now on.

Someone was walking around the side of the house and pausing near the bushes. The dog's high-pitched yip verified that the canine was the size of a squirrel.

"What is it, Martin?" José asked, his voice gruff. "You drive me crazy with all this barking. There's nothing here!"

Martin's shrill bark sent a quick spasm through Heather. *Oh God*, she pleaded, *please don't let him see me!* She had no doubt that she could defend herself in hand-to-hand combat, but she also knew that if the men were armed she couldn't stop one from taking aim while she took down the other. Heather was in no mood to be shot—much less killed.

"I still say he's probably upset about the body." Eduardo's voice floated from the front of the house.

"Come on, Martin!" José bellowed. "If you saw something, sniff it out or shut up!"

Her heart hammering, Heather held her breath and reached

for the record button on her cell phone. It did remarkably well recording her voice notes, and she hoped it would perform at a distance.

"I swear, Eduardo," José continued, "if you kill anyone else this year, I'm going to kill you! I told you not to kill that man!"

"And I already told you he was threatening to tell too much!"

"All we had to do was pass him another ten grand!"

"And how long would that keep him quiet? Look, we've already gone over this!"

"Right! Except now I got a corpse! Why did you bring him here? You should have killed him at your place and put him in *your* freezer!"

"Oh yeah. An apartment. That makes a lot of sense. At least there's privacy here!"

"You think I'm sleeping here with a body in my freezer?" José erupted into a round of Spanish that sounded suspiciously like cursing and then mumbled something about ghosts.

"I told you I'd figure out something—he'll be gone within a week. Meanwhile stay at a hotel and be done with it. Or better yet—at your girlfriend's! Had any luck listening in on her?"

"None!" José barked. "I've barely had a chance to check the connections with you killing people left and right. Come on, Martin! You're wasting my time."

"I swear, I think that woman's up to no good. I don't know why you ever chased her. If she's the one who spotted the print, she might be onto us!" Eduardo's voice trailed off as the two neared the front of the house.

Oh my word! Heather thought. *He's the one who bugged Brittan's house too!* She closed her eyes and pressed the back of her head against the house.

The front door's hostile slamming jolted Heather. She opened her eyes, clicked off the cell phone's recorder, and debated what to do. Once again instinct insisted she run, but her reasonable side suggested she should stay put until the police arrived. Once that happened, José and Eduardo would be so distracted she could slip away unnoticed.

Unless Martin harasses them into another trip outside, she thought. That was the deciding factor. *I need to run while the coast is clear!*

Heather squirmed from behind the lattice and slipped her cell phone into her pocket with her keys. Hunkering forward, she inched toward the edge of the flower bed. Casting a cautious glance past the bushes, she saw no one. Carefully she examined the woods surrounding the back of the house and decided to make a diagonal shot, rather than the backyard path she'd taken here. Because of the angle, her time in the open might be cut by a few seconds.

After another quick glance in all directions, Heather breathed another desperate prayer, sucked in her breath, and bolted forward. Arms and legs pumping, she began cheering her success when she was 15 feet from the woods.

She'd taken two more lunges when Eduardo's surprised voice echoed across the yard, "Stop where you are or I'll shoot!"

As he fired the first bullet, Heather knew she had only one choice—keep moving! Darting to the left and then the right, she didn't think she could run any faster until another projectile whizzed past her head. The gun fired a third time as she exploded into the woods. Tree bark ricocheted off a nearby pine, and bits of bark stung her cheek.

"Stop or I'll kill you!" Eduardo threatened.

Heather's belief in his sincerity propelled her through the thickening underbrush. With another glance over her shoulder, she spotted the man's red shirt near the edge of the woods. Heather knew if she continued to run for her vehicle she wouldn't have time to get in, get it started, and get away. Frantically she searched for a tree with a large trunk that would provide cover. She also scouted the ground for a fallen limb big enough to knock out a grown man.

A sturdy oak provided her first need. One of its stubby, cast-off limbs lying near the base sufficed for a club. Heather scurried behind the tree and gripped the makeshift weapon.

Eduardo's footsteps ominously echoed through the woods, sending a threat through the motionless trees.

Heather swallowed hard and knew she had only one shot. Her first goal was to survive, and her second goal was to keep him from getting a good look at her. All he knew was what he'd seen from behind—a blonde woman of small build. He hadn't seen her face, so he couldn't align her with the Rose later.

Sweat trickled from the base of her ponytail down the neck of her T-shirt. The smells of pine trees and decaying leaves were heavy in the air, not helping to calm her pumping adrenaline. As the man drew closer, his footsteps became slower, more cautious.

Finally he paused. "If you come out now, I won't kill you. But if you make me find you, I have no choice!"

Heather closed her eyes and forced her rapid breath to remain shallow and quiet. When his steps crunched away, her eyes opened. If he didn't step near, her plan would fail. If he walked past the tree, he'd see her if he turned around. She needed to draw him into her trap, and that could only happen if she threw out bait.

"Please don't kill me," she whimpered in a little girl voice.

He halted.

Heather held her breath.

He turned and raced toward the oak.

She didn't wait for him to round the tree before she prepared her surprise. Lifting the limb, she sucked in a deep breath. The second she glimpsed him, Heather slammed the club between his eyes. Eduardo's surprised shriek accompanied his collapse. His gun tumbled from his grasp and toppled several feet away. Heather scrambled for the weapon, snatched it up, and scurried through the rest of the underbrush. She reached the street she'd crossed before. Racing back the way she came, Heather unlocked her Mercedes and tossed the weapon into the passenger seat the second she opened the door. She cranked the engine, gassed the vehicle, sped down the country lane, and hung a right instead of going back the way she came. She planned to drive on this road and take the first highway she came to. A glance in the rearview mirror revealed no one was following her.

"At least for now," she panted. Her hand unsteady, she fished her cell phone from her pocket and pressed Lorna's speed dial number.

Rob paced Brittan's living room while she and Lorna sat on the couch. If the tension climbed any higher, he was certain his skull would split. Not only was Heather's safety in question, Brittan would barely look at him. *Dad will be sorely disappointed to learn I no longer stand a chance with her. He sure likes her,* Rob thought.

Even this morning, Simon had hinted that Rob shouldn't let her get away—*ever*. But the reality was that Brittan was very independent and Rob was very protective. If their major tendencies were rubbing each other raw now, they'd certainly drive each other nuts in the long run.

He paused near the door and gazed at the backyard's breathtaking splendor. Rob had gone to great measures to get acquainted with Brittan. It seemed strange that only weeks ago he'd met her for the first time in this very yard…after pining after her for months. And now it was over like a puff of smoke. Despite his boy-meets-girl fantasies, they'd hit reality like a brick wall.

On top of that, his ear still hurt. Rob touched it and frowned. Those two women were like that Tasmanian devil on speed. Rob hadn't intended to hurt Brittan, only stop her. Apparently they'd decided to take the whole thing to another level. He was sure Zeb would have laughed out loud if he'd seen the whole thing. But good ol' Zeb was gone now.

When Lorna's cell phone rang, Rob twisted toward the couch and clenched his fists.

"It's Heather!" Lorna exclaimed.

Brittan leaned toward her.

"Heather?" Lorna said into the phone. After several seconds, she offered the thumbs-up sign and darted a big smile toward Rob. "Sure. He's here. Yes. I'm sure he'd be glad to talk to you." She extended the cell to Rob. "She needs to talk to you," she explained.

Rob reached for the phone. "Hello," he said at the same time Heather rushed forward with her information.

"There's someone named Eduardo with José."

"Yes."

"He chased me into the woods and shot at me."

"Are you okay? Did he hit you?"

"No, but I hit him," she said through a sly chuckle. "With a big stick—between the eyes. I left him in the woods next to the house. He's unconscious. If you're facing the house, it's the section of woods to the left. He's in a red shirt so he should be easy to spot. He's out cold and flat on his back. I thought you might want to tell your buddies where to find him. If they hurry, they might get him before he wakes up."

Rob rubbed his forehead and shook his head. "All right. Why didn't you take down José while you were at it?"

"He didn't chase me. By the way, I have Eduardo's gun. He dropped it and I took it because I didn't want him to wake up and use it. What should I do with it?"

"Are you coming to Brittan's now?" Rob asked.

"Yes."

"Bring it here. I'll deal with that end of things."

"Okay. And I also recorded a very incriminating conversation on my cell phone, I think. We'll see if it took when I get there."

"We have technology that can amplify and extract voices, so

we'll download it from your phone and see what we can do with it."

"Oh, and Rob? You won't tell anyone about Brittan and Lorna and me, will you? Whatever happens with you and Brittan, we'd all appreciate your keeping our secret. I'm sure Eduardo never got a look at my face. He can't identify me, and no one else in Houston can either. Well, except *you* and my fiancé and Lorna's."

"I'll see what I can do."

"Okay." She sighed.

"I guess we'll see you in a few?"

"Yep. I'm on my way. Can I talk to Lorna again?"

"Sure." Rob extended the phone back to Lorna and realized Lorna and Brittan were gazing at him with curious intensity.

Rob pointed to the backyard and looked past Brittan. "I've got to call in some information, and I'm going to hang out until Heather gets here. She's got something she needs to give me. Then I'll be out of your hair."

He didn't wait for a response. He stepped into the warm afternoon and strode toward the lawn chairs perched halfway between the house and the lake. Before giving in to the desire to relax in one of the chairs, Rob dialed the police chief's cell number once more.

When a gruff voice came over the line, Rob said, "More info. There's a suspect unconscious in the woods to the left of the house. He's wearing red."

"Same anonymous tipper?" the chief questioned.

"Yes."

"Is this by chance the Rose you're dealing with?"

"I never said that." Rob squinted toward the lake that was reflecting a thousand suns on the rippling surface and wondered if the Rose wanted credit for this one. "Let's stick with an anonymous tipper for now, okay?" he said, softening his voice and adding a solid dose of respect.

"Okay," the chief said. "We can sort that out later. I'll notify the team. They're nearly there." He ended the call.

Rob plunked into the first chair he came to and looked across the lake. A sailboat skimmed the water a couple hundred feet offshore. Rob watched as the winds lifted the sails and carried it farther and farther away, just like his relationship with Brittan was slipping from his grasp.

He sighed, lowered his head, and rested his elbows on his knees. Rob's mind churned with what was probably happening at 637 Ivy Lane. He itched to be there, but he knew it was too late and this bust belonged to someone else.

✳ ✣ ✳

José crammed clothing into a leather-tabbed suitcase and followed that with toiletries. Eduardo hadn't returned yet, and José wasn't going to wait on him. He'd barely caught site of the person Eduardo spotted running to the woods. Whoever had been prowling around the house was a small blonde. José never got a look at her face. He figured Eduardo had killed her by now and would be traipsing back with her thrown over his shoulder like some bloodthirsty caveman. He couldn't take the sight of another dead body. One corpse in the freezer was enough. And after today, he was finished working with Eduardo.

"I'm through!" he muttered and tossed his hairbrush into the suitcase. *I never signed up for murder,* he thought. *And I can't take another one.* He zipped his suitcase and nearly picked it up. But when he saw his hands, he stopped. He'd already washed them several times after handling the body, but they were still dirty.

He spun toward the bathroom, turned the water on one degree cooler than Hades, and scrubbed with granulated soap until his fingers and palms burned. Allowing the hot water to run over his aching hands, he gazed at his image in the massive mirror that lined one wall of the ultramodern bathroom. José had surrounded himself with the best of the best in his home, but the eyes that had glowed with pride were growing more haunted by the day. He'd finally stuffed away the guilt of Mosier's death...until he walked into the room and saw Eduardo land the fatal blow on Moe Van Cleave's temple. When the man fell and gasped his last breath, José had been sorely tempted to give the same treatment to Eduardo.

Martin's uproarious barking diverted José's fixed stare. He turned off the water, rubbed his raw hands on a plush towel, and hurried back to his bedroom. Once he secured his suitcase, José planned to grab Martin and leave until Eduardo removed the body. Once the corpse was gone, he'd decide if he could live in this house again. For now he needed to get out before his skin absorbed more death.

Martin's barking grew more ferocious. José rushed down the hallway and emerged into the great room. He dropped his suitcase near the sectional sofa and decided his dog was becoming neurotic. Martin had barked more today than he had in the entire year José had him. Now the Chihuahua sounded like he was losing his mind in the kitchen.

A heavy thud caused Martin to yelp, and José stopped in his tracks. Fingers of terror trailed up his spine and clamped around his throat. Then he realized Eduardo was probably back and scoffed at his fear. "Eduardo!" he called and moved forward. But when he stepped into the kitchen, the first thing that nabbed his attention was the open freezer. Next his gaze trailed to the floor where the security guard lay face down. Martin sniffed the body and went into a new round of growls.

José looked from the freezer to the corpse and back to the freezer, which was taking on the aura of a casket. His pulse pounded in his temples in unforgiving blows. Shaking his head, José backed away from the corpse. A primal roar erupted from his soul. José threw himself toward the front door, shoving anything that got in his way. His final obstacle was a crystal lamp that had once belonged to royalty. It toppled as José lurched the final steps to the front door. He was halfway across the lawn before his dazed mind registered the police cars in the driveway.

THIRTY

 Brittan stood up the second the doorbell rang. "That's Heather," she predicted.

"It's gotta be," Lorna agreed.

The two friends dashed to the door, and Brittan flung it open. Heather stood on the other side. Bark clung to her hair, soil smudged her T-shirt, and long red welts marred her legs.

"Heather!" Lorna exclaimed. Pulling her inside, she wrapped her friend in a tight hug.

Brittan closed the door and then gave Heather a hug of her own. "I've never prayed so hard," she stated as she clung to her friend. An uneasy awareness tugged at Brittan. She'd been less than supportive of Heather's quest for more prayer. Now she wondered if she'd analyzed herself out of a critical source of help.

"I know it was your prayers that came through for me," Heather rasped, her voice unsteady. "I don't exactly *enjoy* being shot at!" She released Brittan.

"But you took him down!" Lorna encouraged and gently punched Heather's upper arm.

"Yep." Heather covered her face with her hands, rubbed her eyes, and then squared her shoulders. "I took him down!" she said with a nod. "My trainer would be *so proud!*"

"Too bad you can't tell him you're using your stuff in the real world," Brittan said.

Hearing the back door click shut, Brittan turned to face Rob. After an absent-minded glance in her direction, his focus was on Heather.

"Hi," Heather said.

"You have a gun and an audio file for me?" he said.

"Yep." She pulled her purse from her shoulder and extracted a black pistol. "I'm sure my fingerprints are all over it," she admitted with an apologetic grin.

"That's not an issue at this point." Rob slipped the handgun into his pocket. "I'm glad you had the presence of mind to grab it." His smile was tinged with admiration and respect.

He darted a glance toward Brittan, who shifted her attention back to Heather. She didn't have a clue what to say or do.

"The audio file is on my cell." Heather removed the phone from her purse's side pocket and extended it to Rob.

He lifted the phone and examined the PC connection portal. "Have you listened to the audio yet?"

"Yes. You can barely hear them, but if you can extract their voices you'll get an earful. Eduardo is the killer, and José is an accessory." Heather touched a button on the phone. "This button will start the recording, but you have to hold it close to your ear to hear it."

"José bugged my house, didn't he?" Brittan asked.

"Yes." Heather pointed at the phone pressed against Rob's ear. "It's on there."

"I can't believe I let him into my life!" Brittan groaned. "It was just that—" She stopped before expounding on her desire for a boy-friend—especially in the face of Heather and Lorna's engagements. In the aftermath of the events it seemed so juvenile. Now Brittan wished she could rewind the last few weeks and start over.

"I should never have agreed to a date with that snake!" she

exclaimed and rubbed the back of her hand where the man had kissed it. "Does he know we're the Rose?"

"I can't imagine how," Heather said and then frowned. "No. I'm sure he doesn't. They sounded like they were suspicious, though."

"If Rob hadn't found the bugs, he might have been way more than suspicious!" Brittan exclaimed.

"Don't be so hard on yourself." Heather rested her hand on Brittan's shoulder. "You didn't know. How could you? You aren't omniscient. Besides, maybe this was God's way of leading us to them. I would have never followed José if it hadn't been for you."

"What do you mean?" Brittan queried.

"I wanted to see if he had a woman in every port," Heather confessed, her voice peaking on the last word. "I was afraid he'd come back around, and you'd, well…" She glanced toward Rob. "That you'd fall for him. I knew if I could prove he was involved with other women you'd drop him. I had no idea I was going to get shot at!"

Brittan removed her glasses and pressed her fingertips against her eyes. "I can't believe all this."

"Do you have the PC download cord with you?" Rob's voice jolted them back to practicalities.

"No." Heather shook her head, causing her ponytail to sway. "It's at home. I can go home and download the file and email it to you."

"That's okay. I can barely hear them. We'll do it at the crime lab. I guess I'll go. I'm heading straight to the station." He snared Brittan's attention. "Can we talk outside?"

"Sure," Brittan heard herself say and wondered what was left to say.

The second she stepped from the cool interior and into May's warmth, Rob said, "I guess it's a waste of time to ask if I can call later?"

Brittan swallowed and shut the door. She lifted her gaze to the spot between his eyebrows. She'd heard that people couldn't tell you weren't looking them in the eyes if you focused there, and she wasn't comfortable looking Rob in the eyes right now.

"What's the point?" she said with a shrug. "Even if we get over the deceit issues, I think having a girlfriend who's doing what I'm doing would drive you to the brink. And the Rose is not going to swear off sleuthing."

"I'm sorry I grabbed you earlier. I've never done that before and probably wouldn't again. I could just see you heading straight into a shootout." He clutched the back of his neck. "I guess I lost it."

"I understand." Brittan crossed her arms. "Lorna and I lost it too."

"In my mind I over-glamorized what you do. I didn't bargain for how worried I'd be knowing you were daring the devil to take you down," Rob said.

Brittan broke her determination to avoid eye contact. The jolt of his blue gaze reminded her of the power of their kisses. But a solid relationship was built on compatibility—not just chemistry. She locked her knees and stiffened her spine.

"Isn't that what you do every day when you're at work?"

"Sometimes, yes." He nodded.

"So how is it so different with me?"

"It's not. It shouldn't be. But—"

"But it is?"

"Yes." He shrugged. "There's something inside a normal, healthy guy that makes him want to protect the woman in his life."

"That's reasonable. But I'm afraid you'll take it too far."

"Yes. Maybe I am and will." He looked away.

"Even if you never grab me again, I can't be in a relationship where I feel smothered. And maybe you don't know how to not be that way?" she prompted and uncrossed her arms.

He lowered his head. "Right now I'm not sure of anything," he admitted. "All I know is that I can't promise you I won't be concerned...and protective."

"And I can't promise that I'll always be cautious. I'm just too... too—"

"Independent," he stated, his voice flat.

"Yes. And so are you, aren't you? How would you like it if I tied you up every time you were going into a dangerous situation at work."

He gazed past her. "I wouldn't."

The silence that ensued broadened the chasm dividing them.

"I really didn't mean to come across like I was baiting you and taking joy in deceiving you."

Brittan sighed and thought about the grace Rob had been extending before Heather called. He'd said he was beginning to understand why she hadn't told him about his father's marriage. "I guess we both pulled the wool over each other's eyes to some extent," she admitted. "I'm sorry too."

His gaze softened, and so did Brittan's resolve. "I really did want to meet you and get to know you. I did talk my dad into buying the house by your place."

She pressed her fingertips against her temple and decided to change the subject before she crumbled. "I hope you won't tell anyone about the Rose."

"I won't unless I have to legally. I've remained silent for months now. You don't have anything to worry about."

"Thanks." Brittan infused her answer with relief and appreciation.

"I guess this is goodbye?"

"It...it looks that way."

He extended his hand, and Brittan slipped her hand into his for a slow shake that could have been unnerving—if she'd let it. She clenched her gut and refused to give in. This was difficult enough without allowing emotions to show. "Like" was easier to overcome than "love," and Brittan would rather end it now before love took over.

She attempted to pull her hand from Rob's and was surprised when he tightened his grip and tugged her closer.

A silent question hung between them, and Brittan read the intent in his eyes. The chemistry she'd been squelching sprang up. Brittan willed herself to back away, but her body refused to budge. When Rob leaned closer, so did she. Once his lips brushed hers, she closed her eyes and relished the rush of tingles.

"It was great to get to know you," he whispered next to her ear before releasing her hand and backing away. "I guess I'll see ya 'round."

"Yep," Brittan croaked.

"By the way, thanks for everything you three did." He jutted his thumb toward the door. "You're amazing."

"Maybe a little too amazing sometimes?" she sadly quipped.

"Maybe." His smile was as defeated as Brittan felt.

The second he began walking away, Brittan stepped into the house. Even though she knew Rob walking out of her life made sense, she didn't want to watch him leave. Sometimes the most logical choice could be the most painful.

He'd drive me out of my mind after a few months, she told herself. Just the thought of it made her feel like she was wearing a straight jacket.

Heather and Lorna looked up from their places in the living room. Both sipped mugs of tea, and Brittan noted hers cooling on the coffee table. Without a word, she picked it up and went toward the microwave. Brittan figured they'd hang out here until the evening news came on. Waiting for the news after one of their busts was always pregnant with anticipation. Brittan didn't have to ask if Heather had called Duke. He was probably already at José's house, snapping shots of the situation. Tomorrow's headline would applaud the Rose's acclaimed work if they didn't stop him. This time Brittan knew they *must* decline credit. Liza Lizard had already suspected that Brittan was the customer who pegged the Mosier print. That was enough of a connection to require that the Rose remained incognito.

I cannot believe I let José pull the wool over my eyes, Brittan fumed as she watched the microwave count down from 60 seconds.

"What are you thinking?" Lorna's question brought Brittan out of her reverie. She jumped and turned toward the doorway where both friends observed her. She knew they wanted to know if Rob was ever coming back. Brittan decided to answer their question and put them out of their misery.

"Rob and I are off for good."

Heather sighed.

"But we liked him," Lorna said.

"I liked him too. But his protectiveness would drive me insane. He followed us all the way to Chicago, for cryin' out loud!" The microwave bell dinged.

"Well, Duke's somewhat protective of me," Heather admitted. "When he found out I followed José to his house and was nearly killed, he *flipped*."

"But I'm sure he landed on his feet and headed straight over there," Brittan said. "And he will be thankful for the story he gets out of it."

"Well, yes," Heather admitted.

"By the way," Brittan added, "we need to tell him not to link us to this case. I'm afraid the hostess at Beynards might connect me to the painting."

"I'll take care of it," Heather agreed.

"Just for the record, Michael wasn't that wild about us going to Chicago Artworks," Lorna said, reverting back to the former topic. "He was relieved when I told him we'd gotten the man's name another way. And really, I've got another layer of stuff to worry about. I'm the mayor's future wife. What if we get caught breaking in somewhere? How's that going to look for Michael? He's already warned me like crazy to *be careful*."

"I can understand that," Brittan affirmed. "But is he putting a vice grip on you to try to stop you? What about what Rob did in front of the house?" Brittan squawked. "Have either of your men tried to hold you hostage to stop you from going somewhere?"

"What all happened?" Heather asked.

Lorna debriefed her, ending with the ear-twisting grand finale.

"Oh, so while I was taking down criminals, you two were taking down Rob?" Heather said over a snicker.

"It was totally over the top," Brittan sliced the air over her head. "But I should have seen it coming."

"I agree it was over the top," Lorna said. "But I seriously doubt he'll repeat it. I think he was desperate. He's a police officer. He understood the danger, and well, we *were* pushing it."

Feeling cornered, Brittan gazed from one to the other. "Are you *trying* to make me feel pressured?"

"No, not at all." Lorna shook her head and stroked her skirt.

"It's just that we can tell he really cares about you. We think you may be making a mistake."

"It's not just *me*." Brittan pressed her index finger against her chest. "We came to an agreement…of sorts…I guess." Her gaze trailed to the chess set on the shelf, and Brittan realized she and Rob never got to play. "Besides," she added, dashing aside the longing for a partner, "I'm beginning to think I'm going through a judgment crisis. I got blindsided by José. The last thing I want to do is jump into something with someone else who's—who's—" She waved her arm and searched for the right word.

"I totally understand." Heather nodded. "But please remember that no relationship is going to be perfect. Duke and I are still working out kinks."

"Humph!" Lorna snorted. "Michael and I have already scheduled some marriage counseling sessions. We had a blowup about three weeks ago that left us both going, 'Whoa! What was *that?*'"

"Hello!" Heather lifted her hand. "My point exactly. If Rob's willing and you're willing, maybe counseling would be a good option for you two."

Brittan sipped her scalding tea and didn't respond. She had nothing left to say and was too bummed to come up with a reply.

Heather glanced at her watch. "Yikes! I've got to get home."

"I was hoping we could hang out here until the news hit," Brittan said.

"Want to come to my place?" Heather asked.

Lorna and Brittan exchanged glances. "Sure," they said in unison.

THIRTY-ONE

"Go Brittan! Go Brittan!" Lorna chanted and shoved her to the front of the group of young women vying for Heather's wedding bouquet. Even though Brittan had no intention of fighting for the bouquet, she stumbled into the line of fire just as Heather released the roses. As if drawn to a magnet, the bouquet whacked Brittan on the forehead. Hands snatched for the flowers and eager debutantes jostled Brittan as she fumbled to catch the bouquet without dropping her sequined bag. It was either claim the bouquet or get trampled!

"I got it!" she bellowed and raised the roses in hopes of ending the competition. *You'd think these women really believed they'd be the next one married if they caught it,* she thought as disgruntled moans chorused from the group.

Heather turned around to evaluate her toss and squealed, "I can't believe it!"

"I made her!" Lorna chimed and hurried forward.

"That's the *truth!*" Brittan adjusted her crooked glasses. "She shoved me straight into the bouquet."

A cheer went up from the sidelines, and Brittan waved the flowers at the crowd. A flash nearly made Brittan groan when she realized the source was a reporter's camera. The media had dubbed

Heather's nuptials "The Wedding of the Decade." More than 2000 guests had arrived to witness the storybook extravaganza. A horse and buggy awaited Duke and Heather, to whisk them away to their honeymoon suite where they planned to spend the night before leaving for Greece.

Duke appeared beside Heather and wrapped his arm around his bride. Like Heather, he'd never looked better—despite his complaints about the tuxedo. Heather adjusted his bowtie in a wifely gesture and then pecked his check. Another flash caught the moment.

"I feel like we're models in a magazine shoot," Brittan groused.

"We are," Heather said through a bubbly giggle. Her pure white gown and gauzy veil made her look angelic.

"You're beautiful enough to be a model," Duke said, his eyes on his new wife.

"Spare us! Spare us!" Brittan teased, but deep inside she was as glad for her friend as she was sad for herself. She gazed down at her tea-length gown, the color of champagne, and wondered if she'd ever be the woman in white. She hadn't seen Rob since the day of José's arrest, and she wondered if any other man would measure up to him. While Rob hadn't been perfect, he'd certainly been fascinating and distracting.

When someone swept away the bride and groom, Lorna leaned closer and said, "This is the reason I'm glad Michael and I eloped. I think the crowd would have killed us before we ever left for the honeymoon!" She pointed to another klatch of well-wishers monopolizing the bride and groom. Heather's engagement ring, sparkling on her finger, was now partnered with a wedding band.

"Oh! There's Michael now!" she said and waved.

The dark-haired mayor came forward and shook Brittan's hand. "Good to see you, Brittan," he said with an easy grin. "You two have never looked more beautiful." Even though the compliment was for them both, his attention was on Lorna, who glowed at her new husband.

Their Caribbean elopement last month was only disclosed to immediate families and Heather and Brittan. The rest of the city found out when the mayor and his bride returned from their honeymoon in the Bahamas. Michael's blatant admiration for Lorna heightened Brittan's loneliness. When the band struck up a love song, Michael tugged Lorna into his arms, and they swayed to the music. That's when Brittan knew she was no longer in their world.

Sighing, Brittan toyed with the bouquet and meandered through the crowd toward the buffet table. *Every gourmet treat known to mankind must be here,* Brittan decided. Her stomach growled at the aroma. She'd barely had time to eat since the rehearsal dinner last night. She slipped her purse's chain strap over her shoulder, juggled the bouquet as she filled her plate, and then found a quiet corner to sit in and enjoy her food. The more Brittan observed the laughter and conversation, the lonelier she felt. The last few months had gone from one exciting climax to another. Now that everything was winding down, she couldn't seem to stop her emotional slump.

After the police arrested José and Eduardo, Duke Fieldman's cover story detailed José and Eduardo's activities while not mentioning the Rose. Brittan read and reread the article until she memorized it. Juan Sanchez, Eduardo's brother and José's cousin, was arrested two years ago for hacking into Houston's banking system. Further investigation is underway to determine if Juan was involved in José and Eduardo's earlier crimes." As she'd wondered dozens of times, Brittan pondered whether Rob had been the one who linked Juan Sanchez's involvement with José and Eduardo's desire to smear the Rose's reputation. Duke's lead article was followed by other pieces linked to the arrests, including a report on Moe Van Cleave's eventual release from the hospital after narrowly escaping death in José's freezer. By plea bargaining he avoided being indicted.

Brittan shivered over the thought of being presumed dead and stuffed in someone's freezer. The tremor jolted her out of her reflective mood, and she gazed at her crystal saucer, empty except for one date wrapped in crisp bacon. Even though her diminishing appetite insisted she'd eaten the other morsels, Brittan wasn't conscious of eating them.

Sighing, she popped the last bite in her mouth and observed Lorna and Michael again. She imagined herself swaying with her own man and couldn't deny that his profile strangely resembled Rob's. She'd assumed that the longer she went without him, the less she'd feel for him...but the opposite was holding true. With each day she thought of him more.

Maybe Heather and Lorna are right, she thought. *Maybe we could work out our differences.*

Even though Lorna and Heather still loved her and were there for her, Brittan knew they weren't as free as they once were. They were no longer "debutantes," and Brittan was seriously wondering if her friends would even continue the Rose activities. She'd barely had four good conversations with Lorna since she got married three weeks ago. She was forever rushing to this meeting or that dinner or lunching with Michael. As Heather's wedding date had grown closer, she was even more occupied than Lorna.

Brittan had gone to her dad's office a lot over the last month. Her father had stopped pressuring her about making an official career decision, and Brittan sensed he took her regular work attendance as indicator enough. *Maybe this is God's way of showing me it's time for a change,* she decided. She'd been praying more than ever in recent weeks and believed she was more in tune with the Lord than she'd ever been. She was learning to listen and watch for His presence daily. As much as she wanted everything to remain the same as it had been the last few years, she also recognized that she and her friends were coming into a new season.

Sighing, Brittan set her empty plate on the table designated for used dishes. Last week, missing Rob had led her to pray about him.

She'd asked God to show her if she should contact him…or to put him in her path if that was His will. So far she hadn't glimpsed him—even though she'd spent all day Wednesday at the lake house.

When she turned from the table, her cell phone emitted a faint ring from inside her sequined bag. Brittan had put it on silent until after the ceremony. Sighing, she pulled the phone from her purse and examined the caller ID. "Rob Lightly" claimed the screen.

She raised her brows and masked the tremor that shot through her. Brittan was simultaneously astounded that he called and stunned that perhaps God was answering her prayers. Deciding not to get her hopes up until she talked to him, Brittan flipped open her phone and answered in a raspy voice.

"Hello, Brittan." His simple greeting warmed her despite her resolve.

"Rob, it's good to hear your voice," she said and hoped she didn't sound too eager.

"Glad to hear that," he replied. He hesitated. "Listen, I need to talk to you about…about some, uh, *roses* that maybe you could help me with."

"Roses?" she echoed and eyed the bouquet she'd caught. Then as if she'd received a download from Rob's brain, she instantly understood. "I didn't think you were…comfortable with roses. I thought you said they had too many thorns."

"Sometimes we need roses, thorns and all," he replied. "Can you meet me at your lake house soon? I can explain there."

"Sure. What about tonight?"

"What about now?"

"Now?"

"Yes. It's urgent."

She glanced at her watch and then up at Heather, who was across the room and still monopolized by the crowd. "I can be there in about 30 minutes. Will that work?"

"Where are you?" Rob asked. "Sounds like you're in a crowd."

"I am. It's Heather's wedding reception."

"Oh yes, right. Her wedding was today. Is Lorna there too?"

"Yes."

"I guess it's too much to ask if she'd meet with me as well. It's important. I know Heather's out, but what about Lorna?"

Her mind spinning with the implications, she spotted Lorna and couldn't imagine both of them ducking out of Heather's reception. But it sounded like Rob needed help with a case and was willing to drop enough info to the Rose to motorize them to action.

"I can't see Lorna and me both bowing out," she finally said. "But I'll come and then share the info with them."

He sighed. "Okay. You do that. That might be…the best anyway," he admitted, his voice getting softer. "Meet me in your garden. I'll be waiting."

Brittan didn't know how to respond, so she didn't. She simply bid adieu, hung up, and took a slow, steadying breath. This could be an answer to her prayer, but then again, it could be nothing more than a case.

She walked toward the exit and debated whether or not to tell Heather she was leaving. Chances were significant her friend was so distracted she'd never realize Brittan was gone. She decided to slip out. If Heather mentioned it later, she'd explain, confident her friend would understand.

Brittan pulled into her lake house driveway within 30 minutes. She didn't bother going through the house, but walked around back, fully expecting to see Rob. She wasn't disappointed. Dressed in his typical shorts and T-shirt, he stood near the shore with Elvis sitting at his feet. Brittan strolled into Eden, dropped her bag in a wooden lawn chair, and didn't make her presence known until she was feet from him.

Discreetly she cleared her throat. Rob turned to face her while Elvis jumped to attention and wagged his way to her side. Brittan bent to scratch his ears, and Rob gently commanded, "Sit, Elvis."

The dog obeyed and immediately calmed down.

"He's okay," Brittan claimed and stroked his silky fur.

"I didn't want him to mess up your dress," Rob said.

"You had him trained, I see."

"Yep. He's a new man," Rob said through a chuckle. "No more mauling neighbors' gardens or trampling small children."

He glanced over her satin dress again and said, "You shouldn't have gotten all dressed up just to meet me." His smile held a tinge of uncertainty.

"Heather made me wear this today."

"She invited me to the wedding," Rob replied. "I was surprised when I got the invitation."

"She never told me she invited you." Brittan stepped to his side and gazed across the indigo lake. The cool waters beckoned her to dip in to get out of the July heat.

"I wasn't planning on going, but then she called me."

"She called you?" Brittan shot a glance toward him.

"Yes. I told her I'd be there, but something unexpected came up at work this morning, and I couldn't make it. I just got off an hour ago. When I talked to Heather, she said she thought you might be…um…open to talking to me." He slowly faced her. "Are you?"

"Wait a minute." Brittan held up her hand. "I thought this meeting was about the Rose."

"It is." He nodded. "But I'm a man who believes in taking advantage of every opportunity."

The warmth in his gaze washed desire through Brittan's every fiber, and she no longer had to ask if God was at work. She'd missed Rob more than she wanted to admit. Never feeling so vulnerable, Brittan hugged herself and wished for his arms around her. She wondered what possessed Heather to tell Rob she'd talk. Brittan hadn't mentioned Rob to Heather or Lorna in months.

Maybe Heather sensed my loneliness, she conjectured and didn't know whether she should thank Heather for matchmaking or be exasperated at her for interfering. Finally thankfulness rose to the top.

"I think we got off to a really shaky start," Rob admitted. "You came into my life at a crisis time when I was really trying to work through some issues. I've been doing a lot of thinking and praying since the last time we talked—"

"Me too."

"And I wanted to tell you again that I'm really sorry I blitzed out on you that day. It's totally out of character for me. I've never done that before and can promise I'll never do it again."

"You've already apologized." She shrugged. "Lorna and I were over the top too." She shifted her attention to his head. "How's your ear?"

Rob touched it. "Super glue will fix almost anything," he commented through a grin. "Except a broken heart," he added.

Brittan's eyes stung. "Is your heart broken?"

"I think so. I can't seem to get my groove back...or think about anything but you." -

Brittan's legs shook.

Rob's demeanor begged to hold her...to kiss her, but he was clearly constraining himself.

"Is there any way you'd give us another chance? I've decided I'd rather have you chasing criminals undercover than not have you at all. I think—"

"*I* think," Brittan whispered, deciding the time had come for his constraint to end, "that it would be *very* reasonable for you to kiss me right now."

His eyes widened as Brittan stepped close and slipped her arms around his neck. "I've missed you so much, Rob Lightly!" she murmured as his arms slipped around her. The kiss that followed swirled the lake, and Brittan clung to him to keep from drowning in the maelstrom. When the kiss ended, she rested her head against his chest, and the two swayed as the waves calmed and the water gently lapped at the sand.

"I know I'm a long way from perfect," Rob admitted.

"Aren't we all," Brittan said. She didn't want to think about all the mistakes she'd made in the last year.

"But if you'll believe in me, I'll continue to grow."

"I believe in you, Rob."

He sighed and rested his head on hers. "That's all I need to hear. I'm playing for keeps. This is way beyond 'like' for me. I'm in love."

"Me too," she admitted.

When he grew silent, Brittan thought he might even be holding his breath.

"We've still got to spend some time getting to know each other better, but really, I'm contemplating marriage."

Brittan closed her eyes and clung to him. "Sounds good," she whispered.

"It's good to know we're on the same page," he said, a smile in his voice.

She relaxed against him and listened to his heart beating with hers until finally a more practical thought barged through the haze. "Hey!" Brittan lifted her head. "What about the business with the Rose?"

"Oh *that!*" Rob said. "I almost forgot!"

"There isn't a case, is there?" she accused and backed away. "You just used that to get me out here."

"No!" He lifted both hands, palms out. "I promise! There *is* a case," he said with a heartfelt laugh. "There's a counterfeiter slipping through legal cracks on technicalities. We know he's guilty, but we've gone as far as we can. I thought maybe the Rose could... well..." He shrugged.

"Do what we do and see what we can find out?"

"Yes. But you have to understand we never had this conversation and tell no one outside the Rose who your source is."

"And you're okay with me slinking around at night…taking care of business?"

Rob nodded, his eyes candid. "I've decided I've got to be. It's the only way I'll get you. I can't change your love for solving mysteries any more than you can change my love for law enforcement. I've decided to accept it and trust God to protect you."

"I've also been working with my dad," she admitted. "He wants me to eventually take over the Shay Publishing Group."

"That sounds way safer to me! But will you be happy?"

"I don't know." She blinked and stared over his shoulder. "It's not nearly as exciting. But maybe I can do a little of both." A faint ring floated from the lawn chair, 20 feet away. Brittan glanced toward it and said, "That's my cell. Sounds like Lorna's ring. They may be missing me. I'd better take the call." She walked away from Rob and retrieved the phone.

"Where are you?" Lorna's question floated over the line before Brittan had a chance to say hi.

"I'm at my lake house with Rob," Brittan admitted as Elvis trotted to her side and leaned against her. "He called so I slipped out."

"Oh." Lorna's simple answer held a depth of understanding. "Well Heather and I were missing you. She's right here. Is it okay if I tell her?"

"Sure. From what I understand, she invited him to the wedding and tried to play matchmaker."

"He told you that?"

"You knew about it?"

"It was my idea," Lorna admitted. "Girl, you've been on the verge of howling at the moon over that guy for *way* too long. We decided it was time to take action."

"Thanks!" Brittan said, her smile all for Rob as he moved toward her side and took her hand. "I mean that! And he's talking to me about wanting some help with some *roses*. Are you and Heather interested?"

"You have to ask? You know how much we love roses!"

"Well lately I felt maybe you two were losing interest."

"No way! Not at all! We've just been busy. Once life settles down, we're on it. At least I know I am. Yep, Heather's nodding her head too."

"Well he would like help *now* on something. But Heather's spending the next month in Greece—"

"I'm not in Greece!" Lorna exclaimed.

"Me neither," Brittan replied.

"Does he want to talk to us today?"

"Yes."

"As soon as I can get away, I'll be there. You're home at the lake, right?"

"Right."

"I should be there in a couple hours. Will that work?"

"Just a minute." Brittan lowered the phone. "Lorna says she can be here in two hours. Does that work?"

"Sure." Rob gave the thumbs-up. "As long as we can get squared away tonight, we're good."

Brittan confirmed the appointment and flipped her phone shut. She narrowed her eyes and pointed at Rob's nose. "Wait a minute, buddy," she teased. "You told me we needed to talk immediately. If the case is *that* urgent, why is it okay for Lorna to wait two hours?"

"When I said *urgent,* who said I was talking about the *criminal* case?" Rob moved in for another kiss.

ABOUT THE AUTHOR

※ ※ ※

Debra White Smith continues to impact and entertain readers with her life-changing books, including *Romancing Your Husband* and *Romancing Your Wife*, The Austen series, and The Debutantes series. She's an award-winning author, including such honors as Top-10 Reader Favorite, Gold Medallion finalist, and Retailer's Choice Award finalist. Debra has more than 50 books to her credit and over a million books in print.

The founder of Real Life Ministries, Debra also speaks passionately with insight and humor at ministry events across the nation. Debra has been featured on *The 700 Club, At Home Life, Getting Together, Moody Broadcasting Network, Fox News, Viewpoint,* and *America's Family Coaches.* She holds an M.A. in English.

Debra lives in small-town America with her husband, two children, two energetic dogs, a herd of cats, and two calves.

To write Debra or contact her for speaking engagements, check out her website:

www.debrawhitesmith.com

or send mail to

Real Life Ministries
PO Box 1482
Jacksonville, TX 75766

or call

1-866-211-3400

More Great Books

by Debra White Smith

✳

FICTION

The Austen Series

Amanda

Central Park

First Impressions

Northpointe Chalet

Possibilities

Reason & Romance

The Debutantes

Heather

Lorna

Brittan

✳

NONFICTION

101 Ways to Romance Your Marriage

Romancing Your Husband

Romancing Your Wife